DOUGLAS SHEA

The Cerberus Effect

1

Four years ago, one billion people around the world dropped dead in an instant. And that is the last thing I can remember...

A long windshield encapsulates me and, far above, the sun hovers and shrinks my retinas. My heavy breath fogs the glass, so I wipe it with my forearm. My bones and muscles ache. Sweat trickles from the temple of my forehead and slides down my cheek. I have no idea where I am... or who I am for that matter. From what I can see, I'm stuck in some sort of small chamber. There's a faint reflection on the glass. I notice my hair is black and buzzed short. A sharp jaw bottoms out my rugged face. Dark brown eyes with tones of amber and speckles of gold stare back at me. The foreignness of my image fills me with panic. A heavy nauseous feeling swirls inside my gut. I feel claustrophobic, and I frantically feel around with my hands as much as the compact space permits. I look for a handle or a knob, anything that can get me out of here. *Got it!* There's a long, skinny lever. I wrap my hand around it and pull it towards me. There's a loud *tssshhh* as the air decompresses and the glass door unlocks.

It's heavy, but with two hard kicks it swings open and I climb out. I had been lying in what seems to be a medical-grade hyperbaric chamber, so I must have been injured. As far as I can tell, I'm fine now. About twenty yards ahead is a fiery airship laid out on the ground with a torn off wing a few yards away from the hull. The flames seem to be fading, so I walk over to examine the crash. *Maybe inside I can find some clue as to who I am or where I came from.*

From within the ripped-open hull I am hit with an unbearable and undeniable stench. Along the inner walls are twelve seats with twelve partially decomposed corpses strapped inside them. Melted and charred skin reveals portions of skulls and some other bones. One of the bodies still has a small flame burning on her uniform. I pat out the fire. There is an American flag patched to her right shoulder and another patch beneath it with three black missiles on it. A couple of the burnt bodies still have rifles in their hands. My desire to continue searching is halted by the sounds of howling in the distance. I jump back out and scan the landscape. It is flat land all around. Grey, sandy dirt and dead grass stretch for miles all around. Up ahead towards the horizon I spot two lurking animals. From this distance, I can't tell if they are wolves or coyotes, but I have no desire of finding out.

Before I leave, I grab an M9 Beretta pistol off of one of the dead soldiers. I'm not even sure if I know how to shoot one of these, but if the animals decide to follow, at least I'll be able to scare them off. Armed and heading in the opposite direction makes me feel a little more secure. After about an hour of walking, my back is sweaty and my face is dripping, but I finally find a road to follow. The asphalt is cracked and broken as if it had been bombed. If I thought anybody could even attempt to drive on this road, I would follow it at least thirty yards out to avoid being seen by any possible enemies. But then again, I have no idea who my enemies are.

The sun is halfway through its descent, and all I see around me is broken road and palm trees. My feet ache. I don't really know what I'm looking for, but if I don't find someone or something soon I'm going to have to build my own shelter.

After another half hour, the road finally leads me to a small town that looks more like a collection of rubble piles and collapsed houses. The only house that still has a complete roof also has an upside down car smashed through one of its broken walls. There doesn't seem to be any signs of human life, so I keep moving forward.

It isn't until I get to the end of the street and past the cluster of broken homes that I see a human being. It startles me at first, but now

I watch as a pudgy man darts through what once must have been a community center. There is no roof, and it is missing two adjacent walls. On one side, there is a pile of rubble high enough to make half of a third wall. The man sees me. I stop and draw my pistol. I aim it at the man who is now hustling over to me.

"How the hell did you survive?" the man asks. He has a round face with blonde hair that parts in the middle of his scalp and falls straight down as far as his jawline. He's wearing a dark cargo vest open with nothing underneath. His belly is sunburnt and dirty. Long blue pants with big, overstuffed pockets and black boots complete his ensemble. "I thought for sure the Fangs would have gotten you, or at least the Cubans."

"What the hell are you talking about?" I keep my gun raised to the man's face. "Do you know who I am?"

"Well, you're obviously a soldier, probably a Brute," he says, and points to my camouflage pants and tan t-shirt. If only I was also wearing dog tags, I might know my name. "We saw your ship go down in Cuban territory. We thought for sure everyone was dead or captured."

I lower my gun. He hadn't noticed it anyway.

"I'm surprised you made it out this far," he says. "Did you see any Fangs?"

"What the hell are Fangs?"

"God, you Brutes are stupid. They send you on a rescue mission, and they don't even tell you what you're up against." He shakes his head.

"I'm not stupid. I just can't remember anything. I don't even know who I am."

"Oh you must have lost your memory in the crash." He laughs. "Well I'm not going to tell you my first name because it's embarrassing, but everyone calls me Reynolds. And you are in Wauchula, Florida." He spreads his arms out as if presenting the town. "Well, at least what's left of it."

I follow him behind the back end of the community center. There is a machine gun attached to the bed of a rusty old truck with no wheels. It's facing a playground of mangled metal twenty yards away. The only thing still standing are short monkey bars. Further beyond the playground, I can see miles of sea grape trees with sable palms looming over them.

"The others won't be back until tomorrow morning," Reynolds says and jumps into the back of the truck. "It's going to be a long night. The Fangs must have picked up on your scent. It's a good thing you found me and my baby," he says, and pets the barrel of his machine gun like it's a dog.

"Are you ever going to tell me what the hell Fangs are?" I say.

"Oh right." He jumps down from the bed. "When the Cubans bombed Florida, their planes released some sort of chemical weapon into the air. Along with the bombings, almost the entire state's population was wiped out. I don't know what the weapon was, but it has had a very different effect on dogs. Instead of killing them like it does to humans, it has made them bigger, stronger, faster..." He uses his fingers as bullet points. "And insanely aggressive."

I'm starting to think this guy is crazy...or maybe I am.

"The Cubans usually stay out of our area because it's so Fang infested."

"Why did the Cubans attack us? How were they able to do that?"

"Damn, you really don't remember much of anything do you? Surely even someone with a little trauma-induced amnesia remembers when a billion people died four years ago?"

I nod.

"Well then you remember that the U.S. lost a good chunk of our population in that instant. Even a Brute can probably figure out that our enemies were quick to take advantage of our heavy losses. I'm no history professor, but from what I understand the communist government had been hoarding U.S. dollars ever since the embargo was lifted. The Cuban people were still starving in the streets, so it didn't take long for the U.S. to place new trade restrictions. On the surface, we were still allies."

Before I can ask another question, he holds up his hand.

"Look, we don't have time for this. It's getting dark and we have to be ready for the Fangs. Ruby will explain more when she gets back."

As if on cue, I hear a howl in the distance.

"Come on," he says. "Let me show you the hiding space." He leads me around to the south side of the building. The adjacent wall has remnants of a roof over it just about big enough to shield a couple people from rain. Draping down from the roof is a large, black curtain that feels like a screen door and reaches down to the ground.

"To keep the bugs out?" I guess.

Reynolds laughs. "No. It's to keep the Fangs away."

"You're joking?"

"No, I'm serious. They have bad vision. To them, this is pitch-black. If we're behind it, they won't touch us."

That sounds crazy, but then again so is everything else. I don't have much of a choice but to trust him.

There are more howls. They are getting closer.

"Let's go," he says, and we run to the back of the building. He climbs into the bed of the truck. It's getting dark, but I can still see past the small playground. My jaw hangs as I watch a stampede of giant dogs running toward us. I see dogs of all different breeds charging, except they have bigger bodies than they should and large, bulbous snouts. There are ones that look like pitbulls, and rottweilers that trample over the smaller ones. But even the lesser breeds bare large teeth and come after us as if they are hungry for human flesh. I pull out my pistol and aim.

"Get the ones I miss," Reynolds says, and fires the massive gun. *Pah-pah-pah-pah-pah-pah-pah.* My ear drums feel like they are going to shatter. The machine gun bullets rip through the bodies of many Fangs. A pile of carcasses forms, getting bigger as he continues to fire his "Baby." But no matter how many he shoots, more keep coming. Several finally make it past the wall of dead Fangs that Reynolds is continuing to build. It's getting dark and the Fangs are quick. I aim and fire several shots, but can't seem to hit them. They are getting closer, and the blaze from the firing machine gun barrel is now my only source of light. I aim for a smaller one that has the face of a pug, but is at least the size of a labrador. I fire. It squeals, tumbling to the ground. After that, every shot I take meets its mark. I kill six that get past Reynolds, but more and more are moving in.

Reynolds stops shooting. "Run!" he shouts, but I take one more shot and nail a Fang that looks like a Shiba Inu right in-between the eyes. A chunk of its head explodes. I run towards Reynolds, who is getting underneath the black drape.

"Come on, get under here," he says, and I slip in next to him. I stand as straight as I can with my back against the wall. I can't see much of anything, but I can hear the growls and snarls of the Fangs right in front of us. *This is insane. They know we're here.*

"Don't worry, Brute," he says, as if he can read minds. "They won't touch us. They're too scared of the dark." From the sound of their consistent angry woofing, I would guess there are only a few left that won't give up on us. One of them jumps up as high as my face and snaps his jaws so close that I can feel his warm breath. I turn my head against the wall, but the unyielding concrete prevents me from retreating further.

"Reynolds, are you sure?" I ask.

He laughs. *How can this guy laugh right now?*

"I promise. They'll all give up eventually. You might as well get some sleep."

"Sleep? Are you insane?"

He laughs again at me. *Maybe in this world I woke up in, I'm the crazy one, and this is all normal.*

"Trust me," he says, as if I have a choice. "Eventually, you'll learn to sleep through this." He's right. After a while, my eyelids become too heavy to keep open.

I wake up in the morning on the dirt ground of the community center.

A large, red English mastiff is blocking the sun from my eyes. I have never seen a dog so big before. Its sharp teeth are showing, and its growl is getting progressively louder. *Where is my pistol?* I must have dropped it. Saliva is dripping from the beast's massive jaws. *Where is Reynolds? Did this thing eat him and now I'm next?* I crawl backwards on my elbows a couple of inches, but this seems to agitate the dog more.

"Yoshi! Heel, Yoshi." A woman's voice calls out, and the Mastiff finally backs away from me. I sigh, and lay my head back down on the ground. A light-brown skinned woman with straight black hair and an unarguably pretty face is leaning over me. Her smile is comforting and almost feels familiar, even though I have never seen her before.

"Sorry about that. She's not used to strangers," she says, and holds out her hand. I grab it and she helps pull me up. She dusts her hands off on her red tank top. I spot a large knife sheathed in a leather holster strapped around her waist, and handcuffs hanging curiously from one of the belt loops of her snug-fitting khaki shorts.

"You have a Fang as a pet? Isn't that dangerous?" I ask.

"Yoshi isn't a Fang. She's the only dog we've seen in a long time that isn't one. I don't know why the gas didn't affect her, but I'm sure glad it didn't. She can take on a smaller Fang all by herself."

"She's a big girl," I say. Even with all the questions I have, that is the best thing I can come up with to say.

She smiles at my awkwardness and cocks her head in Yoshi's direction. "Come and meet the others."

There is a rusted, old truck being unloaded by three men and Reynolds. Two of them are standing in the bed of the truck handing the items to Reynolds and the other. There are pieces of plywood, sacks of cornmeal, a couple of nail guns, and large boxes of ammunition. One of the men unloading the supplies jumps down in front of me. His short, curly hair is graying on the sides, and he wears thick, black-rimmed glasses. Before he says anything, he turns and grabs a fat, green book that is sitting on the open tailgate. He spins back to me and extends his hand. I shake it.

"Have you met Jesus?" he says. He's wearing a green and gray plaid shirt and well-worn work jeans.

One of the others groans. He has a round, freckled face. His hair is almost the same color as his sunburnt face. I don't know if the name Red that is embroidered on his white collared shirt is a jest or a very fitting real name. "Leave the poor guy alone, Wesley. I reckon he hasn't seen another human in a long time. Don't make him wish that he hadn't."

Reynolds chuckles.

The last man in the truck climbs down. He has tanned skin and short, dark hair. There are tattoos all over his muscular arms, including a Cuban flag on his wrist. The man grabs the last sack of cornmeal and flings it over his shoulder.

"*Basura*, religious *basura*," he says. "Try not to listen to him." He then follows Ruby and Reynolds around the east side of the community center.

"That's Marco," Wesley says. "Here, help me grab this." I help him carry a stack of plywood over to where the Reynolds' machine gun is. He lays his book on top of the wood as we carry it. It says *Holy Bible* in gold letters on the cover.

"No one believes me," Wesley says. "A billion Christians die in an instant, ending the peace treaty the Caliphate signed with Israel and the U.S. Now there's a World War with Israel as the main battleground. Don't you see it?" he says hastily, as if to fit as much propaganda as he can in one breath.

"See what? I don't know what you're talking about. I don't even know who I am."

"It's all been prophesied in there," he says, ignoring my ignorance and indifference to the subject all at once. He points with his eyes at the Bible. "The Rapture," he says. "It happened...and we missed it."

We drop the large pieces of plywood on the ground.

"Don't listen to Wesley's fantasies," Red says. "No one knows for sure how or why all those people died, but most people think the Sultan poisoned the water supply somehow...or maybe it was Big Al. In any case, it's pointless to dwell on the past. We need to rebuild and prepare for the future. Bring those over here." He points to the pile of wood. "We're fixin' to build a new wall." We grab the boards and drag them up against the back wall of the building. "I see you and Reynolds were already building your own wall." He laughs. Hundreds of crows are feasting on the piles of dead Fangs that we formed last night. The sight of the carcasses triggers the putrid smell of them, and I wrinkle my nose.

I follow Red around the ruins of the community center, but I can't escape the smell. It doesn't seem to bother the others

"So, soldier," says Ruby, standing beside a fire pit with a large, steel pot resting atop it. "I hear you're pretty good with a gun."

"I do what I can," I say with a smirk.

"Don't be so humble," Reynolds says, and puts his arm around my neck. "He killed six Fangs with only a pistol."

"Impressive," the Cuban says sarcastically. He's sitting at a picnic table to the right of the fire pit with his back turned towards us.

"Alright Red, that cornmeal isn't going to cook itself," Ruby says.

"Yes ma'am," he says, and immediately begins cooking.

"I'm sure you're hungry, Brute. I hope you like cornmeal stew," says Ruby. It hardly seems appetizing, but I nod and smile anyway. I'm starving.

She grabs a stack of colored, plastic bowls from the table and hands one to each of us. Mine is blue and the biggest.

"Bring it to Red; he'll fill you up," she says.

The others beat me to the food line, but there's plenty left. Red is stirring the yellow mush inside the pot.

"Well, I'll be damned. She likes you, soldier," he says, and pours a ladle-full of cornmeal porridge into my bowl. "She gave you the two-scoop bowl." He pours a second scoop into my bowl.

"Maybe she's just nice to newcomers," I say.

"Ha! When we found Wesley, she gave him the half-scoop bowl." I laugh and walk over to the table where Wesley, Reynolds, and Marco are already sitting and eating. Yoshi is sitting next to the table eating out of her own bowl. I'm hoping it keeps her full, so she doesn't come after me for dessert. I sit in between Reynolds and Wesley. Marco is across from us. The seat and table are hot from the scorching sun. Thankfully, a light breeze cools my sweat.

"*Mira,* she gave you the big bowl," Marco says with a smirk on his face, and points at me with a full spoon before shoveling it into his mouth.

"I would give it to him too," Wesley says without looking up from his meal.

"You got a little crush on him, do you?" Marco says and snickers.

"Shut up. All I'm saying is I'm glad we have a real soldier here."

"I'm a real soldier," Marco says. He puts his spoon down and glares at Wesley.

"Yeah," Reynolds says and snorts. "A Cuban soldier."

Marco shoots up off the bench, spilling his porridge. "What's that supposed to mean, *pendejo?*"

Reynolds stands up too, and places his palms on the table "It means you were trained by a corrupt government that resorted to chemical warfare against an ally, and that hardly makes you trustworthy."

"*Cara pinga!*"

"Alright, alright," Ruby comes up from behind. She and Red sit down. "Marco, we're all very glad to have you here. And Reynolds, if Marco was still on their side, he would have killed us all with that machine gun instead of giving it to us."

"I still don't trust him," Reynolds says.

"That's enough," she says and slams her palm on the table. "Sit down, both of you." They both obey her orders. "Now I know we all had a rough night, but we have to get to our new friend's crash site." She looks at me. "I'm sure there's a good amount of weapons, which we can definitely use right now. And maybe we can find out who the hell you are."

"There's also a hyperbaric chamber there. I was in it. I think that's how I survived the crash."

"We definitely need that," Reynolds says.

"I'm assuming it's military grade," Ruby says. "That's almost as good as having a doctor with us."

The scowls on their faces and the lingering tension dissolves with the news of the chamber.

"When do we leave?" Wesley asks.

"As soon as we're finished eating. Reynolds, you'll stay behind. Make sure no Fangs try to eat our cornmeal."

"Yeah, we sure wouldn't want that," I say as sarcastically as possible.

Walking in the blistering heat made the crash site seem a lot further from the community center than it actually is. When we arrive, everyone is in much better spirits. There's not a Fang in sight, and there's a plane full of valuable equipment and weapons. We all jump out, and Yoshi runs around looking for things to play with. I hope she doesn't find one of my old comrade's limbs to chew on. *I wonder if I was close to any of them. Maybe it's better that I don't remember. At least I don't have to be sad that they're all dead.* While everyone goes to look at the hyperbaric chamber, I step inside the broken hull. Now that I'm uninterrupted by Fangs, maybe I can find out something about myself.

"Lieutenant James Federer," shouts Red from outside. "We found your dog tags on the ground."

I dash out.

"I guess you're a lieutenant, James," Ruby says, and smiles. I smile too, but it means nothing to me. I don't feel like a lieutenant, or even a James for that matter. I want to remember, or feel something...there has to be more. I go back inside the airship as the others begin to load the truck up. I walk down the aisle into the open cockpit holding my nose. The bodies of the two pilots remain strapped into their seats. The pilot on the left still has one hand gripped onto the steering wheel. I hear a low static I had not noticed before. A broken voice comes through.

"Lieutenant...erer...is any...there? ...any...read me?"

I climb into the cockpit.

"This is ... control. Can anybody read me?" the voice repeats.

I grab the receiver, "Hello, hello. This is... apparently Lieutenant James Federer. I'm here."

"...Thank God, we thought... dead. What happened?"

"I'm not sure. I think we were shot down. I can't remember what happened."

"Are there any other survivors?...Do you have the prisoner in custody?"

"What prisoner?" I ask.

"The one in the hyper...chamber...a terrorist...he...extremely dangerous..." The transmission cuts off.

"Hello? Hello?" I say, but it's no use. The line is dead.

I hear a footstep on the metal floor. I drop the receiver, and look behind me. Ruby is standing at the entrance of the cockpit with her fingertips grazing her holstered gun.

2

Before I can object, Ruby quickly cuffs my wrists and pulls me outside violently. Her once friendly eyes are now dark with anger, as if I had somehow betrayed her. The fact that she even has handcuffs on her shows how distrusting she is, but I suppose I can't blame her. The world has seemingly gone to hell.

The others all stop what they're doing and gape at us. I almost want to laugh at their dumbfounded faces, but I fear that will only make my current predicament worse.

"*Que pasa* Ruby? What the hell did he do?" Marco says.

"Heck," Wesley corrects him. Marco glowers at him with squinted eyes.

"Both of you shut up," Ruby says, before Marco can respond. "There is no time to explain, and there is certainly no time for you two to continue your endless bickering. Let's finish loading the truck. The Fangs are almost here."

As if on cue, I hear a Fang howl in the not-so-far distance, and it sends an immediate shiver down my spine.

"I reckon Ruby is right. Let's get on with it," Red says.

"Load up the hyperbaric chamber. I'm going to get the weapons out of the plane," Ruby orders and walks passed me, avoiding my eyes. I guess the bright side is that I don't have to help load the chamber, but my wrists are already killing me in these cuffs.

Yoshi starts barking towards the east. I use my hands to block the glare of the sun, and I can now see a stampede of Fangs heading our way.

"Guys, we need to go. Like now," I say. They are securing the chamber in the bed of the truck. Not one of them looks at me or acknowledges me. I can't imagine what they think I did, but they seem to trust Ruby enough to know it must be something terrible...even if I can't remember it.

Ruby comes back out of the crashed aircraft with a large, dark green duffle bag in each hand. I can see long veins streaming down her muscular arms like rivers on a map. Marco jumps down from the bed of the truck. A wet spot is forming on the top of his navy blue shirt near his neck, and his face and forehead are dripping sweat. He helps her stuff the bags in the small crevasse in-between the chamber and the bed walls.

Ruby grabs my arm and pulls me towards the truck.

"Looks like we have more company," Wesley says. He's looking through a pair of binoculars. "Cubans coming from the south."

Marco rips the binoculars out of Wesley's hand and looks through.

"He's right. *Vamanos*."

"Everyone in the truck... Now! We'll let them deal with the Fangs." She grabs me and shoves me into the back seat.

Everyone climbs in except for Marco, who grabs his AR-15 and jumps into the bed of the truck. Ruby turns the key in the ignition, and I hear nothing but a gasping engine.

"Come on, damn it," Ruby says, and tries again to no avail. Fangs of all sizes are so close I can see foaming saliva dripping from their snouts. I see large ones that resemble pit bulls and German shepherds with teeth so sharp and large; they could easily rip through my neck in one awful bite. There are smaller ones that look like pekingese and poodles with inflamed bodies that I know could do just as much damage to my neck. Marco opens fire and takes out an entire line, but there are countless more rows behind.

Yoshi is barking and growling at the coming Fangs as Ruby desperately tries to start the engine. Red fires a Glock pistol outside of the window and even Wesley aims one too, although he hasn't fired a single shot.

"What are you waiting for?" I yell. "Take a damn shot!" I feel helpless without the firearm that Ruby confiscated from me.

Finally catching, the loud roar of the engine brings a tiny sense of relief to my bones. I can feel the tires spinning wildly and flinging up dirt. A small Fang with short, matted hair and a smashed-in snout leaps at Marco from over ten yards away.

The loud crack of Wesley's gun booms in my ear and I see the Fang fall out of the sky. The truck finally accelerates ahead.

"*Gracias*, Wesley," Marco shouts.

"I don't know why he's thanking me. I've just always hated pugs," he says with a smirk.

Ruby looks unamused as she stares into the rearview mirror.

"They're still following us," she says.

"Don't worry Ruby. I reckon we can outrun any Fang," Red says as he buckles himself back into the passenger seat.

"No, I mean the Cubans."

I look behind. Three large black SUVs are gaining on us. The rest of the Fangs are either quickly run over or simply can't keep up. Ruby accelerates, but the road is bumpy and uneven. Marco fires unsteady shots that don't even come close to the oncoming vehicles.

There's a familiar beep of a CB radio followed by static. Then, the static noise is gone.

"Reynolds, do you read me?" Ruby says into the mike. "We have company. Three Cuban trucks are following us."

"And a helicopter," I say.

"What?" she says, and jerks her head around. Her eyes widen. "Reynolds, if you hear me...break out the big guns."

"They never chase us this far," Wesley says. "You think they want the chamber that badly?"

Ruby side-eyes me through the rearview mirror, and I know she's thinking the same thing I am. *They want me.* All she has to do is stop the truck and give me up... but she doesn't. She keeps going. I hear guns firing behind me. I look to see Marco crouching and ducking behind the chamber. He returns a few wild shots without looking.

"Wesley, Red, help him out."

Red fires his automatic pistol out of the window. Bullets crack through the windshield of the SUV on the far left. It swerves hard, flips, and rolls.

The other two keep following. By now, the helicopter has caught up and is trailing right behind them. I see flashes of light as it fires its machine gun. I duck and turn. Ruby pulls Red by his shirt back into the truck, and then makes a hard left turn. I slam my head into the ceiling as we hit a large crater in the ground.

Everything is hazy for a moment, but I think I can see the community center up ahead.

"We made it," Ruby says, but I fail to feel relieved. I can hear the chopper and its machine gun getting closer. Even with Reynolds' machine gun, the community center offers little protection against two trucks full of armed Cubans and a helicopter.

Reynolds is standing in front of the center. I can barely make it out, but he's holding something over his shoulder. He fires a small missile from the long tube and a second later the helicopter is blown out of the sky. My ears are throbbing and everything sounds muffled, but I can still hear the shouts of joy and relief, and a long 'yeehaw' from Red.

The trucks swerve, attempting to dodge the flaming debris raining down above them. They swiftly turn around and drive back the way they came. Marco fires multiple shots until the trucks are out of sight.

After Ruby parks, she comes around and yanks on my cuffs, pulling me out of the truck. Reynolds is still holding the missile launcher with a cheek-to-cheek grin on his face that disappears quickly when he looks at my cuffed hands.

"What the hell is going on?" he says.

"Nice shot," Ruby says, and walks past him. He looks at Red for answers.

Red shrugs his shoulders, "what are you gawking at me for? She hasn't told me a darn thing."

"What did you do to her?" Marco asks, and drives his shoulder into me so hard as he walks by that I nearly fall over. I want to hit him, but that would hardly help my cause. Besides, I doubt I could do much damage with cuffed hands.

"I didn't do anything," I manage to mutter. I didn't mean for it to sound so whiny.

"I reckon you must have done something to piss her off. She isn't the most trusting person I know, but she don't go around cuffing people for no reason neither."

The guys are all surrounding me, except for Wesley. Now, Marco isn't the only one who looks as if he's about to strike me. I grind my boots into the dirt, ready for a blow. Instead, Ruby walks back over to us.

"Red, get started on dinner. The rest of you unload the truck," she orders.

"And what about this *pendejo?* You want me to kill him?"

"Nobody touches him," she says. Her face is hard like a stone. "We'll figure out what we're going to do with him at supper."

With that, she and Red walk towards the fire pit on the other side of the wall. As soon as her back is turned, Marco disobeys her orders and puts another hard shoulder into me as he walks back to the truck. I feel a jolt of pain go down my shoulder and arm, and I almost lose my footing, but Wesley grabs me and keeps me upright. I'm expecting another blow, but instead he just says, "Whatever you did, God forgives you." I think I would have preferred to be hit.

Reynolds looks at me and just shakes his head. He and Wesley then follow Marco to help unload the truck.

None of this makes any sense. *Can I really be a terrorist?* The Cubans did seem to want me for some reason, but I don't feel like a terrorist. If only Ruby and the others would just hear me out. It doesn't seem like I'll be getting a fair trial at dinner. But then again, nothing seems fair in the land of dogs. Although, it does seem that Ruby wants to keep me around for a little while longer. If she wanted to kill me, she would have done it by now.

The guys are coming back with the chamber, so I quickly jump out of the way. I don't need another bump from Marco's heavy shoulders. I walk over to the picnic table to await my trial. I sit alone for a while. I watch Ruby speaking with Red as he makes a big pot of cornmeal porridge. Yoshi is sitting by Ruby's feet, staring into the distance with her ears perked. She seems to always be on the lookout for Fangs. It's getting dark, but thankfully as far as I can see there are none nearby. I don't think I can fight off a Fang with these cuffs on and something tells me the guys wouldn't make protecting me their first priority. I try to listen to what Ruby is saying, but I can't make it out. The look of shock on Red's face, however, gives me somewhat of a clue.

"You don't get to sit over here, *puta*," Marco says from behind me, and I feel his strong grip digging into my shoulder. I feel a rage come over me that feels somewhat nostalgic...

I'm in a yard. There are tall, cement walls around us. A grey-haired man with sharp cheekbones and a thin, black goatee at the bottom of his narrow face swings at me. I feel uncontrollable anger. I barely dodge his fist, and aim mine for his stomach. His forearm easily curtails my attack.

"Focus," he says.

I try a sweep kick to his ankles before he finishes speaking, but he steps over it gracefully and lands a hard downward punch on my face. It knocks me back, and the pain of it only makes my anger greater.

"Focus your rage. Control it," the man says with a calm voice. I leap back up...

Marco is still gripping down on my shoulder. I jump up out of my seat faster than I even thought I could move. I pivot my left foot, and spin my right foot high around, striking Marco in the jaw. His body turns and collapses to the sandy ground. To my left, Reynolds and Wesley are standing nearby, staring at me with dropped jaws. My anger is so overwhelming I feel drunk on it. I focus so that my fists and feet will unleash it all with my next strike. I wait for them to attack, but they don't.

Ruby comes over slowly with her new Beretta pistol out and Yoshi following behind. I steady my breath and calm myself down. Ruby lowers her weapon and helps Marco up, but I swear it looks as if she's about to smile. Instead, she looks at me and points me to the wall with her gun. I comply. I'm in enough trouble as it is, and besides, Yoshi is snarling at me.

I sit on the ground with my back against the wall about ten yards away from the picnic table.

After everyone sits down to dinner, Red brings over a tray full of bowls. He gives me the smallest one, of course, and then brings the rest to the table. He also puts a bowl on the ground for Yoshi, who quickly wolfs it down and then sits in front of me staring and snarling.

"Fine, I didn't want it anyway," I say and slide the bowl towards the fluffy mastiff. It ends up spilling on its side before it reaches her, but she doesn't seem to mind. She laps all the porridge up and then resumes staring at me and showing me her monstrous teeth, as if I didn't know they were there. *So much for appeasement,* I think.

"So what are we going to do with him?" Marco says while taking a break from his meal to rub his jaw.

"I don't know," Ruby says.

"What's going on? What did he do?" Reynolds says. "Did he hurt you or something?"

"No," she says, as if she's offended. "A transmission came in at the airship. It warned that they were carrying an extremely dangerous terrorist on board...in the chamber."

"I knew it," Marco says, standing up. "A Brute can't move the way he does. He's been lying this whole time."

"And a terrorist can?" Reynolds wonders aloud.

"If he works for Big Al he can... or the Immortals," Wesley says.

"I think the engine is running, but nobody's driving," Red says with a spoonful of porridge still in his mouth. He swallows hard. "I mean, a U.S. airship with an Immortal prisoner onboard, flying towards Cuban territory? It doesn't make a lick of sense."

"I agree," Reynolds says. "The Cubans and the Sultan are growing friendly as of late. They wouldn't risk killing an Immortal and destroying any chance for a possible alliance."

I've had enough of this. This is all so absurd. I try and get up, but Yoshi growls at me and I quickly sit back down.

"Guys listen to me," I plead. Everyone looks over at me except for Marco, who is staring inside his bowl and scooping up more cornmeal porridge. "I don't work for Big Al. For God's sake, I don't even know who that is, and I'm certainly not immortal." I have to lower my voice because Yoshi is getting anxious and she looks as if she might pounce on me. "Even if I was working for these people, I don't anymore. Why would I tell you I was in that chamber if I thought I was a prisoner? And why did I wake up dressed like a soldier?"

The only response I get is the far away chirps and wing snaps of cicada swarms. The sunlight finally fades below the tree line and darkness covers the flat land. The only exception being the campsite, which is illuminated by the ring of torches that Wesley had lit. I can't help but wonder if there are Fangs prowling about. I shudder at the thought. At the moment, protecting ourselves from a Fang raid seems much more important to me than figuring out who the hell I am.

"We want to believe you, bud. But how can we?" Reynolds asks.

"Nightshade," Marco says almost inaudibly and pushes his bowl away. He stares at me as if I have a secret and he knows it.

"What?" Ruby says.

"He's one of them. I'm sure of it. It's a secret organization in the U.S. of highly-trained assassins and spies. They're kept so secret the United States government denies they even exist. They specialize in deceit. They were behind the coup in Mexico City that allowed the States to annex Mexico and a string of assassinations all over the Middle East that unintentionally helped the Caliphate."

"If they're so dang great, and if the Brute is one of them, how in tarnation did he manage to get captured by the likes of us?" Red scoffs.

"He didn't. That's how the Nightshade works. The whole entire thing is a ploy. The airship, the transmission, the Brute with no memory, even the hyperbaric chamber. It was all an elaborate trick to get to us. To find out who we are and how strong we are."

"If that's true, they sure are gonna be disappointed. Seems like a whole lot of effort for jack shit," Red says.

"Maybe, but that's how they operate. They go to extreme lengths even for the smallest bit of information about their enemies."

"Oh come on. This is ridiculous. Surely you guys don't believe this! Do I look like an assassin to you? I really don't remember anything," I plead.

"That proves nothing. They would wipe your memory to make your character fully authentic. A man who doesn't know he's lying believes he is truthful, and a man who doesn't know he is a highly-trained assassin believes he poses no threat."

"You mean to tell me, I'm working for a secret organization and I don't even know it?"

"You wouldn't be the only one. There are probably thousands of operatives out there waiting to be activated or extracted. Ruby, he is a ticking time bomb. Either he will kill us all or the Cubans will come back for him and kill us all. We need to kill him now," he says and stands up.

Ruby looks at me with inquisitive eyes. "Either way the Cubans will be back," she says softly. "We need to be ready when they get here."

Marco looks as if he's about to object, but Reynolds beats him to it.

"We need to head to the North."

"There are too many Fangs," she counters, almost desperately.

"Ruby..."

There's a rustling noise in the darkness. Everyone is quiet. Yoshi's ears are perked up and she is staring out into the blackness. She's growling a bit. She barks and darts towards the noise. Everyone gets up, grabs their guns, and follows her... except for me. I get up and watch from a distance. I'm no use without a gun and my hands still bound.

"What is it girl?" I hear Ruby say.

Suddenly, I feel a gloved hand cover my mouth from behind and a cold, metal barrel pressing against the temple of my forehead. Whoever is holding that gun slowly pulls me backwards, out of the glow of the flames and into the darkness.

3

The gloved hand is so tight on my mouth that I struggle to breath, but I don't want to make any sudden movements. I don't know how careful this person is with his finger on the trigger. So I let him take me wherever he wants to go. He keeps leading me backwards.

Ruby must have been right. The Cubans came back to kill me. They must know who I am. I only hope they will leave the others alone. Even if they have me pegged as the enemy right now, they're my only friends.

The moment he lets go or looks away I can possibly fight him off or escape, but so far the man holding me has been very vigilant. He's keeping his grip and the barrel of his gun pretty tight on me. I hear gunfire close to where the others might be. The man loosens his grip for a split-second.

Big mistake. Now's my chance.

I grab his hand and twist it out and down. He shouts in pain and swings the butt of his pistol towards my head. I duck and keep twisting his arm. I swing my leg around and kick him to the ground. If I keep twisting I'll break his wrist, but my whole body freezes as a jolt of electricity goes up my spine. There are two other men in dark clothing standing nearby. One of them pokes at me with a long baton with blue sparks coming out of the end. More electricity runs through my veins and I feel completely paralyzed. I fall and convulse on the ground as the current flows through my entire body. All I can do is watch the ground moving underneath me as they carry me and put me in the back of a truck.

They place me on a little bench that runs alongside the inner wall. It takes some time, but the numbness finally goes away, and as I regain the ability to move, I prop myself up. The ceiling is uncomfortably low and I have to bend my neck. On the bright side, my kidnappers finally remove my handcuffs. It feels good to have them off, but the rest of my body is aching.

There are two men sitting across from me in dark blue and black uniforms. Their painted faces match the colors of their attire. There are two others in the front seats dressed the same way. One is driving, although I don't know where to. One of the men sitting across from me has his neck bent forward, like mine. The other sits comfortably straight and is holding an M-16 rifle in his thick arms and pointing it at my chest. It doesn't scare me though. I doubt he will pull the trigger if he wants information from me. I want the same thing from them; although I wouldn't hesitate to kill any one of them if the rifle was in my hands.

There are no windows on the walls, but I can see well enough through the front windshield and the small windows on the back double doors to know that we're driving on a dark highway. Every once in a while, the driver swerves hard to dodge a large crack or break in the road ahead. The two men across from me just stare straight ahead. It's annoying me.

"Where are you taking me?" I ask even though I'm pretty sure I know where we're going and I doubt they even speak English, but I just want them to stop staring at me.

The taller one smiles. I don't know if it's because of the contrasting paint, but his teeth look really white.

"We're heading north," he says. "Someone wants to see you," he says with no distinguishable accent.

"Who wants to see me?"

For the first time, they take their eyes off of me and glance at each other with furrowed brows. The taller one's gaze returns to me as the truck makes another hard swerve.

"You don't know?" he says, sounding less Cuban every time he speaks. Perhaps Marco was right and Nightshade has come to extract me, but I don't want to reveal any information to them. I need to find a way to escape.

"I don't know anything. I don't even know who I am. Are you Cubans? Do I work for you? What did you do to my friends?"

The taller one laughs, but the shorter one continues to stare blankly at me. I can't even tell if he's looking at me or just zoning out at this point. This is slightly concerning, given that his gun is still pointed at me, and the driver continues to swerve.

"Just relax, we're not Cubans. Mika will explain everything else when we get there. As for your friends, we didn't do anything to them. The Cubans attacked. They were going to kill you. We had to get you out of there."

I hope the Cubans didn't kill my friends in that case. It seems they won't stop until they find me.

"Am I your prisoner?"

"Not exactly."

"What the hell does that mean?" I didn't mean to raise my voice.

The taller man seems surprised and a little annoyed; although I don't know why he should be given the circumstances.

"It means we're ordered to bring you back to Mika by any means necessary, but you're not our prisoner."

"If I'm not your prisoner, then why is the mute pointing his gun towards me?"

"Excuse my partner, but we know your capabilities. And given how things must seem, we didn't want you...reacting poorly."

I smirk. He's right. I was planning on killing them the first chance I got, but now I need them. I lean towards the shorter man.

"I wish you would point that damn thing somewhere else."

His eyebrows raise and he looks at the taller man who nods his assent. He then lowers the weapon and rests it across his lap. I let out a long sigh of relief. I look at the two in the front. Neither of them has said a peep and I wonder if they too are also mutes.

"That's Rob, and Samson is the one driving. I'm Jackson, but you can call me Jax. And the shy one we call Mo the Mute."

"If you can't tell me my name, why do you think I give a damn about your names?"

Jax smiles.

"Like I said, Mika will explain everything when we take you to him. He is—"

"I'm not going. I need to go back to help the others."

"That's impossible. I'm under strict orders," Jax says and Mo the Mute points his rifle at me again, until Jax waves his hand and he grudgingly returns it to his lap.

"I have to go back for them. You said I wasn't your prisoner. I'm going whether you like it or not."

Jax sighs and Rob looks back for the first time. Jax nods at him, and Rob lightly smacks Samson on the arm and then motions his thumb backwards. The truck slows down and does a wide U-turn. I stare at Jax with curiosity. *Well that was easy.*

"My orders are to get you to Mika alive. So if you're going, we're going with you."

"I don't need your help," I respond before he finishes.

"Maybe not, but it couldn't hurt. And I'm not going back to Mika empty-handed."

It seems it's going to be harder to get rid of these guys than I thought, but if Ruby is still alive maybe they can be of some use...for a time. I'll figure out a way to lose them after I get her and the others back. As much as I want to find out any information about myself, I'm not so sure Mika or these men are trustworthy.

"Just don't get in my way," I say.

"We won't, just don't try to escape... and don't get yourself killed. Mika will have my head."

"And why should I care about that?"

Jax snorts. "Because we're on the same side."

"Is that so?"

"We work for Mika; you belong to him."

"I don't belong to anyone," I say, liking this guy less and less.

"You really don't get it, do you? Mika is a hero. When the war started, the U.S. sent most of its forces to fight overseas. It left us vulnerable to attack. U.S. officials refused to listen to Mika when he warned them, so he built his own army. Now we are the only thing keeping Big Al from moving further south and taking over the rest of our land."

"Enough of this," Samson says. "We don't have to convince him of anything. You belong to Mika and we are taking you back to him one way or another. If you try to escape, I will kill you myself."

My hands clinch into tight jagged balls. Jax is watching me.

"Let's everybody calm down. Like I said, we're all on the same side. We need each other," Jax says and looks directly at me. His eyes are dark and wide with deep wrinkles around the edges, where the face paint couldn't penetrate. "Whether we like it or not."

I lean my head back as much as I can and try to rest. We must have gotten pretty far from the community center while I was out.

Maybe I really do need them. If they help me rescue Ruby and the others, perhaps I'll owe it to them to help complete their mission. Plus, it would give me a chance to talk to this so-called hero and see if he actually knows me. I think of what Marco said about Nightshade. Maybe this too is all part of some elaborate scheme...

"What's my name?"

Jax just grins.

"You don't know, do you?" I say.

"Actually I don't."

I figured for sure he would at least attempt to lie.

"Well, not your real name. I know your code name."

"Well? Don't keep me guessing."

"You're not going to like it," he says and for the first time, I see a hint of a smile on Mo the Mute's face.

"It couldn't be any worse than your names," I counter, and Mo's smile quickly dissipates.

"They call you The Naked Lady," Jax says clearly trying to hold back his laughter.

"You're joking."

Jax and Samson both lose it and Mo the Mute has a big grin on his face. Rob looks back with sympathy.

"I wouldn't be too upset." Rob's voice is higher than I would have expected. "The Naked Lady is an extremely deadly flower. Even when I was still in the Army I had heard of you. Everyone heard stories of how many people you killed in Turkey and Syria. Granted, we did all think you were a woman," he finishes with a grin, and the others laugh even harder.

I close my eyes and take comfort knowing that Ruby would kick all their asses if she was here. I hope she is still alive. I can't wait to tell her and the others that I'm not really a terrorist. Maybe we can join forces with Mika when all of this is over.

"Why do you want to rescue them so badly?" Jax says and for a moment I wonder if he can read minds. "You've only known them for a day."

"My memory only goes back a day. As far as I can remember, they are my only friends."

"Some friends," he says with a snicker. "They had you cuffed when we got there."

"You don't understand. Ruby heard a transmission while we were searching my crashed airship. They thought I was dangerous."

"You are dangerous."

"But not towards them, damn it. I'm not a terrorist."

Jax looks as if he's about to say something, but catches himself.

"What was I doing on that plane anyway? It was heading towards Cuban territory, why? Was I on a mission?"

Jax squints and looks at Mo the Mute for help, but I know he won't be saying anything.

The truck is slowing down. The headlights shine on a cement wall and illuminate the community center up ahead. Something outside moves quickly in front of the vehicle and then disappears as fast as it came.

"What the hell was that?" Samson says.

"Fangs are out tonight boys. Let's make this quick," Jax says.

"What are we looking for?" Rob says.

"Survivors first, anything left behind second. Maybe we can figure out where they went."

"I don't suppose you'll give me a weapon? We wouldn't want anything to happen to me now would we?"

Jax smirks. "If I had a weapon to give you...I still wouldn't give it to you."

When the truck finally stops, Mo the Mute opens the back doors. He shines the flashlight on his rifle outside for a moment and then leaps out.

"Samson, stay here and keep the truck running," Jax says before he too jumps out. I follow right behind him.

"Close the door, man" Samson says, and Mo the Mute listens. He and I follow Jax around to the passenger side of the truck where Rob is waiting.

"You and Mo check the south side. The Naked Lady and I will check around back. Lights out, we already have their attention," he says and then pounds the hood of the truck with his fist a couple of times. Samson immediately turns off the headlights and Mo the Mute switches off his flashlight.

"How are we supposed to see anything?" I say. The compound is pitch-black now. The torches that were lit earlier have burnt out and the sky is cloudy, covering any light the stars and moon could offer.

"Your eyes will adjust. The Fangs' won't. Let's move," Jax says. Mo the Mute and Rob are already gone.

I follow slowly and carefully behind Jax towards the pick-up with a machine gun but no wheels. The black air is thick and humid, but the songs of nearby crickets conceal the sound of my heavy breath. As I go, I search the ground around me for any signs of the others, or God forbid, dead bodies.

I reach out and touch Reynolds' machine gun that he had protected us with. He accepted me so quickly. I hope he's still alive. As much as I don't want him or the others to be prisoners, I hope that the Cubans have kept them alive. Of course, how long will that last once they find out the others don't know where I am? Damn Jax for capturing me. We're wasting our time here. We need to head south. I need to find them before it's too late. Perhaps it already is. It never really goes how you think it will. They're probably already dead. I need to look out for myself.

"Find anything?" Jax asks from behind me. It startles me. Hopefully he didn't notice.

"Nothing," I say.

He sighs. "Me neither. We better get the guys. The Cubans must have taken them in for question—" I hear the snarl before I see the large, furry Fang leap at him. It's attached to Jax's back as he flails his arms around, attempting to get it off of him. I hear him shout in either pain or fear. He stumbles and crashes to the ground. I stomp on the beast's back as hard as I can. The Fang is unfazed, and keeps its jaw clinched on Jax. I look around for the others, but they're nowhere in sight. There's a tire iron on the ground near the jeep. I grab it and strike at the Fang's spine until it finally lets go of him and turns to snap at me. I raise my arm back, but before I can strike its snout another Fang tackles me to the ground. The salivating Fang has the mouth of a pit-bull, only much larger. I push at its neck with my hands as he bites repeatedly at my face like a raging fiend. The drool is dripping all over my face. I reach out my hand, trying to grab the tire iron I dropped. It's too far, and I can't hold off the Fang with only one arm for much longer. Extending my hand out as far as it can go, I feel the metal on my fingertips and grab hold of the tire iron. I smash it against the Fang's humungous snout, but all it does is make the beast angrier. It opens its jaws and leans in for my face. There's nothing I can do, but close my eyes. I wait for the ending bite, but instead hear a loud squeal and I feel its weight come off of me. I open my eyes and see another Fang fighting with it. It has orange fur. It's not another Fang. It's Yoshi!

The Fang is too strong for her and is able to toss her over. It latches violently onto her shoulder and Yoshi yelps loudly. I dash over and strike the Fang in the back over and over again. When it finally lets go of her, Yoshi takes the opportunity to bite down hard on its throat. Dark blood gushes out and the Fang goes limp. I help push it off of her. Even though Yoshi is hurt, she still manages to stand up on her hind legs and wrap her paws over my shoulders. She licks my face and my hands disappear in her shaggy mane as I scratch her back.

Jax is standing behind her. I realize now how it must look. He raises his gun at her. He thinks he's saving me.

"No!" I shout.

4

"I haven't seen a dog in such a long time," Jax says as he lowers his gun. "Come here, boy."

Yoshi is now sitting next to me. She stares at Jax with a tilted head.

"It's a girl."

"Come here, girl," he says while reaching out his hand and pretending like there's something in it for her. She stays put and looks at me. Apparently she is as untrusting of him as I am. I pet her behind her big, floppy ears as she pants and large drops of saliva fall to the ground from her mouth.

"How is she not affected by the virus?"

"I don't know, Ruby—"

Yoshi barks loudly at the sound of her name.

"Where is she, Yoshi? Where's Ruby?"

She barks again.

"Take us to her, girl."

Yoshi takes off around the south side of the wall. Jax and I follow her. She takes us to the Fang shield and then darts several yards out from the wall. I can only see her silhouette moving in front of me. She stops next to something on the ground. Yoshi sniffs it and lies down next to it with a whimper. It's a corpse. I inch towards it. It must be Ruby. I can hardly bring myself to look at it. The body is mangled and twisted.

Jax flicks on his flashlight and shines it on the body. I can feel my heart stop in my chest, and my breath is held tight.

It's not her. It's a man. I breathe a long sigh of relief and my heart thumps again. The body lies in a pool of blood. His neck is badly bruised and cut open in the front. His legs are twisted and broken, and a bone is sticking out of his shin. He was tormented before he was killed. Even his face is unrecognizable, but the Cuban flag tattoo on his arm is the only thing on his body that seems untouched. There's not even a drop of blood on it. I can't look at Marco's mangled body any longer. It's not that I don't have the stomach for it, but the thought of the others enduring the same fate angers me so much that I'm beginning to feel lightheaded. I clench my fists and think of the grey-haired man from my only memory. He says, "focus."

I concentrate on the word. My heart slows a bit and the darkness around me becomes less hazy. I wonder if Jax hadn't kidnapped me would I have been able to save them or would it be me in that puddle of blood.

Yoshi walks forward, barks once, and points her head to the south east. She then looks back at us. Her eyes are glassy. Her face seems sad, and if she wasn't a dog I'd say she'd been crying. Jax turns his light off.

"They must have captured the rest of them. They only killed this one because he was a traitor. The others will be questioned."

"What makes you so sure?" I ask. I don't want to get my hopes up, and him be wrong.

"Because they need to find you. They will torture and question the others before they kill them."

"We must head south then."

"And deliver you right to them?" Jax says.

"We have to rescue them"

"We came all the way back here for him," Rob says creeping up from behind us. Mo the Mute is with him. "He has his proof now. They're all dead. We have to get him back to Mika. We've wasted enough time already."

Jax is silent for several moments. If he sides with Rob, I will not go with them...at least not without a fight, and I know Yoshi won't either. Even if we manage to escape, what chance will we have against thousands of Cuban soldiers and even more Fangs along the way? But I'll take my chances if I have to.

"A good captain must listen to the advice of his men. But if he always followed them, he wouldn't be much of a captain. There is a Cuban military base maybe forty miles south of here. We will check it out. If it is too guarded, we will leave. If there is no sign of your friends, we will leave." I smile, but then he grabs my arm and stares into my eyes. "And if I think, even for a moment, that you are going to try and escape, I will chain you up and drag you back to Mika myself, understood?"

I lose my smile and nod. Yoshi snarls. Just when I was beginning to think I would let them bring me to Mika after we rescued the others, he throws that threat at me. Now I know I will leave them as soon as I can.

"Come on girl, let's go find Ruby," I say.

Once again, I find myself sitting on the hard bench in the truck. It's uncomfortably quiet the whole way south, except for an occasional whimper from Yoshi when the truck hits a bump in the road or makes a hard turn. She barely fits in the aisle between the opposite benches and she struggles to sit still the whole way. Every time we pass a mile marker she yelps and wags her tail, as if she knows she's getting closer to Ruby. Maybe it's blind hope, but I'll take it as a good sign. Perhaps somehow she can sense that Ruby is still alive.

We get there surprisingly fast. Rob gives Samson a nod that I would consider suspicious and he parks off the road a good distance away. He turns off the headlights. I can see a complex ahead. There are several buildings and large cylindrical basins spread out inside of a barbed wire fence.

"Is this a military base or a water treatment plant?" I say.

"It appears to be both," Jax says and nods ahead. The complex is only lit in some areas, but I can see a couple of armed soldiers walking past a basin. They disappear into darkness after a few moments.

"So what's the plan? Cut through the fence and waltz right in?" I ask dryly.

"If you have a better plan now is the time to share," Rob snaps back.

Yoshi starts barking and whining. She's staring at the back door of the van unable to sit still.

"The dog stays here," Jax says "We don't need him making any noise."

"Her," I correct him again.

"Samson you stay behind. Keep the truck running. I don't plan on being in there for very long," Jax says.

"Stay," I tell Yoshi and try to push her back, but it's no use. She's too heavy and determined. Instead, I open the door slowly and try to get out while blocking her from escaping, but this too turns out to be ineffective. She leaps at me. The doors slam open as she pushes me through them and out of her way. I fall hard on the ground. She jumps off of me before I can grab her and takes off towards the base.

"Damn it," Jax says as he hops out of the truck with his rifle.

"Well, you could have helped," I say as I grab his extended hand. He pulls me up and shrugs. Rob and Mo the Mute are now standing beside me. Mo the Mute is holding his rifle and Rob has one strapped across his back. He's holding a pair of steel cutters.

As we march closer to the complex, I see a couple more soldiers. They could be the same ones as before. They are both carrying PP-90 submachine guns in their hands and each has a pistol and a knife cased in their belts. I wonder why they are so well-armed. Aside from our small group, there probably aren't any people for hundreds of miles and the barbed wired fence is enough to keep out the Fangs.

Jax stops when we are close to the fence. We hide near a row of hedges. Ahead there is a one story building with a light above the double doors around back. The two soldiers are walking in our direction now. I hear one talking in Spanish. The other one stops to light up a cigarette for a moment and then they continue walking our way.

I hear a pattern of short bursts of vibrations. It's not coming from the soldiers. It's right in front of me. Jax frantically searches his body with his hands. The Cubans are closer now. A few steps closer and they will be able to hear it too.

"Shut that damn thing off," I want to yell, but that won't help either.

The Cubans stop at the corner of the building. The one with the cigarette looks in our direction. I lower myself, but I can still see him staring out towards the hedges. He takes a long hit on his cigarette and then flicks the butt towards us while letting out a big cloud of smoke from his mouth. He pats the other one's shoulder and they walk around the east side of the building.

When I can no longer see them, I hear a metal thud that sounds like a door closing. I let out a long breath. Jax finally finds the phone in his pocket. He pulls it out and reads it for a moment. We all stand behind him waiting. He puts the phone away and then stares off, as if contemplating something.

"Jax?" Rob finally says. "What is it?"

"Nothing, let's move."

We creep passed a long stretch of the area that was completely lit up. I quickly realize that part of the fence we're passing is a gate. I run faster and bump into Mo the Mute.

"Go, go, go," I say. "It's opening."

We barely make it to the other side and away from the light before the gate is fully open. A black utility vehicle with blacked out wheels and windows so dark that I can't see a thing inside, drives out through the gate.

"Did they see us?" I ask quietly. We're hiding behind what seems to be an old, abandoned car that is smashed into a tree stump. Someone shushes me. It must be Rob. The vehicle passes us and turns towards the way we came from. If they see our truck, the base will be alerted and we will all be caught.

"Let's go," Rob says as he darts past me and towards the gate.

"No, wait," Jax says but it's too late. Rob creeps through the gate and turns left.

"Shit," Jax says and quickly follows him. I'm tempted to stay back, but then I'll have no way in and they definitely won't try to rescue my friends without me. Mo the Mute and I barely make it in before the gate slides closed and locks behind us. We take off towards the others before I can even look to see if anyone has spotted us. I figure I'll hear an alarm soon if they did. We follow a road of gravel and dirt that starts out straight east, but then curves south at a watch tower.

There's an open garage to our right. It's dark, but I can see large trucks behind smaller, off-road vehicles parked inside. Mo the Mute follows me past a sidewalk that splits several buildings and seems to cut the base. First into two, and then into many more pieces with each turn it makes. We continue ahead and I hear a whisper coming from inside a dark, awning-covered area to my right.

"This way," it's Jax and Rob. Underneath the awning is a maze of tall cylindrical tanks with large pipes flowing in and out of them. I follow them through. The spaces between some of the pipes are so tight that we have to go through them one at a time. Mo the Mute is so thickset he gets stuck, but I'm able to pull him out. We finally make it to a set of heavy, metal doors with small, glass panels above the push bars. The doors are next to each other, but one leads outside to a sidewalk that follows along a couple buildings and turns past a basin. Through the window of the other door, I can only see darkness.

"Let's go," Jax says. He goes through the door that leads outside. The metal hatch echoes loudly through the awning-covered room as he opens the door. Rob and Mo the Mute quickly follow, but I wait. I stare into the darkness of the other door, wondering what's inside. I feel as if something is drawing me towards it. Maybe I can come back to it... but right now I must follow the others. Jax seems to have an idea of where we can find my friends.

I put my hand on the door, but before I can push the bar I hear a muffled voice outside. It's unfamiliar and speaks in Spanish.

"Stop right there," it says. I don't know how I understood it, but I quickly take my hand off the door and lower myself. I peek through the window. There's a yellow light flashing against the next building.

I hide against the little bit of wall in-between the two doors. Maybe they didn't see me. There's shouting outside. Swiftly, I inch my way to the other door and open it, carefully making my way into the darkness. I close the door behind me as gently as I can. It makes a slight clicking sound, but I doubt they can hear it outside.

The metal grate floor guides me to the left and makes a clinking echo with every step I take. Fortunately, it is drowned out by the constant humming of large pumps below. Metal boxes line the wall on my left. Each of them has electroluminescent displays and it's enough light for me to see down the long hallway ahead of me. It stretches almost fifty yards and then takes a hard right turn and continues along a long wall full of dark windows.

I follow that wall as quickly but as quietly as I can. All of the displays have either red or blue numbers. Most of them are fluctuating, but some stay the same. Halfway down the walkway is a metal staircase... maybe I should hide down there between the pumps.

I wonder if Jax and the others will tell the Cubans there was a fourth in their group. At least I know Mo the Mute won't talk and Jax won't unless it benefits him in some way. But how long until Rob says something? He might betray me out of spite. After all, he was the one who didn't want to come here. Of course, maybe the Cubans saw when we came into the base and were just waiting for us to come out from underneath the awning. Maybe they know exactly where I am, and besides, hiding here won't get my friends back. Even if I stayed here it would only be a matter of time before they found me. I have to keep moving. I make it to the end and turn the corner. Cupping my hands over my eyes, I stop and attempt to see what's inside the windows, but it's too dark. I follow the pathway until a make it to a small door with a knob. It takes me into a small alley that intersects adjacently with a long, carpeted hallway. It's dimly lit, and there are rooms and offices on both sides. Some are open and some closed, but all are dark inside. Only from the lights of the hallway can I see anything. On one side I pass a room with a large, oval shaped table and chairs all around, and on the other side is a room filled with countless rows of cubicles and desks. I keep walking forward.

There is a foul smell that intensifies with each step ahead. I can now hear a faint whimpering. It sounds like a dog. It must be Yoshi! Did they already catch her? Or maybe she snuck in and has found Ruby. I walk faster, but I'm still careful to stay quiet. If Ruby and the others or Yoshi is imprisoned here there might be guards on watch. If only Jax had entrusted me with a weapon I would be a lot more confident. *Focus*, I tell myself.

The stench is so strong now I can barely stand it. I breathe through my mouth, but now I can taste it. It tastes how I would imagine a dead rat would taste. I come to an open entryway to my left. I hold my nose as I enter the room.

Fangs...

I jump back at first and nearly run back the way I came, but then realize they can't get to me. Rows of cages line the walls and over fifty pairs of red eyes stare at me from within them. The cages rattle and shake, as all but two bark and growl at me. Some smash their heads against their cages over and over again, trying to get out. Some try to force their snouts through the metal bars to the point of their skin ripping, which doesn't seem to stop their frenzy. I try to shush them, but it's no use. It only seems to make them madder. Some of them are so big they barely fit inside their confines, and all I can do is hope the doors are strong enough to hold them. There are two larger crates separate from the rest. Inside are the two biggest Fangs I've seen yet. Almost the size of small horses, they have giant muscular heads that resemble pit bulls. Their massive shoulder muscles are pulsing out of their skin and covered in jet-black fur. Their eyes are the color of blood but, unlike the others, these two are calm. They just stare at me, and a feeling of dread filters through my bones.

"*Callate la boca!*" I hear a voice shout from the hall. I look for another exit, but there are none. I have to hide somewhere. At the end of the room, there are boxes and empty crates. I squeeze behind them and crouch down. I peek out. The two calm Fangs are still staring at me, and all the rest are barking ferociously in their cages.

In the midst of the barking and howling, I hear the shouts of the Cuban guard getting closer. He speaks in Spanish, but again I'm able to comprehend it. He enters the room yelling and cursing. He is in a dark green uniform with a Cuban flag patched on his upper arm. There are other badges too, but I don't know what they are. He has short, curly hair that is as black as the two calm Fangs.

"Loco, Max, shut these dogs up," he says and unlocks the cages of the two larger Fangs. The doors burst open and the great beasts immediately dash towards me. My heart sinks and I hold my breath.

The Cuban man puts his fingers in his mouth and whistles loudly. The Fangs instantly stop at the end of the row of cages.

"Where are you going? There's no more food back there," he laughs.

Both of the monsters stare into my eyes. The hairs on the back of my neck are standing straight up. Big globs of spit are forming a pool on the ground beneath their jaws. Their teeth are so large and sharp that they make Yoshi's look like a Chihuahua's.

"Shut these damn Fangs up," he says. The two turn around and each of them walks slowly along each row of Fangs, lightly growling and staring into their cages. Like a wave, the other Fangs quiet and calm themselves as the alphas walk by. Some let out small whimpers and lay down, but all of them look away or cover their eyes with their paws. The room is quiet when Loco and Max make it back to the guard.

"Back in your cages," he says and they follow obediently. He locks them up and leaves the room. They are still staring at me, but at least all the others are quiet. I wait a few minutes. Hopefully, it's enough time for the guard to go back to wherever the hell he came from. I get up slowly to test the Fangs. They stay quiet as I tread through the aisle, but I can feel them watching me. As soon as I leave the room, they all start barking and wailing again.

"*Puta pendejo*," I hear the guard yell from down the hall. I immediately take off, heading back the way I came from. I find a stairwell to my right. The guard is yelling at the Fangs as I rush down the steps. It gets darker the further down I descend, and I have to slow myself. I can't even see the steps ahead of me or how far it goes down. I trace my hand along the wall for balance. At the bottom, large double doors appear out of nowhere and I nearly smack my head against them. I push in the long metal bar handle softly, but it still makes a loud, clanking sound as the door unlocks. I open it cautiously and peer out. There's a small open space. No one seems to be around. I step in and close the door behind me. Up ahead is a wall of concrete, interrupted by a tan-colored metal door. There is a small, plastic window in the middle of it, but it's too dark to see inside from where I'm standing. To my right is a desk with a sleeping computer monitor and a couple of disheveled papers and folders. There's a cup of coffee sitting next to the keyboard and steam is rising from the top. Someone was just here. They could be returning soon.

I step to the small window. There is a tiny knob on it. I use it to slide the plastic frame open. Inside, there are three men slouched on a bench. They look sickly and beaten. I don't recognize them until one looks up at me.

"Brute?" Reynolds says. It seems he's sore as he gets up and comes to the window. Wesley and Red follow him. All three of them stare at me through the space between us. They look scared and defeated.

"I'm here to get you out," I whisper. "Where is Ruby?"

They look at each other with confused looks. They still don't trust me and probably blame me for their current predicament.

"I'm here to help. How do I open this door?" I look around. There's not even a handle or a knob.

"The computer over there," Reynolds finally says, but his voice still sounds skeptical, as if I'm trying to trick him or something. I hurry over and grab the mouse. The screen lights up. It's asking for a password.

"What's the password?"

They look at each other for answers. Red shrugs and Wesley shakes his head.

"Quickly, I need an answer!"

"I'm not sure. I think the guard's name is Julio. That's all I know," Reynolds says.

I type in "Julio". *Incorrect password* pops up on the screen.

Damn.

I look around on the desk and shuffle through some of the papers. Nothing of importance sticks out to me, until I come across a photograph of a dark-haired smiling man at a park with a leashed German shepherd by his side. I flip it over. Handwritten on the back it says "*Pepe tronco del barrio.*"

I type in "*pepe.*"

Incorrect password.

I type in "*pepe1.*"

A new display pops up.

"Got it!" I say. The entire screen looks like a blueprint of the building. Or is it the entire plant? Big circles show what I'm assuming are the tanks on the upper left of the screen. There are long, green lines that turn and intersect with each other and lead to diagrams of the pumps, but I don't see anything that looks like a prison cell. I hit the escape button and the window minimizes. I see several icons, and the same picture of the smiling man with his dog is the background of the monitor's display. Below the picture and to the right corner of the screen is an icon of a door. When I hover over it with the cursor, it says *abierto* below it. I double click. The door unlocks loudly, and Reynolds pushes it open.

"Thank God," Wesley says. They all stagger out.

"What now?" Red says.

"We can go back the way I came from," is the best answer I can offer.

"That way is no good," Reynolds says, and I now realize that door too has no handle or way of opening it from this side. "We can head down that corridor."

Before we move, I grab Reynolds. "Wait, where's Ruby?"

"She's gone. They sent her away."

"Where?" I shout.

"Shhh. To Mika as part of a prisoner exchange."

I smile and breathe a long sigh of relief.

He raises a single eyebrow at me. "We have to get her back. Mika doesn't mean to free her. He means to execute her, just as the Cubans will execute the poor sap Mika is giving them."

"Who?"

"I don't know. They called him *La Dama Desnuda.*"

I wrinkle the corners of my eyes and wince slightly as I translate for him.

"The Naked Lady," I say.

5

The smiling man wasn't smiling anymore when he found me freeing his prisoners. He reached for his holstered gun, but I kicked it out of his hand before he could aim it properly. I followed with a punch in the mouth, so hard that from now on he'll be smiling with a few less teeth.

Samson will suffer the same fate or worse if he doesn't do exactly as I say. I swing open the driver's door of the parked truck and lead with the Glock 22 I took from the knocked out prison guard. He's surprisingly calm as I press it into the temple of his forehead. I watch his eyes shift slightly to the right. Now both of us are staring at the combat shotgun he has laid out on the passenger seat.

"Don't even think about it," I say and push my barrel harder against his skull. "You seem to know better than I do what I'm capable of, so don't think I won't kill you right here."

Samson looks ahead, but then again to the right as Reynolds throws open the passenger door and grabs the shotgun. He points it at Samson.

"Better do as the Brute says," Reynolds says with a smirk.

"Brute?" Samson laughs loudly. "If only."

"Get out of the truck," I say and pull him out by his arm. He falls to the ground at the feet of Red and Wesley.

"Why are you doing this? I knew we shouldn't have helped you."

"I was your prisoner all along." I say no more. I don't want Reynolds and the others knowing that I am The Naked Lady. I'm not sure of anything right now, and I certainly don't know how they will react. I point my gun at Samson's face. My finger is ready to pull the trigger.

The only thing I do know for certain is that the whole thing was a lie, an elaborate ruse to hand me over to the Cubans without a fight. Clever really or at least that's what I have to tell myself so I don't feel so foolish for believing them. In one move, they would have traded me to the Cubans and had Ruby for themselves. But why? Why does everyone want Ruby and I dead?

I tighten my finger on the trigger.

"Wait," Wesley says. "No sense in killing him."

"You're right," I say and pull back my pistol. "I'll leave him to the Fangs."

"No, I mean if we want to get Ruby back we might need him as a bargaining tool."

"He's right," Reynolds says.

"He's just their driver," I reason.

"Whatever we do, I reckon we do it quickly," Red adds and points to the base behind us. I can see dozens of soldiers hustling about the base, and a continuous red light is flashing throughout. Even worse, there is a whole army of Fangs inside the base. They are grouped and ordered, and they march towards the gate like a well-trained militia. Red is right. It's time to go.

I nod my head towards the rear doors of the truck. Wesley and Red grab Samson and throw him in the back.

"Reynolds take the wheel," I say and get in the passenger seat. Wesley is sitting on the bench in the back next to Red, who now has the shotgun and is pointing it at Samson across from them. As Reynolds reverses a bit, I can see the gate opening behind us and a swarm of Fangs emptying out of the complex. Reynolds begins to move forward and the back door pops open as we roll over a bumpy root or rock.

"Wait," I yell. "Yoshi is still out there."

"Yoshi!" Wesley and Red shout and whistle.

"Come on, girl," Reynolds says under his breath as he takes the truck onto the road and accelerates.

"There she is," I say. She is dashing towards us. Before I can tell

Reynolds to slow down, I see the host of Fangs right behind her. They are gaining on her, and if we slow down they will overrun us as well.

"Come on, Yoshi," I yell and climb into the back. "Faster, girl."

I pull out my new gun and aim towards the Fangs behind her. It's almost impossible to keep my arm steady on this bumpy road. I don't want to miss and hit her. My heart is beating so fast I feel as if it's going to burst out of my chest. It's getting hard to breathe, and everything is becoming a blur.

Focus...

I take long, deep breaths. Everything slows down, and becomes clearer than ever. I take perfect shots one after another. I see the bullets strike several Fangs right in-between the eyes. They fall over, but are quickly replaced by others. No matter how many I kill, there are still more right on Yoshi's heels.

"Yoshi... No!" I yell.

A Fang that looks like a papi-poo on steroids jumps on Yoshi's back and clinches its jaw around her neck. It hangs there, swinging back and forth as Yoshi continues to charge forward. A Rottweiler Fang, almost the size of Yoshi, leaps at her shoulders and finally brings her to a halt as it sinks its teeth into the top of her head. She cries out as she falls to the ground, and within a second I lose sight of her within the swarming pit of wild Fangs.

I shoot a couple more even though I know it's pointless, and Red fires the shotgun into the crowd, blasting several of them to bits. It hardly makes me feel better. I just want to kill every Fang there is. I sit back down in the passenger seat. Reynolds tries to wipe his eyes without me noticing, so I stare out to the highway ahead and pretend I don't see his grief.

Everyone is quiet for a long time, until Samson finally breaks the silence.

"Mika won't trade your girl for me, you know?"

"Boy, you ain't the smartest fella are you?" Red says. "That's the only reason the Brute hasn't shot your face off yet." He once again

46

points the shotgun at Samson.

"Might as well kill me now. If you deliver me to Mika, I'm dead anyways. I failed a critical mission. The deal was a token for a non-aggression pact. A friendship between Mika and Cuba, but without your Brute... it failed."

Reynolds looks at me, and I'm sure the others are staring too.

"Oh, you didn't know your mysterious friend is the infamous Naked Lady?" He chuckles. I knew I should have killed him.

"It doesn't matter, I reckon," Red says. "The Cubans want him dead, they want us dead, and now they want you dead; and so does Mika. We're all in the same sinking boat here. And that'll be enough talking from the likes of you."

"If we're all the same, why are you pointing your gun at me? Don't you get it? The plan fell through. They don't have The Naked Lady. The Cubans won't deliver Ruby to Mika. They will bring her back and kill her themselves, assuming they haven't already."

"Then we need to stop them on the way and take her back," I say.

"I don't think they'll give her up without a fight," Samson says. "The only way we survive is to give up The Naked Lady."

He gives a smirk to Red, who seems unamused.

"Maybe we can trade you for her," Wesley says.

"Now that sounds like a plan we can all get behind," Reynolds agrees.

"Yee haw," Red says in the most unenthusiastic tone possible.

We continue up the highway. It cuts us through another deserted town; although I wonder how deserted it really is. Maybe there are other survivors like us. The rising sun turns the sky bright purple and orange. Until now, I didn't realize the severity of my exhaustion. I shake my head and take a deep breath. I have to stay alert and on the lookout for Cubans. A fight with them could be disastrous, but we have to get Ruby back before they kill her. If Samson is right, they should be coming back on this road, but if he's wrong then I hope we can catch up to them before they reach Mika.

"So, The Naked Lady, huh?" Reynolds says.

"Have you heard of me? If so, please feel free to share with the class. To me it's just a stupid name."

"I've only heard stories really. You helped end the civil war in Turkey when you killed the Grand *Mufti* of the rebels. In the States, you were considered a war hero. Well that is until the new Sultan of Turkey revived the Ottoman Empire and declared war on Israel and the West. The U.S. was once again embarrassed for aiding their future enemy, and no one had heard about you since. There was a rumor that you went to work for the empire and joined Al-Menzanii when he invaded New York, but I never really believed it."

"First I thought I worked for Nightshade, then Mika, now possibly Al-Man...zayni."

Reynolds laughs. "We just call him Big Al."

Through the side view mirror, I can see a single Fang chasing the van. He looks like he was once a greyhound before he became infected. It's fast. It keeps up with us for a while until Reynolds accelerates. He must have seen it too.

"There's a war going on out there, and we're stuck here fighting dogs," I murmur to myself. "Why does Mika want Ruby dead anyway?"

"They used to work together," Reynolds says and swerves past another large crack in the road. "When war broke out overseas, most of the U.S. forces were immediately sent to defend Israel and Europe. Our own defenses and even the government became, at best, a skeleton crew. With all the fighting going on halfway across the world, no one believed the new Caliphate could muster enough strength for a full attack on the U.S."

"But they did."

"Big Al hit New York first. The assault was quick and painful. What remained of the U.S. forces were pushed as far west as the Mississippi, and as far south as New Jersey. What stopped them from coming further south were Mika and his militia. Ruby and many others rallied to his seemingly worthwhile cause. She became one of his top lieutenants. Mika was soon strong enough that he separated himself from the U.S. and even refused their help in fighting Cuba. He said he didn't need their help, and he was right. The Cuban military's own chemical warfare created the Fangs, and now Florida is so overrun with them it has kept them from advancing any further."

Not for much longer, I think. It seems the Cubans are learning how to use the Fang population to their advantage now.

"When the Fangs were beginning to migrate as far north as Gainesville," Reynolds continues. "Mika decided to seal off Florida completely to keep both the Fangs and the Cubans out of his territory. He began to build a wall. Ruby protested. She tried everything she could to stop him, but he wouldn't listen. She had a daughter named Miranda living in Wauchula with her grandmother. After the Cubans attacked, Ruby had hoped Miranda was still alive, and she refused to let Mika finish his wall no matter what it took. So she came to me, the only weapons and explosives expert she knew, well...at least knew of. When she came to me I...I just had to help her. Besides, I had a cousin living in Florida when the Cubans attacked. I understood what we risked losing. So I built her a couple bombs. These weren't like the movie set explosives I was used to. I gave her enough power to take down that wall, and I even helped her plant them. We set them and took off south. When they went off we were already miles away, but could still see the explosion. It was magnificent. I'm still proud of that one."

"There were a lot of people working on that wall when it exploded," Samson says. Turning my head, I see that he is now crouched in between us. I had thought he was sleeping.

Reynolds has nothing to say back. He's quiet for a long time and just keeps his eyes on the road.

"I am sorry, but that wall had to come down," Reynolds says and looks at me as if seeking approval. I awkwardly nod.

"Many people died on that wall. And for what? Who did you save? I don't see anyone," Samson says.

"We never did find Miranda. We did find Wesley and Red, and Marco came to us later."

"Big deal," Samson says.

"Screw you pal," Red says.

"What about your cousin?" I interject.

"Who Bo? Nah, I went to Bradenton. It was completely razed to the ground. Not a sign of life anywhere."

"Maybe he escaped and went to another town."

"I doubt it. Even if he did survive the air raids, he would have been killed by Fangs or starved to death. Bo wasn't the most resourceful person in the world."

"You'd be surprised. The threat of death can change a man."

"What do you know? You don't even remember anything."

That's not true. I remember seeing Ruby for the first time. I remember her long, black hair shining in the sun as she leaned over to help me up. I remember her almond colored skin contrasting against her pearly white smile. I remember she only has one dimple, but it's a good dimple. I remember her cuffing me, but not wanting to escape or break free because I wanted to stay with her and the others because they were the only friends I've ever had as far as I can remember, and the only people I can make sense of the world with.

"We have to get Ruby back," I say.

"Speak of the devil and she shall appear," Samson says and points ahead.

Parked on the opposite side of the road is the black utility vehicle we saw leaving the gate of the Cuban base last night. Its headlights are still on and all the doors are wide open. No one appears to be inside or around. Reynolds pulls up in front blocking its path, and we all rush out.

Reynolds and Wesley look inside the truck. I look all around, but there's not much to see. The town we passed before has been long gone; now all I see are miles of buttonwood and a mixture of tall cypress trees and silver palms lining both sides of the road. There seems to be no sign of Ruby or any Cubans, until I finally notice a red piece of cloth hanging on a branch at the threshold of the woods. I walk closer. No way I could forget the red tank top that hugged Ruby's thin torso and curvy chest so well.

"Guys," I say holding up the torn piece of cloth. Samson looks at it with a blank stare as if it means nothing, but the others recognize it instantly. Without having to say a word, we immediately enter the woods. It's humid inside the dense brush and we tread as fast as we can. I'm in the lead, but I can tell by his heavy breathing and weighty steps that Reynolds is close behind. I'm assuming the others are after him, but I keep my eyes ahead. I bob and weave through the branches and low hanging palms. It becomes much cooler as we move further beneath the trees. Exhaustion is threatening to overwhelm me, but I force myself to keep moving, staying alert for any signs of Ruby. If they hurt her...I swear I will kill them all.

We finally make it to a wide path that curves and then splits the trees. It leads to an opening in the forest with a series of large ponds separated by muddy medians. I stop in front of the largest pond. After a few moments Reynolds, Wesley, and Red finally catch up.

"No sign of them," Wesley says somberly. He is still carrying his Bible along. I pay no mind to it and scan the open area around the ponds. I see nothing, save for what appears to be a log or branch swaying in the wind on the opposite shoreline of the southernmost pond. I focus my eyes and shield the bright, white sun with my hand.

"*And the light of the sun will shine seven times brighter like the light of seven days,*" Wesley quotes.

Something stretches out and extends above the log-shaped figure. *Jesus,* it's an arm: a hand reaching out for help. Without thinking, I run towards the median between the two ponds, but my boots begin to sink into the muddy ground making, it almost impossible to run any further. I forgo the boots and I dive into the water, swimming as hard as I can towards the other side. I can hear shouting as my head bobs in and out of the water.

Maybe I misjudged the size of this pond, or maybe it's because I haven't slept in over a day, but I'm only half way there when my arms and legs start feeling extremely fatigued. My strokes are turning into frantic splashes. I gasp for air every time I raise my head out of the water with each choppy stroke. My vision is shaky and blurred, but I can see the shoreline getting closer, and Ruby is there...reaching out to me. At least I hope it actually is her and not just a mirage born from my incessant need to find her combined with this damned humidity.

I push forward with what little strength I have left in my arms and legs. I nearly choke on the hot air as I finally make it to the shore and crawl through the sandy mud towards Ruby.

Sunlight gleams off her hazel eyes as I kneel over her. I hold her face. There is bad bruising across her cheek and chin.

"What happened?" I try to steady my shaking voice as I frantically search her body for more wounds. Her shirt is torn, exposing her entire midriff. There is a gash on her lower abdomen that pulses out crimson liquid every time she exhales.

"You've been stabbed," I stammer. I take off my shirt and, using both hands; I twist it and wring out as much water as I can. I press it against her wound, feeling my heart sink as she writhes and clenches her teeth. "Ruby, where are the Cubans?"

She breathes in short, little bursts.

"I ran...they followed me here. I tried fighting. There were four of them...the big one...he pinned me down. He tried to pull my shorts off... so I spit on him and jabbed him in the throat." A slight smile appears on her face, but it's gone as fast as it appeared. "He couldn't breathe, but before I could shove him off of me, the bearded one stabbed me." Her eyes well up into little, light brown pools, and I feel a twinge of self-loathing for thinking they're beautiful that way.

"I...I couldn't help it. I let them hear me scream. I...let them hear my pain."

"It's okay," I say and use my thumb to wipe the only tear she let escape.

"We're going to get you out of here and fix you up in no time."

"No. We're dead. We're all dead...the soldiers were chased down and torn apart," she says with a slight quiver on her lip.

"It's okay. There are no Fangs around, and we have guns in case they do come."

"No," she says. Her face is losing color, and she seems as if she can barely hold up her eyelids. She raises her hand up again and points to the sky. I realize now a large shadow engulfs us. I look up above me. A locust-like creature the size of a large horse spreads out its wings, completely blocking out the sun and the sky as it descends on me with sharp talons. Its eyes are as red as the fresh blood on Ruby's abs.

6

For the first time that I can remember, I am truly terrified. My whole body trembles as I shield Ruby and stare at this giant beast with a face like a locust and long, black hair. Sharp, lion-like teeth appear, ready to devour me. Its talons, as sharp as meat hooks, reach for me. A loud, crackling boom reverberates around me and the beast shrieks. Reynolds fires the combat shotgun once more and the beast struggles to flap its immense wings. It twists and turns and snaps and screeches at Reynolds, but finally flutters and crashes to the ground before reaching him.

"What the hell was that?" he says. The skin above his upper lip is glistening.

I pick up Ruby and hold her in my arms. "We have to get out of here," I say.

"You won't hear an argument from me."

The creature twitches and flaps its wings, but they only wither and break apart as they smash futilely against the ground. We force our way through the thick median as fast as we can.

"What in Sam Hill was that?" Red says when we finally get back to them.

"*And he opened the bottomless pit, and behold locusts came upon the earth,*" Wesley says.

"Whatever it is, it's infected just like the Fangs. Ruby says there are more," I explain. Ruby is in my arms with her head lying on my chest. She is drifting in and out of consciousness.

"How badly is she injured?" Wesley says and grabs my arm.

"She's got a knife wound in her belly," I say, still feeling slightly sick.

"How bad? I reckon I can sew it up if it's not too deep." Red lifts up my shirt from her stomach and examines the bloody wound. "I don't think the blade punctured any organs. If we get her back to the community center, I can patch her up. Time in the hyperbaric chamber will probably do her some good too, but we have to hurry. She's losing a lot of blood."

I agree. I want to get as far away from this place as possible. If any more of those giant locusts shows up, we don't stand a chance. The trees are up ahead. My arms are tired. I can see veins protruding along my forearms and up towards my biceps. It would be much easier if I could just fling her over my shoulder, but I don't want to upset her wound any further. I just want to get her back so Red can fix this as quickly as possible.

Thick mud envelops my boots and threatens to entrap me with every step. My legs ache and my feet are cramping. Ruby rouses slightly and points to the sky behind me.

"No, don't do that now. We're so close," I say, but I can't help looking behind. I'm blinded by the bright rays of the sun, but when my eyes finally adjust I can see a swarm of infected locusts, that might even be bigger than the first one we encountered, flying straight towards us. My heart sinks so deep in my chest that I'm no longer sure if it's still beating or even still there for that matter.

"Faster," I yell. "They're coming." I dash past everyone ignoring all the pain in my arms, shoulders, and legs. I'm ahead for only a moment. Soon Wesley, Reynolds, and Red speed by me. I can hear the locusts getting closer. Dozens of wings flapping and fluttering reverberate through the airwaves like a fleet of helicopters advancing into battle. The swarm blocks out the sun as they swoop down towards me. I'm almost there. My whole body is dripping with sweat. I'm afraid I might let Ruby slip out of my grip, but I hold onto her as tight as I can.

Right behind me I hear a shriek so loud I think my eardrums might burst. I feel the hot breath of one of the creatures on my neck and I leap forward as far as I can through the entrance of the woods. Twisting myself in the air, I'm able to crash to the ground on my back. I feel root and rock scrape against my skin as I slide into the forest, but I keep hold of Ruby on top of me. One of the giant beasts folds its wings and tries to fit itself in-between the trees, crawling towards us. The top of its insectoid head has yellow markings that make it look as if it's wearing a crown.

Reynolds fires another thunderous shot at the infected locust. The beast is thrown back and lets out a hideous scream of pain as it crashes to the ground. More of them circling above us over the tree line match its scream, as if they feel it too. The deafening chorus of screaming bugs wakes Ruby out of unconsciousness. Her eyes widen.

"Wesley, grab Ruby," Reynolds commands. "We need to get to the truck."

Wesley hands his Bible to Red and picks her up off of me. I would object, but I know I can't carry her any further without rest. Reynolds pulls me up with his free hand and Red hands me the Glock that slipped out of my waistband when I fell. We continue through the forest in the shadows of the great beasts above. Their wide, spinning circle follows us as we move. It's humid inside the darkness cast by the trees and beasts, but at least my back and shoulders are protected from the scorching sunrays. Every time there's a break in the trees, one or more of the locusts attempt to swoop down, only to flee back to the swarm with a screech when it realizes it has to close its long wings. It seems they aren't used to being this big, and perhaps they haven't been for very long. What once was their home, they are now too big to fit into.

Suddenly, they all scatter. I realize I'm not the only one watching them. The others are stopped in front of me looking up.

"What happened? Where did they go?" I wonder aloud.

"I reckon they finally gave up."

"*One woe is past. Behold, still more come after these things,*" Wesley recites. Ruby looks as comfortable and peaceful in his arms as she did in mine, and I'm ashamed to admit that I'm jealous.

"Locusts don't give up until they've eaten everything in sight," Reynolds says.

"Let's keep moving," Wesley says.

"For once I agree with you," Reynolds says.

We keep moving. Palms, loose branches, and random bushes of thorns scrape my skin. Roots and long vines try to trip me with every step, but I continue to dodge through every new obstacle, hoping each time to see a break in the trees and the truck parked ahead. The way out seems much longer than the way in.

I can hear trees and branches rustling above and behind me. A loud thud quiets the susurrus and I turn quickly. A giant locust stands over me. Its enflamed eyes seem to examine me. Its wings are folded in on its back, making its body look even bulkier and possibly more hideous. It hisses loudly at me. I spin around, but another loud thud ahead stops the others in front of me. Another one lands on each side...and now we're completely surrounded. The humongous insects creep towards us, forcing each of us backward until we're huddled in-between them like easy prey.

I aim my gun at the one in front of me. I doubt it will do much against the thick skin of its chest. It looks as if it's wearing a breastplate of armor. I wish I was the one holding the shotgun, but maybe if I shoot it in the crown it will be enough. There are still many more circling above. I don't think we have enough bullets for them all. The one in front of me steps closer with its long, sharp legs. My finger tightens against the trigger. I aim right in-between its hideous red eyes.

"Don't," Ruby whispers, so weakly that I almost didn't hear it. "Don't attack them."

"What? Have you lost your mind?" Red says. His freckly face is covered in sweat. "Shoot the doggone thing."

"They killed the Cubans when they shot at them. They left me alone. Drop your guns."

"This is a bad idea," I say as the monster steps closer to me.

"Has she ever led us wrong?" Wesley counters. Reynolds drops the shotgun, without a second of hesitation. Red and I look at him in disbelief, and I'm tempted to pick it up. I look at Ruby. She is staring at me.

I lay down my pistol on the ground, feeling like a fool. She better be right. I can smell the creature's breath as it lets out a haunting hiss in my face. It smells like grass and dead things. Its mouth is big enough to take off one of my limbs with one bite, and its talons can impale me and rip me to shreds with ease. I stay as still as I can, offering no resistance. I attempt to show no fear, but the perspiration pouring from forehead and my palpitating heart is proving me a liar.

It stands up on two legs and towers over me. It could crush me in an instant, but instead it spreads its wings as far as the neighboring trees permit and launches itself back into the sky. The others quickly follow suit and disappear into the circling swarm.

My long-winded exhale joins the same song from the others, but no one dares says a word. We just pick up our guns and keep marching forward as fast as we can. Thankfully, it isn't much longer until the end of the collection of trees is finally in front of us. The SUV and the truck are still out front, and Samson is leaning against the black SUV, smoking a cigarette and watching the sky.

I quickly remember how hot and bright it is as we leave the shade of the trees and the fleeing swarm.

"We could have used your help," Reynolds says. I disagree. I doubt he would have listened to Ruby. He might have gotten us all killed.

Samson flicks his cigarette onto the road and he pushes out puffs of white smoke from his nostrils.

"We should take this. There's more room and gas, plus it has weapons," he says, and I now realize he has a submachine gun hanging from a strap around his neck.

Reynolds sneers at him, and now I know I've officially been replaced as the most untrustworthy of the group.

"Relax," Samson says and tosses a water bottle at him. "There's more in the truck."

"Fine, but I'm driving," Reynolds says and gulps down the whole bottle in no time. Wesley and I lay Ruby down in the back seat before taking drinks of our own. The water is warm, but still extremely refreshing.

Wesley stays in the back with Ruby and I sit in the middle row with Samson, but not before noticing the stockpile of firearms in the back. I grab ammo clips and an ankle holster for my Glock. Red takes an AR-15 before climbing into the passenger seat while Reynolds maneuvers a U-turn to get back on the main road that leads north.

"Where are you taking us wise leader?" Samson says. His black, curly hair is so thin that I can see his scalp in several spots.

"We're going back to the community center in Wauchula. Healing Ruby is the priority. We'll decide where to go next when she's better."

"Great idea. Take us back to the place where everyone knows we are."

"Samson's sarcasm aside, I reckon he's right. We can't hope to survive there very long."

"Ruby is tough. She'll heal quickly," I say.

"She's also stubborn. You know as well as I do she won't leave," Samson says and Reynolds stares at him through the rearview mirror.

"I know more about Ruby than you think. Let's not forget my boss is her husband."

Husband?

"Ex-husband," Reynolds snaps back.

"According to what law? What judge sat over their divorce? Who decides the end of a marriage in No-man's land?"

"The fact that he wants her dead, for starters," I chime in.

"He doesn't want her dead. He wants her back."

"Well, he can't have her," Reynolds says.

"Oh don't worry. You can keep your little crush..."

Crush?

"...he doesn't want her as a wife anymore after she destroyed his precious wall. But he still wants her back safe in his territory instead of chasing ghosts in this wasteland."

"Miranda," Ruby whispers in her sleep.

"She's dead. Everyone knows it, except for Ruby," Samson says.

"What do you propose?" Wesley says.

"We return to Mika," his voice is suddenly louder.

"I thought he wants you dead, and all of us dead for that matter."

"Not true, that's just what she wants you to believe. On the contrary, he would welcome those who bring her back. Even you, Naked Lady."

"And you get the prize for bringing both Ruby and The Naked Lady back to him, huh?" I say.

Samson shrugs and tries to hide a smirk. "For Ruby, maybe. You're just a bonus. The others and I were sent to get Ruby. The Cubans intended to retrieve you, but grabbed her when they realized you weren't there anymore. We were outnumbered, so Jax had to improvise. We decided to take you and try to make a deal. It was nothing personal. We didn't want to give you up to the Cubans, but it was the only way to get Ruby back."

"And I suppose a possible alliance with the Cubans had nothing to do with it either," I say sarcastically. "How did you even know who I was? Or that I would be there?"

"Mika is not stupid. He knows every move the U.S. is doing. He probably knew your mission long before you did, and he monitors all transmissions coming from American airships. He knew you went down, and he heard your voice on the radio. It was only logical that you might have found your way to Ruby's little fort."

So I am a U.S. agent. But I still don't know why I was in the hyperbaric chamber, and why the incoming transmission warned that I was a terrorist, or where the hell my airship was going...Mika has answers. Going to him doesn't seem like the worst idea, even if it will help Samson.

"Why don't we put Ruby inside the chamber, secure it in the back of your pick-up truck, and we'll all drive to Mika together?" I ask

Reynolds.

"Are you off your rocker?" Red says. "We bring Ruby to Mika without her say and she'll be carving our tombstones with that big ass knife of hers."

"Maybe when she—,"

"Out of the question," Reynolds says before I can finish. "We let her heal, and then see what she wants to do."

"And when she's too stubborn to leave?" Samson says.

"Then we will stay by her side."

"And surely die by it as well..."

We pass through what remains of a town dotted with small shacks that line both sides of the highway. Further inland, the land is mostly huddles of rubble that stretch for a mile or so. There are big letters spray-painted on the boarded-up doors of a few of the makeshift houses. "*Help us*" one says in red letters. "*The blood dogs are coming*" says another in white paint. "*God is dead*" reads the last house we pass. Scrappy bushes and trees are all we see the rest of the trip.

It's mid-afternoon when Samson chuckles to himself.

"The fort of the last Floridians," he says.

The community center is up ahead. I see the fire pit and my stomach rumbles. I never thought I would be so excited for Red's famous cornmeal soup. Even the sight of buzzards picking apart Marco's remains can't ruin my appetite right now.

Reynolds parks next to his old pickup truck.

"I'm going to start boiling some water," Red says. "Ruby, we're going to get you fixed up, okay?"

I help Wesley carry her into the shade cast by the community center wall. We lay her on the grassy dirt, and Reynolds balls up an old, blue blanket and rests her head on it. She's so still now that if I didn't notice her chest slightly expanding as she breathes, I might mistake her for dead. Wesley pulls my blood-drenched shirt off her wound. The gash still oozes blood, but not as much as before.

After a few minutes, Red comes over with a bottle of clean water and a first aid kit. When Red pulls out the needle, I notice his hands are shaking. Before I can object, Reynolds throws me an old, grey shirt with a hole near the armpit to put on and then nods at me.

"Come on. Let him do his thing. We can start cooking dinner."

"I think someone else should be doing that," I say, indicating towards his still shaking hands.

"Relax, he just gets nervous when people are watching him. He's patched me up several times." He shows off a long scar on the inside of his bicep, and pulls the collar of his shirt over to reveal another on his upper chest. "Trust me. I wouldn't let him go near her with a needle if I didn't think he was good."

There's a big, grey garbage can on wheels with a lid on it near the fire pit. Inside, it is half full with yellow cornmeal, and a clear scooper sitting on top of the mound. Reynolds grabs a large, metal pot.

"Two," he says. I put two heaping scoops into the pot. He pours some clean water into it, and then puts it over the fire,

"I have a surprise. Don't tell the others yet. I found it in the truck." With a smile, he pulls out a slab of dried bacon meat. My eyes widen, and I can feel my mouth watering as he rips up the meat and drops it in the pot. I mix it in with a long, wooden spoon. I hear stomach growls, but I'm not sure if it's Reynolds' or mine.

"You can't be serious," Samson says coming up from behind us. "You guys are over here smiling and drooling over this slop? And here I thought I was sick of rations." He crinkles his nose.

I scowl at him. "Be happy you're getting anything at all."

"Damn Cubans had to ruin our mission. In Mika's militia, officers and their men get to eat whatever they want when they complete a mission. The whole way down here, Jax and I debated what we were going to have when we brought Ruby back. I should be eating steak and mashed potatoes right now...maybe with some buttered asparagus. Jax wanted to waste our meal on pizza." He laughs. "Not even a pizza with anything good on it, just a plain cheese pizza."

"That does sound good right now," I say.

"I just hope they didn't kill him," he says softly and looks at his feet.

Red and Wesley come over.

"Does my big, freckled nose deceive me, or is that pork I smell?" Red says with a smile.

Reynolds laughs. "I found some in the truck. I figured I'd share." He winks at me.

"You are a mighty fine human being," Red says and takes in a deep breath. "Well, I cleaned her wound and stitched her up nicely. The preacher here even said a prayer for her too. Once we get her fed, we can put her in the chamber."

"I'll do it."

Reynolds looks at me queerly for a moment, but then nods.

I sit next to her with two bowls, and the smell of food wakes her up a bit. I'm able to help her eat most of the bowl before she rests her head on my leg and nods off again. My porridge is cold by the time I get to it, but I don't care. I don't know if it's the meat mixed in or how hungry I am, but it's delicious. There's not a drop left in my bowl when I'm finished.

Red and Samson are eating seconds at the table when Wesley and Reynolds come over. Wesley bends over and scoops her in his arms. "Up you go," he says as he lifts her up. Reynolds and I follow him around to the other side of the wall where the chamber is.

In front of it lies a humungous Fang, as big as the calm ones I saw at the Cuban base. It raises its swollen head and shows its sharp teeth when it spots us. Its red fur matches its red eyes. It was once an English mastiff.

"Yoshi," Ruby whispers.

7

What once was Yoshi no longer exists. This creature has Yoshi's face, only more fat and swollen and its body is almost twice the size it was before. Engorged muscles look as if they are going to rip out beneath her skin and fur. Her eyes are storming with fire. Yellowish, bubbling foam swells up between her spike-like teeth, and her growl stops us in our tracks. No one moves a muscle.

"Yoshi," Ruby says again. The colossal Fang stops growling, hides her teeth, and tilts her head. Ruby reaches her hand out, and Wesley takes a step forward. Yoshi shakes her whole body, and once again she growls and shows her enormous teeth. She attempts to stand, but instead retracts her hind leg and falls on her front side.

"She's injured," Reynolds says.

"Bring me to her," Ruby says.

"I don't think that's a good idea," I say, but Wesley doesn't listen. With slow, careful steps he carries Ruby over to her old friend. Yoshi shakes her head and snarls so loudly that Wesley takes a step back.

"It's okay baby. It's me," Ruby says in a soft voice.

Yoshi tilts her head again, but this time with a squeaky whimper. Ruby reaches out to her. Yoshi lifts her head to the sky and howls so loud I wonder if the Cubans can hear it all the way at their base. Her tail wags a bit as Ruby places her hand on top of her head. Ruby stares into Yoshi's big, red eyes. Ruby is crying.

"Put her in with me," Ruby says.

"What?" I say. She must be delirious. Even if Yoshi hadn't become a human-eating Fang, they would hardly fit into the chamber together.

"Are you nuts?" Red asks incredulously. "We can't put you in there with a Fang."

"Do it," Ruby says.

"Ruby, we can't," Reynolds pleads and steps forward. Yoshi leans up and snarls at him. He quickly lifts his hands and retreats a couple of steps.

"Trust me. I'll be okay."

Wesley gently places Ruby inside the chamber.

"Come on girl," Ruby says. Yoshi winces, struggles to stand, and limps towards the chamber. She climbs in and Ruby wraps her arms around her. I don't think this is a good idea, but Ruby's smile is so big that I keep my mouth shut. I wonder if my face is as pale as Reynolds'. "Don't worry," she says as Wesley closes the door with woman and Fang together inside.

The four of us stay, looking inside the glass at them. I have my hand on my gun, and I'm ready to use it if Yoshi makes any move that could be harmful to Ruby. But it isn't long until woman and beast fall into an oxygen-induced hibernation. We finally leave them to their rest and join Samson by the fire. It's hot enough without the flames, but it seems to be keeping the mosquitos away.

"It's a terrible idea to keep one of those things around. Even if it is fond of the girl," Samson says. He has a half full bottle of rum that he must have gotten from the trunk of the SUV. He hands it to me after taking a swig. I take a big sip. It's spicy and harsh. It feels warm going down my throat and into my stomach.

"It seems it only wants to protect her," I say and hand the bottle to Reynolds.

"Yes, but how long until it sees one of us a threat to her? Say the wrong thing or take a wrong step and it will kill you...no matter what Ruby says," Samson reasons.

"I reckon he's right. I loved Yoshi as much as the next guy, but that thing is no longer Yoshi. It's uncontrollable."

"No it's not. They can be controlled," I snap back. Eight narrowed eyes look at me.

"Say again?" Red says.

"The Cubans. I saw it. They had trained Fangs, well-trained ones. They were terrifying, but calm. It seemed like they were specifically bred to lead the other Fangs."

"What do you mean?" Reynolds says.

"They were bigger and calm. All they had to do was walk by a wild Fang, and it would submit. A single trainer ordered two of them to calm down more than fifty wild ones, and they listened."

"If they can use all the Fangs in Florida as a well-trained army, there will be no stopping them," Reynolds says.

"Too bad you and Ruby blew up that wall, huh?" Samson says. "We have to get to Mika and tell him."

"Ruby won't leave."

Red hands me the bottle and I take another drink. My head is already reeling.

"Does she really think her kid could possibly still be alive?" I say.

"Her daughter used to come here every day after school. She used to write letters to Ruby telling her that each afternoon she arrived hoping her mom would be there to surprise her. Ruby would try to make plans but the war was always in the way. A mission or a battle would inevitably come up. By the time she finally got here, it was too late. Florida was destroyed. Ruby believes if Miranda is still alive out there somewhere, she'll come here looking for her."

Samson has no response for a change. None of us do. I just stare into the flames. Swirls of orange and red rise up into the air, before transforming into a harsh, grey smoke. I wonder if Miranda is really still alive, or if Ruby is just holding onto some false hope. Even if she was, what chance could she stand on her own against millions of Fangs? Although, if she is as tough as Ruby perhaps it wouldn't be such a long shot.

When the fire begins to diminish and the moon is floating high above us, the bottle of rum is nearly empty. We all stumble our way to the SUV and stuff ourselves inside, except for Reynolds, who chooses instead to sleep standing up behind the Fang shield. He says he's used to it, but reclining in the car seat seems so much better to me. It feels good to finally rest.

Three uneventful days pass. Aside from a stray Fang or two, no real danger threatens us openly, but we stay alert. The following morning, we are sitting at the picnic table eating more cornmeal for breakfast. It's a bright and oddly quiet morning. The only sound is the slight howl of a breeze that chills my skin. I realize that I haven't heard a bird singing or even an insect chirping.

"Ruby is looking much better," Red says and sits down next to Reynolds with a full bowl. "I think we can wake her and the dog in a day or two."

"Fang," Samson corrects him. "If it were up to me, we'd keep them both locked in that thing until we get them to Mika."

"I hate to agree with him, but that's not the worst plan," Red says. "Waiting here any longer is asking for trouble."

"And leaving is much better?" I ask. "How do we even know if he's telling the truth? Mika might want to kill us all." I spoon my last bit of cornmeal gruel into my mouth. I must admit, I'm starting to like the taste. I don't think Samson has gotten used to it though. He hasn't even taken one bite. He gets up and throws his spoon down on the table. It bounces off and falls to the sandy ground.

"I'm tired of this wasteland. And I'm tired of eating dirt soup. I'm going hunting," he says. He picks up his submachine gun and walks towards the woods behind the community center.

"Maybe he'll bring me back one of them big locusts to cook," Red says.

"If we're lucky, he won't come back at all," Reynolds says and spits on the ground.

"Probably won't. Who knows what other unholy creatures have been infected and are lurking around those woods."

"We might need him though if we run into trouble in Mika's territory," I say, but really I just like having his suspicious ass around. No one seems to question my loyalty anymore. Samson was smart to grab a weapon while we went after Ruby. I doubt they would have let him have one otherwise.

"We don't need him; we have Mika's wife," Reynolds points out and spits again. He leaves the table and goes to the hyperbaric chamber.

Wesley finally looks up from the Bible that he's been reading all morning.

"He might be more afraid to leave this place than Ruby is. *Love is patient, love is kind,* but sometimes it blinds a man from the right choice," he says and stares at me. I awkwardly look away.

"Well, don't tell him what that book says about divorce. I reckon he won't like it," Red says and saves me from Wesley's knowing stare. He buries his face back in the Bible and shuffles the thin pages back and forth.

Hours later, there are thick, dark clouds coming from the south west. They conceal the burning sunrays and bring with them a cool breeze that dries my sweat. I can't help but chuckle when I see Samson return empty-handed with a big scowl on his face.

"Give me that big wrench again," Reynolds says from underneath his pickup truck. I grab a wrench that is lying on the hood and place it into his outstretched hand. I'm helping, well more like watching Reynolds try and fix a leak in his carburetor.

"I'm guessing now you'll enjoy some of my famous porridge," I hear Red say to Samson.

"Give it to me," Samson says.

"You better hurry. A storm is coming," I say to Reynolds as he finally slides out from under the hood.

"I need to flush it," he says.

I can see rain coming down hard on the ghost town to the south and moving in our direction. It's loud as it falls on the abandoned houses and stores.

"Hail," Reynolds says. "Hail," he says again louder for the others to hear. Red looks back, and then he and Wesley cover up his pots and trashcan of cornmeal with lids. They stretch a big blue tarp over it all and pin the corners to the ground.

"We'll have to wait it out in the SUV," Reynolds says. Samson is now standing next to us, staring at the oncoming storm. He seems to always have one hand grasping or grazing his submachine gun. He points it ahead, as if he can fight the storm with bullets. Reynolds almost trips over himself as he grabs his shotgun from underneath the wheel of his pickup. He also aims it towards the oncoming storm. I immediately think it might be locusts, but instead I see a man coming our way.

The man walks with a heavy limp, dragging his right foot with every step. His arm dangles at his side uselessly. He must be injured, but he moves oddly fast towards us. If he's in pain, he doesn't show it.

"Not another step, sir," Reynolds calls out to the man, but he keeps moving towards us. The hailstorm trails him almost by the step.

"Please stop," Reynolds says. "We will fire."

I reach for the pistol strapped to my ankle and point it at the figure. He keeps moving towards us like a mad man. His lips are moving, but only muffled grunts come out. Across his chest, there's a large tear in his blue shirt. His black pants are tattered and worn, and I can see he has only has one boot on. I recognize his uniform. I squint. I recognize his face too.

"Jax," I whisper. His face is swollen and his lips blue and cracked, but his eyes are blazing red, forced wide open by his lack of eyelids.

"What have they done to you?" Samson yells out so loudly he sounds like a monster himself.

Jax's crimson eyes stare blankly ahead as he moves uncomfortably close to us. Large pieces of hail thump and crack against the ground behind him.

"He's no longer Jax," Samson says and opens fire. Reynolds and I follow suit and Jax's body flails and falls back onto the ground. His body convulses there for a few moments. It isn't until the hail reaches him that he finally lays still.

"Into the truck," Reynolds shouts.

Reynolds and I climb in the front seats as fast as we can. Wesley and Red are already sitting in the middle row.

"Samson," I yell. He's still outside, staring at his dead friend. "Come on. Get in!" He finally hustles over and climbs into the back seat. As soon as we close the doors, hail is already pounding the roof.

"What the hell was that?" Red says. The question is cringeworthy.

"He was my friend," Samson says and almost chokes on his words. "They infected him."

"I didn't even know that was possible," Reynolds says.

"It is possible. We've seen it before. In Jersey, the Caliphate used a similar weapon. After they saw what it was doing to dogs here, they must have experimented with it and learned how to use it on humans." He sounds as if he's about to cry. I really hope he doesn't. No one here is fit to console him, except for maybe Wesley.

"Does it say anything in that book of yours about zombies?" I say quietly to Wesley.

"He's not a zombie!" Samson shouts.

Some comfort I am.

"If they can now infect any animal and humans too who will be able to stop them?" Red says.

"That...thing wasn't exactly threatening. Look how easily we killed it," Reynolds muses.

"His name was Jax," Samson corrects him.

"One of them is hardly a threat perhaps, but what about a hundred or a thousand of them coming for us?" I counter. "If the Cubans and the Caliphate can turn their captured enemies into weapons, we don't stand much of a chance." I can't even consider the thought of being infected myself. If Jax and Samson had their way that would have been me we just killed. That realization makes me no longer feel bad for Samson. In fact, I want to kick him out into the hail and put a bullet through his head.

"Maybe the Cubans didn't infect him?" Wesley says.

"What are you saying? We just shot him for nothing?" Samson says.

"Maybe he was just injured or sick," Red says.

"What about his red eyes? He definitely had red eyes," I say.

"I mean perhaps he was infected another way. Maybe he escaped the Cubans and was bitten by a Fang on the way here," Wesley says.

"Is that possible?" I question.

"This isn't a movie," Reynolds says.

"It happened to Yoshi," Wesley says, and everyone shuts up. "If the Cubans had infected him they wouldn't only send one, they would send an entire army of them."

"Maybe he was a scout, maybe an army is coming next," Samson says. We all look behind us, except for Red. Thankfully, there is no army coming yet.

"Guys," Red says. He's staring at the hyperbaric chamber. "If Wesley is right...then Ruby is infected."

"What are you talking about? She wasn't bitten," Reynolds says as if he is personally insulted.

"She said she was stabbed," I say.

"No, she was bitten. She told me when I was stitching her up. I promised not to say anything. I didn't think it mattered."

I look at the chamber. I can hardly see it through the hailstorm. Large chunks of ice smash and shatter against the glass of the chamber. It looks like it's rocking back and forth, but I can't tell if it's just my imagination.

A chunk of hail the size of a softball slams through the rear glass of Reynolds' pickup truck.

"My God," Wesley says and another hail chunk takes out the side-view mirror clean off.

"This storm is going to destroy our vehicles!" Reynolds says.

"And the chamber," I say and, without another thought, I open my door and throw myself out into the hail. I shut the door behind me, quieting the objections and questions from the others. Thousands of icy rocks fall and detonate around me like enemy mortars. Many smaller ones break and bruise my skin as I rush towards Ruby, not knowing if I'm going to rescue her or kill her.

8

I'm lying on the ground face up. There's no more hail, but dark, bluish-grey clouds are still struggling to imprison the sun to no avail. Bright rays escape from the cluster of clouds. My head is throbbing, but I manage to lift it. The chamber is still ahead of me. It looks like I never made it to Ruby. The door is swung open and the glass portion has a fist-sized hole in it, along with chips and scattered cracks. A red light is flashing inside. I sit up and look around. My eye eyesight is hazy, but it seems to be slowly returning to normal. *Where is everyone?* The SUV is empty and so is the truck. It seems as though Ruby and Yoshi escaped. Maybe the others are hunting her down now...or maybe she is hunting them.

It's quiet. The only thing I hear is a slight whisper of the wind. I attempt to get up, but stop when I see the great beast once again standing in front of me. Yoshi stares at me. Her muscles are swelling from her chest and legs.

Slowly, I bring my hand down my own leg, but before I can grab my pistol, she charges and pounces on me. She knocks me flat on my back and pins me down with her incredible weight. Saliva drips from the sides of her snout all over my cheeks and nose. She lowers her freakish head to mine. With one bite from her massive jaw, she could rip half my face off. She stares into my eyes. Her eyes are...not red. They are a yellowish-brown.

Her mouth opens wide, and her big, wet tongue slithers across my face again and again. As disgusting as it is I can't help but laugh, which makes her tail wag and her tongue lick even more.

"There he is," I hear Ruby say. "Yoshi heel!"

Yoshi finally jumps off me and dashes over to Ruby in only a few strides. Thankfully, Ruby's eyes aren't red either. They're hazel, like they always were, but the reflection of the sunlight makes them appear pale yellow. There is a long line of discoloration across the muscles of her abdomen, where her wound once was. I didn't think a wound as big as hers could be healed so fast. It's no wonder that everyone wanted the hyperbaric chamber so badly.

She smiles at me and reaches out her hand. It's soft, but strong enough to pull me up. She turns from me. "Guys, he's over here," She says.

Moments later, the others emerge from behind and inside the walls of the community center. I pet Yoshi on her head as she pants and wags her tail some more.

"She's not infected?" I ask. I don't understand how it's possible.

"Not anymore and neither am I," Ruby says.

"How?"

She shrugs her cinnamon-colored shoulders and looks at the chamber.

"Apparently a dose of highly concentrated oxygen is the cure," she says.

"We've been looking all over for you," Reynolds says. "We saw you get hit in the head with a fist-sized chunk of hail. You should have heard the thump. I thought for sure it would knock you out, but instead you just wobbled off. I guess you came right back to where it hit you."

"I guess. I don't remember anything."

"Oh shoot, not this again. Do you know where you are?" Red says with a smirk.

"Yes of course," I say and smile at Ruby, but she looks at Reynolds.

"Now that you're found we can get ready to leave," he says almost angrily while looking back at Ruby.

"Where to?" I ask.

"To Mika's country," Ruby says.

I don't know how Samson was able to convince Ruby to leave, but I'd rather not ask. I just nod my head.

"We'll have to take the SUV. We have just enough gas to get us to the fuel station in Plant City. Pack lightly. It will only take us a few hours to get to Mika's territory," Ruby orders. "Red, we should eat before we go."

Ruby grabs my arm and leads me towards the picnic table while Red starts cooking and the others load the SUV with supplies.

"They told me you're The Naked Lady," she says almost whispering.

"So they say, but I have no recollection of it."

"Samson says Mika won't kill you, but he doesn't know Mika like I do—"

"You're married to him."

"Only in his country, but regardless of what Wesley says, that means nothing to me. The same way his child meant nothing to him. Nevertheless, I do know him well and he knows you well. He will kill you if you come with us." She stares at me with big eyes. She must see the confusion on my face. "The U.S. used you many times to thwart his missions and silently kill some of his generals."

"I thought they were allies."

"On the surface perhaps, but enemies with a common enemy are still enemies. The U.S. of course would deny any involvement every time, but Mika is a suspicious man. He will arrest you the moment you step into his country and surely execute you after."

"Samson has been lying to me since I met him. There is no evidence I am who he says I am."

She says nothing for almost a minute and turns away from me.

"After we fill up you can follow the highway to Clearwater. Once there, finding a boat shouldn't be difficult. You'll need to go as far as Louisiana to get past Mika's territory."

"No. I want to go with you. I'm not—"

"It's not an option. I'm sorry," she says definitively and walks towards the SUV. I sit at the table and watch her gracefully tell the others what things she wants and doesn't want loaded into the vehicle. Yoshi follows her every move. *This isn't fair. I worked so hard to rescue them and save her, just to be dumped off at the nearest exit.* Reynolds says something I can't make out and Ruby laughs and touches his arm. *What does she see in him? Doesn't she know who I am? I am The Naked Lady. I suppose that's precisely the problem. I have to stop thinking about Ruby. Maybe going to the U.S. will be a good thing. At least I'll be able to find out who I really am. Who knows, maybe I'm happily married and have a family. The only problem is...I want Ruby. How can I just leave them? They're my only friends in the world. And besides, I have this inexplicable urge to meet Mika. I feel like some purpose is calling me to him. Maybe he knows more about me than they'll allow me to believe. I have to get there, if not with them then some other way.*

After a rushed lunch, we all squeeze into the SUV. Reynolds drives and Ruby is in the passenger seat. Yoshi is squeezed in-between Red and Wesley, and of course the newest members of the group are in the back. One will be deserted, the other will be rewarded.

Reynolds take us north on the broken asphalt of the highway.

"So tell me Samson, does Mika still have that horrible cat?" Ruby asks.

Samson smiles. "You of all people would know that Mika hates cats. I suppose you were trying to test me to see if I actually work for him? Fine, I'll indulge you. He has two pet ferrets: Milo and Laney. They sleep with him in his barn on Chickering Lane. His mother's name was Miranda and so was his daughter's. And his wife's name is Ruby."

It gets uncomfortably quiet.

"You've been gone a long time now. You don't recognize me, because I was in the North fighting Big Al for our freedom while you were blowing up a wall that could keep it."

Surprisingly, no one has a response.

"I suppose though," he continues. "You were right to do so."

She looks back at him, suspecting mockery.

"I won't pretend I care about you or your ragtag team of warriors here. And I don't pretend to believe there are any more survivors in this godforsaken state. Nevertheless, our territory is getting smaller and smaller with every battle. Even battles we won we would still have to flee. The wall would only seal us in."

"Why would you flee if you won?" I say.

"Like I said, Big Al has the same chemical weapons the regime in Cuba used against Florida. Why do you think I shot Jax so fast? It wasn't the first time I've seen an infected human. The battle of Bergenline Avenue was easy. We had Big Al's forces outnumbered and outgunned. Before we overtook them completely, they gassed a part of our unit. It didn't seem to do anything though. Our medics cleared everyone, and we had few casualties. It was almost too easy. We heard of several other victories throughout northern New Jersey, and even the U.S. was managing decisive victories in Pennsylvania with the National Guard. It looked like the invasion was coming to a halt.

"We set up camp on 57th street. The very next night, the men who had been hit with the gas started acting strangely. I remember this young guy. We called him 'Choir Boy' because he was better at singing hymns than fighting. He barged into our tent that night. Usually it was to complain that we were being too loud and drunk, but this time his eyes were red and he slurred his words so bad we couldn't understand him. If we didn't know any better, we would have thought he was drunk too. Jax suggested he might be having a stroke, but again the medics checked him out and said there was nothing wrong with him. A day later, it became worse. He and a few others became violent and berserk. They were uncontrollable and they even killed a fellow soldier. They ripped the man to shreds. I saw them with my own eyes eating the soldier's flesh like hungry animals. We finally gunned all the Berserkers down, but the infection continued to spread through our camp until we had to leave. We heard the same story from other militias as well. Soon all of Jersey and Pennsylvania were lost, and our territory had gotten smaller."

"Well, at least Big Al's did too," I say stupidly.

"Not true. The Caliphate doesn't fear the infected. They create them and use them as a weapon, just as the Cubans are learning to do. Soon we will be surrounded by Fangs and Berserkers, and this war will be lost."

"We have to get word out that hyperbaric chambers can cure the infection," Reynolds says.

"There are only a few hundred working ones left in the world, and hail just broke one of those," Ruby says. "Even if we managed to track down all of them, how could we possibly hope to cure them all? The infection spreads and works faster than the cure."

"Besides I don't reckon a Fang or an infected human, present company excluded, will willingly get into a chamber to be cured."

Reynolds pulls off the highway and onto a long, straight two-lane road with acres and acres of farmlands on either side. Occasionally a house or a far-off barn passes by. They all seem empty and a couple are just piles of rubble.

"Do you think anyone is out there?" I say looking at a small, dark house surrounded on all sides by flat fields.

"They're all gone," Samson says.

"Maybe someone out there survived. We did," Wesley says. "Maybe we can help them."

"What do you propose we do? Search the whole state? There's no time. The best way to help is to get the message to Mika," Samson mocks.

"And what's he going to do? Build another wall?" Reynolds says in an angry tone. "We should stay and continue to look for survivors."

"What good is it to survive in no-man's-land?" Ruby combats Reynolds' anger with a soothing voice. "We all might as well be dead if we can't win this war."

"And how do we do that?" I say. She looks back at me.

"We need to unite the country. We won't win divided," She says looking into my eyes. Is she trying to tell me something? Perhaps she wants me to convince the U.S. to unite with Mika.

Like a sudden whirlwind, my head is swimming with a memory. It feels more like deja vu than a memory and I try to hold onto it. *The grey-haired man with the black goatee and narrow face is sitting in front of me. There's a long, metallic table in-between us. The room is white and oddly bright. The walls to my left and right are mirrors. The grey-haired man is in a blue military suit...or is it beige?*

"Focus," he says. I realize my hands are restrained to the table. My heart is racing.

"Focus," he repeats. I take deep breaths until my heart rate slows. "You did well today. Tomorrow will be more difficult. Remember, we have to unite this country at all costs. Do you know what that means?"

What did he mean? I can't remember anything else. *'Unite this country at all costs'* I focus on the words. Was that my mission before the crash? Maybe Reynolds was right and my ship was sent to rescue them, or maybe we were supposed to capture Ruby and bring her to Mika as a gift. Surely that would help ease tensions between the two countries. I try to grasp for more of the memory, but it's making my head hurt. Either way, whatever the mission was it failed. And now Samson will get credit for bringing Ruby back. I'm still wondering how they convinced her to go. Maybe they showed her Jax's body. It certainly makes me want to get out of this hellhole.

"Will Mika ever want to unite?" I ask.

"I don't see that happening," Reynolds says.

"If Mika cares about his people like he claims he does and not just about the power, then maybe," Wesley says.

"If he really cared about the people, he wouldn't have walled his own daughter out," Ruby mumbles.

"Here we are," Reynolds says. He pulls the SUV into a small and old, but untouched by war, gas station. There are only two aisles, each with two pumps, and there is a small store that doesn't look big enough to even have a bathroom. Reynolds parks next to one of the pumps, and I rush out around the back of the store to find some privacy. There is a small strip mall ahead of me that also seems unscathed by war or bombs. I know there is no one out there, but I still shield myself against the wall of the food mart as I relieve myself. I feel silly. There is no one for hundreds of miles. *I can piss wherever I want.* I turn around and wiggle my hips so my stream goes back and forth.

"Having fun?" Ruby says behind me and Yoshi barks.

"Oh..." I say and quickly turn back to the wall with red cheeks. She laughs and I zip myself up.

"A little privacy please," she says with a smile and lays her assault rifle down into the grass.

"Right...yes, I'm going," I say.

I walk back around. Reynolds is standing next to the vehicle with a nozzle in his hand, and Wesley has the computer panel of the pump torn off. He is playing with wires. Samson is at the edge of the lot by himself, staring at the deserted town with his gun in his right hand and a burning cigarette in the other hand.

I jump back as Red comes busting out of the food mart as if he just robbed it. His arms are full of beef jerky sticks. He smiles at me.

"Jackpot," he says. "The only thing not expired."

I follow him and open up the trunk door. He drops the pile and then grabs a handful of sticks. He hands me one. I unwrap it and scarf it down quickly. It's salty and good, but really I'm just thankful to eat something other than cornmeal.

"Okay, I think I got it," Wesley says. "Try it now."

Reynolds has a beef jerky stick hanging from his mouth. He puts the gas pump nozzle in the tank. He triggers it multiple times. There is a clicking noise.

"It's empty," Reynolds says.

"How's that possible?" Ruby asks coming up behind us. Yoshi is right beside her. "This is the pump we used last time."

"Must be the other one," Red says pointing to the first pump in the other row. "I reckon the Fangs haven't figured out how to use the pump yet."

"Try it then," Ruby says unamused. She grabs a jerky stick for herself and one for Yoshi. The jerky is gone as soon as it hits Yoshi's tongue.

Reynolds moves the SUV to the other pump, and Wesley once again attempts to hack the computer on it.

"You sure you want to leave us in Clearwater?" Red says.

I don't want to leave at all, but all I muster is "I guess so."

"Damn it," Samson says as he walks over to us, reeking of smoke and tobacco. "I was really hoping I could bring back both Ruby and The Naked Lady. I'd probably get promoted to Mika's personal guard. What an easy gig that would be. Everyone loves him. I wouldn't even have to do anything, and I heard they eat steak and potatoes once a week."

Maybe I'll turn myself in and join his personal guard myself.

"I think I'll take my chances on my own."

"Where will you go?" Red says.

"To the U.S. Maybe I'll find out who I really am."

"Okay try it now," Wesley says. Reynolds sticks the nozzle in the gas tank, but again all I hear are empty clicks.

"Impossible," Ruby says. Yoshi barks. Ruby grabs the nozzle from Reynolds and squeezes the trigger. It clicks. She tries a few more times to no avail. "These were full the last time we were here."

"Has Mika started coming down this far?" Reynolds asks Samson.

"Not that I know of, and I doubt he would know of this gas station in the middle of nowhere anyways."

"Maybe there are other survivors like us," I say feeling vindicated. And to cement my victory, the sound of noisy truck engines rumbles nearby.

Suddenly, we're encircled by at least six lifted trucks with big, swamp-treading tires. All of them have camouflage paint and big, round tail pipes. Their engines sound like a swarm of a thousand locusts. It seems pointless to reach for my weapon, but I do it anyway. I'm not the only one. We each hold up our weapons as the trucks circle closer and closer towards us

9

At last, the hefty, lifted trucks come to a stop. They park in a wide circle around us. When their doors open, at least thirty men in long white thobes come out holding AK-47s. They completely surround us. Most of them wear red and white or green and white checkered ghutra scarfs on their heads and around their faces, leaving only their eyes showing. They also wear black headbands with strange, white writing on them.

The only one without a weapon and without a ghutra is the one that approaches us. He has black curls covering his head down to the tip of his ears. His nose is long and bumpy, but as he smiles it hardly seems unattractive anymore. He looks no older than twenty five and his olive skin is heavily-tanned by the sun.

"My friends," he says with open arms and a desert accent. "We come in peace. Please lower your weapons. My men are only armed for defense. It's not every day we see other people around here."

We all look at Ruby. She nods and lowers her gun, and we all follow her lead.

"I see that we may have used all the gasoline here. My apologies, but if you will accompany us back to our camp we would be most delighted to get you filled up. It is some miles away, so we will tow you. Is this acceptable?" he asks Reynolds.

Ruby scrunches the corners of her lids. "I make the decisions here. You will address your questions to me."

"My apologies, I meant you no disrespect. However...it is not our custom for men to take orders from women."

"I don't care what your custom is – "

"I mean no offense. I want us to be friends. It is merely a precaution, so as not to provoke an incident with my men." He waves his hand as if to put his armed men on display. He looks at Reynolds. "If you will allow me to direct any questions towards you, I can permit you access to our camp and give you any provisions you require."

Reynolds looks at Ruby. She looks mad, but she nods anyway.

"Very well," Reynolds says.

"Wonderful," he says and claps his hands together. "My name is Amalek. If you would be so kind as to leave your weapons in your vehicle, we can go."

We all look at Ruby again. She hesitates.

"We are a peaceful community," Amalek assures us. "We do not allow weapons within our gates. Please, you will be safe."

Ruby finally throws her gun and her knife in the SUV and the rest of us follow reluctantly.

"Yours as well," Amalek says to Wesley. He looks down at the Bible in his hands. Before he can object, Ruby puts her hand on his forearm.

"You'll get it back after they fill us up."

Wesley hesitates, but then finally kisses his book and puts it in the SUV.

"Come, ride with me. My men will take care of your truck."

We climb into the extended cab of his truck, and Amalek takes the wheel. Yoshi hops up to ride in the bed.

"What brings you this far north?" he asks as he pulls the truck out of the gas station lot.

"We are trying to make it to Mika's territory, where it is safe," Reynolds says. He is squeezed in-between Amalek and Ruby.

"Safe? Mika is surrounded on three sides. It's war here too, but all we fight are dogs. The whole world is at war. Our community is the safest place to be, you will see."

"What about food and supplies? You'll have to run out eventually."

"Gas maybe, but we have become very self-sufficient. You will see.

The others war with each other. We want nothing to do with it."

"Then why do you wear the mark of the Caliph on your forehead?" Samson says.

"Yes, we pledge our allegiance to the Sultan of course. He is the Mahdi, but his war is far from us."

"Big Al is just up the road."

Amalek laughs. "Hardly. And Al-Menzanii is only one king out of ten in the Ottoman Confederacy. We do not align with him. And besides, as I told you, we are peaceful."

"Well, we thank you for your help," Ruby says.

"It is nothing. We Floridians need to stick together and help each other. Besides, we didn't leave you any gas. If we had known there were others, we wouldn't have taken all of it. For the life of me, I don't know why my men love these monstrous trucks." He smiles. His teeth are perfectly straight and without blemish.

We drive north for some time. It isn't until we pass a sign that says Dade City that Amalek turns off the highway. It is hardly a city. Long roads with crumbled strip malls and leveled neighborhoods make up the city proper. We drive through it all and then head down a long, empty road. We pass a pack of Fangs that stare at us at first and then chase us for a while, until Amalek's men make sport out of shooting them from their trucks.

We finally arrive and enter through a tall, barbed wire gate with a fence that surrounds a mobile home park. Inside, there are several homes being built or rebuilt by men who are dressed similar to Amalek's men, only their faces are uncovered. There are small boys riding bikes down the thin streets or playing in yards. It is eerie, but good to see a community so alive and untouched by war and devastation. I can't help but smile at seeing so many people who aren't trying to kill me.

The main road curves slightly and leads to a long, clubhouse building. Amalek is gloating about the farmlands they have to the east. He says everyone has jobs and contributes to the community. Some children run in front of the truck, and Amalek slams on the brakes. He cranks down his window.

"Out of the way, little ones," he says in Arabic, but somehow I understand. He smiles and continues driving towards the clubhouse when the young boys scatter away.

"Our community is growing," he says. "In just a few generations, we can repopulate Florida again."

"Yes, and every man and woman and child will wear the banner of the Caliphate," Samson says, annoyed.

"Should we hold up the flags of Mika instead?" He says kindly. "Should we pay homage to the one who attempted to wall us off with dogs? This land is unclaimed and unwanted. We make the best of it and besides, everyone has a choice to follow Imam Mahdi or not. It is not for you or me to decide what's in a man's heart."

We park to the right of the clubhouse. There is a lake behind it and a few small boats scattered on the glimmering water. There are men casting out nets on a couple of them. Some of the other trucks park next to us, but the one towing our SUV veered off several minutes ago. Ruby seems to have only now noticed this, as she looks about nervously.

"Come inside and eat with us. You cannot buy or sell here unless you choose to wear the mark of the Mahdi, but we will gladly provide you with anything you need. Come, eat and drink with us."

"Some choice," says Samson as we walk into the clubhouse. Yoshi waits outside and rolls around in the grass by the lake.

Inside is cool and smells of roasted lamb and grilled onions. There are many smiling faces. To the left of the main foyer is an open cafeteria, where woman cook and serve dozens of men with happy faces. Opposite the cafeteria is an empty room with an empty floor and an altar at the end.

There are people in the foyer talking amongst themselves, and stop to gawk and whisper about the outsiders, but only for a moment. It seems once they realize we are with Amalek, they continue their conversations without issue.

Compared to them, we are severely underdressed. In contrast to the women who are covered from head to toe with only their faces showing, Ruby might as well be naked. It's no wonder all the men and women stare at her with either hateful or lustful eyes I can't tell. Amalek stops us before we enter the cafeteria.

"Please, please let us give you fresh garb before you eat," he says. He leads us to a small wardrobe room with a single woman inside surrounded by rows of plain-looking clothes.

"What is this you brought me, Amalek?" the short woman says in Arabic. I pretend I do not understand and smile at her.

"Fellow Floridians. They're starving. Dress them appropriately so I can bring them into the cafeteria."

"Head bands too?"

"No, no not yet," he says and then smiles at us.

"Fadwah will give you new threads," Amalek says so we can all understand. "Then, I beg you join us for dinner as our honored guests." He bows with a grin and leaves the room. Fadwah grabs long, white and cream-colored thobes off the racks and holds them up to our bodies as if to measure us. Her face is round with dark, almond-shaped eyes. Even with her loose black tunic it's easy to tell she is fat. She finally decides on a thobe for me. It's white and spotless and flows down to my ankles. It's surprisingly cool and comfortable. I want to laugh seeing the others dressed the same, but I'm too disappointed in the long, black tunic that now covers all of Ruby. I can take some solace in the fact that I can still see her face. Even these people with their strange customs would have to admit it would be a crime to cover her beautiful face.

"Looking sharp," I say to Samson, but it does nothing to diminish the scowl on his face.

"I tell you the truth, I like these outfits. Maybe I wouldn't be so sunburnt all the time if I had one of my own. Do you think they'll let us keep them?" Red says.

"They are comfortable," Reynolds says. "But I don't think going to Mika's dressed like this is a good idea."

"Why should that matter? Is Mika so intolerant of other people's customs?" I ask.

"As long as we don't wear those headbands he can't question our allegiance, right?" Wesley says.

"Allegiance?" Ruby says. "Let's not forget, we don't align ourselves with Mika. We are going to warn him of the increasing Cuban threat, and that's it."

"What will we do after?" Reynolds asks.

"Why don't we just go eat for now? I'm starving," I say. It's only half a lie. I seem to be the only one who notices Fadwah is listening to our conversation, and I doubt it's wise to let her hear any more of our plans. Ruby must understand, because she glances at Fadwah and then back at me. "You're right. I'm hungry too," she says.

When we leave the wardrobe room, Amalek is outside waiting for us. His face brightens as he sees us.

"Much better! I trust you find your new threads adequate?"

Even if I didn't, he seems so happy I don't think I would have the heart to tell him no. Instead, we all give him approving nods and smiles, except for Samson.

"Come my friends, let's eat." He leads us into the dining hall.

There are long tables crowded with men eating and talking. The opposite wall to the entrance has a handful of women cooking on stoves and ovens and prepping dishes for the men on the free counter space. It almost seems like Ruby shouldn't be allowed to sit and eat with us, but aside from a couple of surprised glances, no one says a thing when we sit down in what seem to be the only empty seats left. Almost immediately after we sit down, multiple serving women lay out large platters of roasted lamb, seasoned duck, and steamed vegetables. All the aromas make my stomach rumble. They fill our glasses with tea to wash it down; although I'm sure I'm not the only one who would rather have a beer. I keep that to myself.

"I could get used to this," I say as one of the women cuts off pieces of lamb and duck and put it on my plate. Ruby gives me a look that says 'I would kick you under the table if Wesley wasn't in-between us.'

Although Samson didn't wait for approval to eat, Amalek says "go ahead dig in."

The lamb is tender and tasty and the duck is juicy and delicious. There is more than enough for all of us, but Samson and I still eat as if there's not and it's a race for seconds. The men surrounding us talk in Arabic as we stuff our faces. I try to keep my eyes on my food as I listen.

"Amalek, it is bad enough that you brought outsiders here, but to let them eat our food is wrong." I look up, but it's hard to tell who spoke. They all have thick, black or grey beards around their smiling lips and look at us with exaggerated admiration.

"It is not wrong to show friendship and hospitality. They are our friends," Amalek says.

"They are enemies to the Caliphate. They do not wear allegiance to the Great Sultan," a man with a curly, black beard that dips down to the center of his chest says. He looks no older than thirty, but has several grey hairs at the edge of his beard. He notices me looking at him, and he smiles. I smile back and hope he doesn't realize that I understand.

"Enough," Amalek says. "They will have a choice of allegiance soon enough. For now we will show them kindness. When Imam Mahdi comes to lay claim to the West, will he not ask if we multiplied his kingdom? What will you have me do? Offer them death or allegiance now, before they have even witnessed the pleasures and benefits of the latter? Surely they would choose death. And what is the point of ruling the West if there is no one left to rule?"

"You are wise, Imam Amalek," another man says.

"I see you are enjoying your meals," Amalek says in English with a hearty laugh. "You have barely said a peep. All that we have is yours. We hope you will enjoy your stay." Then in Arabic, "and soon they will see what happens to non-believers." He smiles. Ruby and the others smile and nod graciously back, except for Samson and me. I don't think he understands, but I believe he suspects what I now know: that we have to get out of here as soon as possible.

"How is our vehicle doing?" I say. "We appreciate you giving us food and filling us up, but we have to be on our way now." Ruby looks at me as if she has the urge to kick me again.

"Nonsense," Amalek says. "You have not seen our whole camp yet. Besides, you must be tired. You can leave in the morning after a good night's rest."

After lunch, my stomach feels like it's going to explode. Amalek takes us in his truck and drives us around the camp. I'm biding my time until I can be with the others alone and let them know that Amalek's friendliness is not what is seems. Their fenced-in camp is much bigger than I had previously thought. We drive past open pastures and farmlands on both sides of the road.

"We farm wheat, corn, potatoes, strawberries, and we have some of the best fisherman always casting their nets in our lake. We have everything and anything we could possibly need."

"It's almost as if you knew the Cuban attack was coming," Samson says.

"We also have two schools for our children and almost 500 people within our gates now," Amalek continues.

We pass a long, black barn that sits eerily by itself in an open field. It looks more like a prison then a barn.

"Have any Fangs ever breached your fences?" Ruby asks before I can ask about the barn.

"Only once and my men killed it swiftly. As you know, they are well-armed and well-trained."

"Who would have thought you could keep Fangs out with just a fence, and not a wall?" Red says and chuckles.

"Did it bite anyone?" Ruby asks.

"Yes, one man. His name was Rasheed. He was a good man and an even better fighter. But the Fang snuck up on him. It bit him on the leg. If it had been a mere dog bite a few stitches might have sufficed, but the infection spread uncontrollably. It is unfortunate. He was my friend."

When we finally make it back and the clubhouse is in front of us, the sun is beginning to set. Fireflies the same color as the sky are sprinkled over the streets.

"It is time for the call to prayer. Let me take you to your house," Amalek says and turns down the main road.

"Well, I'll be. We get our own place?" Red says.

"Yes, of course. Surely you are tired from your travels. A good night's sleep in a warm bed will give you strength for your journey ahead." He smiles.

Amalek drops us off in front of a small mobile home at the end of an adjacent road. From it, I can still see the clubhouse. Many of the campers are gathered there now, all dressed in white. Yoshi runs over to us.

Inside the house is small and there are only two beds and a sofa, but it is nice having a roof over our heads, even if it is only for one night.

"We have to get out of here," Wesley says, and for the first time, I agree with him.

"Don't worry. We'll leave tomorrow," Ruby says.

"Hopefully after breakfast. These people sure do know how to cook," Red says and pats his belly.

Outside, a loudspeaker plays a man's voice singing and speaking in Arabic. It is calling all the followers of the Caliph to come together and worship.

"No, we have to leave now," Wesley says adamantly. "I don't trust them." Ruby looks at him as if he's crazy.

"These are the nicest people we've met in a long time. I may not like wearing that robe, but it would be rude to leave unannounced. All they've shown us is hospitality and kindness," Reynolds says.

"He's right," Ruby says. "We shouldn't offend them, and sleeping in a bed sounds pretty good to me." She spreads her arms out and falls backwards onto the queen-sized bed in the open room to the right. Yoshi jumps on the bed, and Ruby wraps her arms around her and strokes her back.

"What sleep?" Samson says. "I can't sleep with this noise." The loudspeaker is still blaring the Caliphate's praises. "I want to know what's in that barn. Amalek is hiding something."

"I'm with you. I won't be able to sleep either," I say.

"I'm in too," Wesley says. "Let's find out what Amalek is hiding in that barn."

When it gets dark, Ruby, Yoshi, Red, and Reynolds stay behind as Samson, Wesley, and I sneak out the back and head down the road that cuts through the farmlands. We escape the light of the torches that surround the clubhouse and continue down the dark road. I wonder if we should have tried to find our weapons first.

I'm sweating by the time we make it to the barn. Wesley leans over and takes a deep breath.

"I'm too out of shape for this," he says.

The barn is even more ominous in the dark. It looks more like a giant, metal furnace than a barn. Before I can look inside one of the window slits, I hear the roar of a truck engine.

"Someone's coming," I say and we quickly hide behind the side of the building. All three of us peek out and watch a lifted truck park in front of the barn. Two men climb out of the truck. They are talking, but I can't make it out over the sound of the loud engine in idle. The headlights are still on. They walk towards the back of the truck and pull a live ram from the bed. It's fat with a shaggy mane and thick horns that curl around on both sides of its head. The man who was driving pulls the ram by a leash and the other follows him in front of the barn. It isn't until they get to the front of the building that I can make out what they are saying. They too speak in Arabic.

"The outsiders are nice," the one holding the ram says.

"Do you think they'll choose to stay with us?" the other man says.

"They would have to be fools not too." He yanks on the chain leash and the ram comes to him. Both of them push the ram forward into what I initially thought was a large, black door, but is actually two large, black screens draped over an open doorway. The ram bleats and cowers, but the men push it through where the screens meet and overlap. It looks as if it isn't the first ram these men have pushed into the barn. I can hear the ram bleating inside. Then I hear what sounds like a man grunting and groaning inside. He sounds like he's in agony.

"Rasheed, share with your friends," one of the men outside shouts. Now I hear more men inside as if they are trying their hardest to speak, but all that comes out are horrible groans and squeals. Then I hear a hideous scream, and the men outside begin to back away towards the truck. The terrified bleating of the ram stops, and I can hear what sounds like flesh being torn apart.

"Berserkers," Samson says.

10

"Wake up," Wesley says. "We have to leave. Now!"

Yoshi perks her ears up and barks, but Ruby rubs the back of her neck to calm her down as she wakes. Her hair is disheveled and her eyes are droopy.

"Why in tarnation do we have to leave now?" Red says while stretching out his arms.

"They are holding infected humans here," I say much calmer than Wesley, who is pacing back and forth and biting on his fingernails.

"For what purpose?" Reynolds asks, as if we would know somehow.

"Probably to use them against Mika, just as Big Al did in New Jersey," Samson says shifting from one leg to the other, and moving his hands from his pockets, to crossed arms, and then back to his pockets again.

"Let's not jump to conclusions," Ruby says. "Amalek said a friend of his was bitten by a Fang. Perhaps they don't want to kill him in hopes of a cure."

"Which we now know is as simple as prolonged exposure to higher concentrations of oxygen," Reynolds says.

"There are more than one, and they are locked up in cages and fed like wild beasts," Wesley says.

"Well, maybe we can help them. We can tell Amalek the cure in exchange for his hospitality," Reynolds says. "It's only fair. I feel bad as it is mooching off these people."

"No, we need to leave and get to Mika as soon as possible. I don't trust them," Samson says.

"They've given us no reason not to trust them," Ruby says firmly.

"They've shown us nothing but courtesy and have helped us tremendously. The least we can do is tell them of the cure. Maybe they will be grateful and help us against the Cubans. We need to stay at least until morning. It would be a great insult to leave in the middle of the night. Besides, they still have our SUV."

Maybe she's right. Amalek has shown us terrific generosity and I have to admit the thought of sleeping in a warm bed instead of fleeing all night does sound tempting. But knowing Berserkers are within the camp's fences still makes me uneasy. The knot in my stomach that I haven't felt since I woke up in the chamber days ago has returned in full force, and maybe even grown a bit.

"Let's get some sleep. We'll leave in the morning after breakfast," Ruby says.

"There's no way I'm sleeping with Berserkers in this camp. I've made that mistake once before and I woke up to the sound of my friends being eaten alive. I won't let that happen again. I'll be on watch," Samson says.

"Suit yourself," Ruby says and lies back down on her bed with Yoshi. Reynolds lies on the couch, Red on a pile of sheets and blankets on the floor, and Wesley and I share the second bed in the room adjacent to Ruby's.

My belly is full for the first time that I can remember, and I have a comfy bed and roof over my head, yet I'm hardly comfortable. I keep shifting from lying on my side to my back or flat on my stomach. I keep folding my pillow and then unfolding it back and flattening it out, back and forth for at least thirty minutes until I finally give up and climb out of bed. I should stay. I don't know when the next time I will have a chance to sleep in a bed again. Wesley doesn't seem to be having the same trouble getting to sleep as I do.

It's quiet and dark as I walk through the small living room. I can see a silhouette of a person standing outside of the sliding glass door on the back porch. I walk through the kitchen and slide the door open. I use my hand to clear away the cloud of cigarette smoke. Ruby looks at me and takes another drag.

"You smoke?" I say.

"Only when I can't sleep," she says.

I lean against the wooden railing of the tiny porch and stare out ahead. From here, the barn looks like a little, dark speck. I wouldn't have noticed it if I didn't already know it was there. I wonder how many infected are locked up inside. It would be kinder to just kill them like we did to Jax. His face looked in agony, with an unquenchable bloodlust and hunger in his crimson eyes. But maybe they can be healed, and maybe Amalek will let us go if we tell him the cure. But what then? Everywhere we go there will be war and death. Perhaps it would be better to stay here.

"What happened to us?" Ruby says. "This country I mean. We were once the strongest nation the world had ever seen, but now we are divided and conquered."

"We lost millions, didn't we?"

"We lost millions in the first two world wars, but we persevered and became a super power. Then we turned into Ancient Rome. We became a country of entertainment and nothing else. Actors, singers, and sports stars lived like kings, while those who had fought to protect them starved in our streets and couldn't even get proper healthcare. Our farmers and builders couldn't make a decent wage, but it didn't matter as long as we were entertained. For God's sake, we couldn't even eat without watching television, we couldn't shit without social media, and our children couldn't play without a controller in their hands. There was no more room for thought or learning. Just like Rome, we were built on hard work, blood, and sweat but we turned fat, lazy, and thoughtless and then...we were conquered on all sides."

"There's still hope."

"I once thought Mika was that hope."

"He still can be. We must convince him to unite with the U.S."

"You don't know Mika. He's more stubborn than me."

"That's why you want me to go to the U.S." I say.

"Yes, I want you to go to the president and convince him to join with Mika."

"I hate to sound like Red," Samson says as he comes out from behind the side of the house. He chuckles when I jump slightly. He puffs on his cigarette and adds to the cloud of smoke I've been trying not to breathe in. "But are you off your rocker? You have a better chance of converting Wesley to atheism."

"Maybe, but we have to try," Ruby says softly. "Try to get some sleep." She squeezes my forearm. I turn to watch her walk back inside admiring how she steps with grace and authority at the same time.

"I see why you guys like her," Samson says, watching her as well. He takes a final hit of his cigarette and then flicks it into the grass as he exhales. "I like a girl who is sexy and tough. I'd let her boss me around in the sack." He laughs.

"Shut up."

"I'm joking, relax. I don't want to seduce her and ruin your little love triangle. Besides I have a wife."

"You do?" I say, shocked at the notion that anyone could stand him long enough to wed.

"Well...I did. She died with everyone else. I know they say 'till death do us part,' but I will never love another woman."

We're both quiet for a long while. A half moon is attempting to shine through a cluster of dark clouds in the distance. The clouds brighten for a moment as lightning flashes within them.

"It's funny," he finally breaks the silence. "She used to drag me to church sometimes. I hated all of it, the singing, the boring sermons, and most of all having to be friendly to people. It was miserable...But now I would give anything, even my own life, to spend just an hour in church with her again." He's silent for a moment and then chuckles. "I must have been so annoying. I would complain the whole service and play on my phone. Half the time I would fall asleep, but Alyssa didn't care. She would listen intently to the preacher, and she would sing all the songs more than dutifully. Her voice was terrible, but I would kill a man to hear it again."

"I bet she would have loved Wesley. Who knows, maybe he's right about the whole Rapture thing," I say and laugh.

"He is right," he doesn't laugh or smile.

"I didn't take you for a Bible thumper, Samson."

"Oh, I believe in God. I just hate him. He stole Alyssa from me. She was mine, and he took her." His voice quivers, but only for a split second. I don't know what to say.

After a few moments of silence, he walks back around the side of the mobile home. I can't help but wonder if I had a wife or a family before I lost my memory. Maybe I had kids, and siblings, and parents. Maybe they're all waiting for me back home...wherever that may be. Or maybe they all died too. Perhaps Samson is right and God does exist, and maybe he took my family too. I have to find out.

I go back inside and lie down. The bed is comfortable. It makes me realize just how tired I really am. I try not to think of Berserkers or Fangs or gods. Instead, I try to picture what my family might have looked like. I picture a boy and a girl playing in a big yard. They smile and laugh and run to my wife. She hugs them and laughs with them. She's faceless at first, but when I focus, her face is familiar...it's Ruby.

It feels like I've only been sleeping for a minute when the loudspeakers boom with the call to prayer. A raucous thumping on the front door follows moments after.

"You've got to be kidding me," I say as I climb out of the last bed I'm probably going to see for a while.

Reynolds beats me to the door. A familiar man with a thick, black beard and hooked nose is standing at the threshold. I remember him eating with us yesterday.

"You are all invited as special guests of...Imam Amalek...to...p...p...prayer," he says staring at Ruby as if he's never seen a woman before, or at least one that wasn't completely covered. He shakes his head and stares at the ground "P...p...please come to the clubhouse."

"Maybe if we pray hard enough they'll give us our truck back,"

Samson says after the man leaves.

As far as I can remember I've never prayed a day in my life, but maybe I used to. Perhaps I should pray for my family, or maybe God will tell me if I have one. We all get dressed, and again I am disappointed to see Ruby's body so covered. It bothers me, not only because it's aesthetically a travesty, but I hate to see Ruby forced to cover up and be silent.

It is still dark out when we leave the house. We join many men in thobes and Caliphate-sponsored headbands walking along the streets towards the clubhouse. Some of them look at Yoshi and walk faster or cross to the other side of the street. I can't blame them; I was terrified of her when I first met her.

When we arrive, everyone is gathered outside of the clubhouse near a fenced-in court that was once used for tennis. There is a group of men surrounding Amalek, but as soon as he sees us he excuses himself and comes over.

"Good morning, my friends," he says with a great big smile. He wears a short, rounded skull cap patterned with sky blue and white. Amalek looks at Ruby and frowns. "I'm sorry, my dear. My messenger was supposed to inform you that you and your dog must participate in Adhan from the comfort of your own house. Forgive me for the embarrassment, but it is for your safety I assure you."

"Why? What's going to happen to her if she stays?" I say angrily.

"Please, please take no offense. As you yourselves know, we men are sinful, sometimes lustful at heart. It would be most distracting for men to pray with such a lovely woman present."

"So, it's not for her safety. It's for yours," Wesley says.

Amalek blushes and smirks. "Most of our women pray at home, but some pray in the sanctuary inside. You are more than welcome to join them if you wish."

"I'll go back to the house. I have nothing to pray for," she says and turns around.

"Maybe a daughter—"

She snaps back around. "How did you know I have a daughter?"

"A mere guess," Amalek says staring at her with a stony face.

"Come on Yoshi," she says and turns back to the house. Yoshi follows her. I want to join her, but Amalek leads us inside the court. A large, Persian carpet has been laid out on the ground. The rest of the men pour inside and stand shoulder to shoulder in front of Amalek. We stand in the back near the fence.

Amalek looks at the crowd of men standing in front of him. There is a golden statue erect at his side. It is at least two feet taller than Amalek, but looks like him. It has curls on its head that go down to its ears and a long, bumpy nose. Amalek looks up to the sky and stretches out his arms.

"Oh peoples," he says in Arabic. "When you hear the sound of the Adhan you must fall down and worship the golden image of the Great Sultan. Whoever chooses not to worship him and take the mark of his name and his god upon their forehead or upon their arm will pay the ultimate price." If I still had my gun, my hand would be on it.

"So pray," Amalek continues. "Pray that our new friends will make the right decision at the right time. And pray that our Caliph, who the Great Prophet foretold about 1500 years ago, in advance, will crush our enemies until all of the earth will worship the Majestic One." The last words caused all the men to prostrate themselves before Amalek and the golden sculpture.

I look at Wesley. I wonder if he can understand them like I can. He looks as uneasy as I feel. His face is pale, and he's silently mouthing what I can only assume are Bible quotes. The others just seem amused, as if they are taking in some culture. I would feel a lot more comfortable if we were armed.

Amalek is still standing with his face pointing to the sky and his arms open, as the sun rises behind him. A man from the front row of prostrate men gets up and stands next to Amalek, looking at us. I recognize him. He was the man at lunch with the long, black beard with a few white hairs peppered at the bottom of it.

"Imam," he says in English. "It is, as you say, the law of the Caliph that all men must surrender to him and pledge allegiance to his Caliphate. Those who do not must be sent to the furnace to be cleansed. These men do not bow down to the image of the Caliph. They insult us with their presence here."

"I really want to kill that man," Samson says to us.

"Yes," Amalek says loudly. "All men must serve the Great Sultan...but at the right time."

"The time is now. The choice has been laid out before them. Even you, Imam must obey this mandate given to us by the Mahdi."

Amalek's face turns to white, and he frowns. Suddenly, I am very aware of the armed men standing outside of the gate. The men in front of us stay face down on the ground however. Amalek's face hardens as he looks at us.

"You must choose now," Amalek says. "Worship the Caliph and prove yourself loyal to the empire and you will be given every comfort and freedom within our borders, or refuse and suffer an infidel's death."

"Some choice," I say, not loud enough for Amalek to hear.

"I hate my own God, why the hell would I bow down to yours?" Samson says, definitely loud enough for Amalek to hear. Reynolds looks worried and surprised. The armed guards have already come through the gate and are surrounding us. I'm not sure how we can escape this. Reynolds looks at me. I raise my eyebrows and shrug my shoulders. As much as I don't want to, it seems more logical to bend the knee now and figure out how to escape later. Before I could step forward, Wesley beats me to it. I thought for sure he would be the last to bow.

"We will not worship your false god or your false king," he says and the man standing next to Amalek gasps. "*That terrorizes the four corners of the earth with war and destruction.*"

I sigh.

"Blasphemy," the man with the white-tipped beard yells and shakes a finger at us.

"You offer us subjection under the guise of freedom and destruction hidden behind fake smiles and friendliness. We don't want your peace filled with lies and bullets," Wesley says loudly and firmly.

"Then there is no other choice," Amalek answers. "You must die." The armed men aim their rifles at us like a firing squad. "Take them to Rasheed and his friends. I'm sure they're hungry."

The thin clouds hardly shield us from the blistering sun as we walk down the main road. My forehead is dripping with sweat. We are bunched together like cattle heading for slaughter. Several men with AK-47s follow us and behind them are a dozen other onlookers. I look at the house we stayed at last night as we pass it. *Run Ruby* I want to shout, but I can't take the chance of ruining the small possibility that maybe they forgot about her. Even if it's just for a moment, maybe she can escape. *Look outside Ruby. See what's happening and run, damn it.*

"What does it matter anyway?" I scold Wesley. "It was just a statue. We could have pledged allegiance and escaped later."

Wesley looks at me queerly. "We may live in a world without honor, but at least we can die knowing we didn't bow down to these assholes." I don't know which is more shocking; the fact that Wesley just cursed, or the fact that he's right. I suddenly feel ashamed that I even thought about giving in to them.

"Go ahead, grovel at their feet. There's still time," Samson says and drives his shoulder into mine as he walks past me. I need to find a way for us to escape. I stop as I see the barn ahead. The walls are made of steel with small windows covered with thick, metal bars. I can only see darkness inside. The long, screen curtains hang down from golden rings at the top of the entrance. One of Amalek's men strikes the small of my sweaty back with the butt of his rifle, and I keep walking forward. Perhaps I should just run. A bullet in my back sounds better than being torn to smithereens by Berserkers. If it were men inside I could fight and kill them, but these are much faster and stronger than ordinary men.

"How many of them are in there?" I say to the armed man behind me. "Maybe you can go inside and find out for me." He quickly responds and smashes his rifle butt into my back so hard, it makes me fall to my knees and grunt in pain. Samson laughs and it infects me until I laugh as well. If there is only a few and they send me in last, I might have a chance to survive. Samson and Reynolds should put up enough of a fight to tire them out. One of the men picks me up by the arm and pushes us all in front of the curtained entrance. I stare at the long drape that looks like they made it out of lanai screens. I can't help but laugh that a Berserker can eat a man alive, but can't walk through a screen door.

That's it! I can use the curtain against them. Two lifted trucks with chrome rims pull up beside us. Amalek and the man with the white-tipped beard climb out of one. Out of the other comes a single man who circles around and yanks out a half-naked woman by the hair. She falls to the ground. Her hands are bound.

No! Ruby, damn you. You were supposed to escape. Three others pull out Yoshi from the back of the truck. She has a large, metal muzzle over her snout. A metal pincher collar is around her neck and her legs are bound like a lamb for the slaughter. They carry her and drop her in front of us. Yoshi stares at me with wet, brown circles. She looks sad and defeated and I'm sure we all look as pathetic as she does.

The other man grabs Ruby by the arm and walks her over in front of us. She doesn't fight back. It seems she has already tried and lost. Her eye is swollen, her lip is bloody, and she has several bruises on her arms and legs.

I will volunteer to go in first. I will kill the Berserkers. Then, I will kill Amalek and each and every one of his men.

11

"Soon the Great Sultan will conquer the whole world and there will be peace forever," Amalek says to us and his men. The sun shines above him and the humidity is so thick I almost wish they didn't rip my thobe off. It's hard to listen to Amalek's rhetoric. I need to figure out how I will use the curtain against the infected. Maybe I can tear the whole thing down and let the Berserkers escape, but that's likely to get me shot, and those thick, golden rings at the top don't seem likely to budge.

"There will be no nonbelievers left alive," Amalek continues. "But until then, the Caliph is most gracious. He offers life to those willing to pledge allegiance to him and his kingdom. It is a regrettable thing when one refuses that free gift of life, but it is our duty as humble servants to give them their choice." He looks up to the sky for a moment and then to his men. "Send the girl and her dog in."

"Wait, no," I shout and reach for Amalek, but two of his men grab me before I can get to him. "Send me in first," I demand, not caring about the spit coming out of my mouth. Amalek looks at me calmly. A droplet of sweat rolls down his temple and he raises a single eyebrow.

"Please, send me in first," I say.

"I'm sorry. The girl must die first." He turns to his men. "Untie the dog and send them in."

"At least loosen her hands too," I beg, as two men cut the rope around Yoshi's legs and then quickly retreat away from her. Amalek shakes his head and watches as his men push Ruby towards the entrance. Yoshi cries as she follows at Ruby's side. If only my eyes were weapons, I could kill Amalek with my glare. I know he must feel me staring at him, but he pretends that he doesn't. "You will die, Amalek. By my hands!" I yell louder than I've ever yelled and yet he looks forward unwavering. His men grab me tighter and pull me back.

Ruby stops at the entrance and turns to look at us. If she has any fear, she does not show it. I want to run to her, but I know I'll never make it. They will gun me down. Her eyes meet mine for a moment, but then she looks down at Yoshi. Yoshi whimpers as if she was still a puppy and her tail hangs between her legs. Ruby turns and walks slowly behind the curtain with Yoshi by her side.

Through the small, barred windows on either side of the curtain I can see her silhouette as she walks deeper inside. Then, I see three more move hastily towards her from opposite corners. I hear Ruby scream, followed by strange grunts and shrieks. I can't watch any longer. I fall to my knees and stare at the dirt in an unfocused trance of rage. Everything is becoming hazy as my anger takes over.

I hear a man whispering to Amalek. "Didn't we only send one of them inside?"

I look up to see Amalek shoo the man away. Inside the windows, I see four figures...no five...five figures huddled together. Yoshi howls desperately. When there is no longer movement or noise from within, two men lift me up by the arms.

I will kill all of you! I yank my arms free and grab one of the men by the back of the head. I pull his head down onto my incoming knee so hard, that he falls backwards. I spin to the other and block his thrusting rifle butt and plant my right fist on his face. He stumbles back and fires his gun into the dirt uncontrollably. Blood gushes from his cheekbone and before he can balance himself, I kick him in the chest. He falls to the ground. Amalek looks terrified and I start towards him, but before I can take another step I feel a rifle butt smash the back of my head. Suddenly, everything around me is distorted. My head is pounding as I'm being dragged through the dirt towards the barn.

A hazy whirlwind of colors and sounds swirls inside my head. I hear shouts, but I don't know who is shouting or what they're saying. Whoever was dragging me drops my arm abruptly and runs away yelling. I hear gunfire.

What's happening? Did Reynolds and the others start to fight back as well?

The entrance to the barn is right in front of me. I look behind. It looks like everyone is running around and fighting. Wesley is running towards me, at least I think it's Wesley. My head hurts and I'm dizzy, so I lie on my back. The sky is cloudless and bright. Suddenly, I'm being carried again. To where, I don't know...

...The next thing I know, I'm indoors. My head is pulsating as if someone is squeezing my brain. I look around. I'm sitting on a small, plastic chair in the middle of a two-story stable. My arms are tied behind my back with a thick chain. White sunlight is shining through big windows along a wooden walkway above me. The boardwalk leads to a door , and past it are moldy stairs that lead down in front of me. I can feel a lump growing on the back of my head.

Why did they bring me here? I can't help but wonder. Did they restrain me to make it easier for the Berserkers?

I hear a squeak and then the door above me opens. A short, round man waddles out. He looks down at me and says something, but I can't make it out. When he makes it to the bottom, he grabs a stool near the wall and drags it in front of me. He sits down. His face is leathery and sunburnt. He smiles at me. His teeth are too far from each other and crooked. He wears brown pants and a grey, collared shirt with short sleeves. His top buttons are unbuttoned enough to form an upside-down triangle of hardened red skin. To the left of the triangle is a sewn-on name tag that reads *bob* in cursive letters. He stares at me for a while without speaking, as if he's studying me or waiting for me to speak. His eyes are black and beady.

"Do you know who I am?" He finally says in a raspy voice, so low that I almost can't hear him.

"Bob with a lowercase 'b' I presume?"

His smile disappears instantly, but I'm happy not to have to look at his awful teeth anymore.

"No, Bob was the first man I ever killed," he mumbles. I have to lean forward to hear him. "I wear his shirt everyday so I never forget it." He laughs. "After so many men you tend to forget their faces, so I keep something from each of them. My name is Mika."

"You're lying," is the only thing I can think to say. How could someone like Ruby ever have loved and married such a tired, ugly-looking man? The thought angers me.

"Believe me or not. It makes no difference," he says and lets out a condescending chuckle. "I rescued you from a hell of a gruesome death. I deserve gratitude, not accusations of deception."

I have to try my hardest to keep the thought of Ruby being torn apart by Berserkers out of my head.

"The least you can do is tell me who you are."

I remember the dog tags that the others had found.

"I'm James. Where are my friends?"

"They're safe. Wesley took a bullet in the arm, but no major damage."

"What about that snake, Amalek? Did you kill him?"

"Unfortunately the Imam escaped, but he won't survive long out in the wilderness. Despite what he may have said, the people here weren't survivors like you. The Caliph sent them several months ago. He was going to keep sending people over until they could attack me from the south. The buffoon underestimated my intelligence. I knew they were here. I knew they would try and make allies with Cuba as well. That's why I tried to beat them to it, but Jax's incompetence screwed me over.

"Everyone has said your name was James, and that you are just a survivor who wandered into Ruby's camp. I am inclined to believe it, as even Samson has confirmed this. But then the question still remains: where is The Naked Lady? The others; their stories don't add up and hence..."

"...why I'm tied up."

"That's right."

"Even if I knew where he was, I wouldn't remember." I twist and roll my wrists. It seems the chain is getting looser, but I can't tell if I'm just imagining it. My skin feels like it's bleeding, but that might lubricate the chain and help my wrists get free.

"If you can't remember, isn't it possible that you are him?"

I swallow hard and stare at him with my best poker face, as I keep rolling my wrists.

"You see, like the Caliphate, the U.S. government has also underestimated my intelligence time and time again. They see me as just a redneck militia leader. After all I've done to protect this land and these people. They still don't respect me, and they still try to kill me. I know you are The Naked Lady and they sent you to kill me." He pulls out a magnum revolver from his back waistband and rests it on his leg.

"Even if that was true, I have no memory. I'm not who I used to be."

"Don't give me that 'I'm a new man' bullshit. I know all about Nightshade."

"I don't know what you're talking about."

"Don't insult me like everyone else has," he shouts and waves his gun around. I squirm, as if I could somehow dodge a bullet. "I know how your organization works. It's all about deception. The crash, infiltrating Ruby's group, even your memory loss are all lies to get to me."

I laugh. "Don't flatter yourself. Are you so paranoid and vain that you think I would risk my life, lose my memory, fight Fangs, and eat cornmeal stew for days just so I could get to you?"

He smirks. "Not you. You're just a cog in their never-ending schemes, used over and over like a murderous tool. Think hard about it. You remember, don't you?"

"I don't remember anything," I lie. I do remember the grey-haired man telling me to unite the country. Could he have possibly meant killing Mika to accomplish it?

He stares at me with unflinching eyes. "If I had to guess, I'd say it was Ira-ish. He would try the most elaborate schemes just to get to me, but I've always been one step ahead. He of all people should have known to respect my intelligence. Tell me, did he plan for you to be my chained prisoner?" He forces a loud, mocking laugh.

"Yes," I say with a grin and loosen my bloody hands completely out of the chain. I leap at him and swing the chain over his head and around his neck before he even has time to realize what is happening. I swoop behind him and pull the chain against his neck with both hands. He hacks and chokes and tries to grab the chain with his fingers to pull it off, but it's a pathetic attempt. His eyes are bulging and his face is becoming even redder than it already was. Within a moment, my mission will finally be complete.

Ahead of me, across the open stable, a set of double doors open and a single person comes through. But it doesn't matter, they can't stop me. I've been training for this for too long.

"Ruby..." I say. She stares at me with her big, haunted eyes. I slacken the chain, and Mika drops to his hands and knees gasping for air. Ruby runs over to him. Three armed men come in behind her and look at Mika with widened eyes. One of them is Samson. Then they look at me with a heavy chain hanging from my hand. They hustle over and Samson is the last one to aim his gun at me.

"Drop the weapon," the one standing beside Samson shouts at me, but all three of them have made the mistake of getting too close. I instantly form a plan of attack. I can kill everyone in the room with this chain. I was trained to do so. My memories cascade inside my head like a flood. It's overwhelming. My eyes water and I take a sudden, deep breath. I remember many things since I joined Nightshade, but not all. My memory has been wiped several times over at varying degrees. Sometimes it was wiped to forget a certain piece of information, and other times the entire mission. For this mission, I remember all of my training. Every detail, every action and possible reaction was meticulously planned out, so that I would be sitting in front of

'Mika with a chain around my hands. I can remember entire days dedicated solely on escaping from chains and ropes around my wrists. I remember planning to sabotage the aircraft to look like we were attacked, and then I remember jamming the syringe into my arm and releasing the Nightshade compound into my veins, to wipe my memory until the right time. It was the only way to be truly believable. Even if the mission was compromised and I was captured and tortured I couldn't reveal any information, not even my identity, because I couldn't remember. The only thing Operation Sleeping Willow didn't prepare me for was...falling for Ruby. It is good to see her face again, but I don't know how she is still alive. I saw her with the Berserkers. Could it have been a trick? Was Mika one step ahead of me the whole time? I look at him writhing in pain and struggling to breathe. *He certainly doesn't seem to be ahead of me.* I can't help but smirk.

"Put the weapon down now. I will shoot," the armed man yells with spit coming out of his mouth.

"No, wait," Mika says. If it was hard to understand him before, it's almost impossible now. Ruby helps him stand up. "Put your weapons down." Samson looks relieved, but the others look at him as if he is crazy. "If he still wants to kill me, I will die and there's nothing you can do to stop him. But he won't."

I drop the chain. He's right. I won't kill him...for Ruby. I can't stand that she won't even look at me.

"Let me kill the one who almost took my life," Mika says. He grabs his revolver that he had dropped when I attacked him, off the ground. Samson and the others finally lower their weapons. He rubs his bruised neck with his free hand, and flashes me a wolfish smirk. He aims his gun at my face and then steps behind me.

"No!" Ruby shouts, but two of his guards grab her. "Don't do this! You said it yourself, he won't kill you."

There's nothing I will do. I could kill them all if I wanted to, but I won't. The mission is over. I failed.

"You almost killed me because I fell for your lies," he says calmly. He kicks the back of my legs and I fall to my knees. I close my eyes. "You almost got me killed!" he yells louder and clearer than I thought he possibly could. The bullet exploding out of the chamber is louder than he is, but I muster all the strength I have not to flinch, even though my heart feels like it is free-falling into my stomach. It's not me who falls though. I open my eyes to see blood exploding from Samson's neck. His lifeless body collapses to the ground. Ruby covers her dropped jaw with her hand.

12

"Damn it Mika! Why the hell did you do that?" Ruby yells. He lets out a raspy laugh and sticks his gun back into his waistband. He shrugs his shoulders "What did you want me to do? He lied to me about the Naked Lady, and I almost died because of it. I expected you to lie, but he was my soldier, sworn to protect me."

Why would Samson lie for me? He could have taken credit for bringing me in. I should have killed Mika when I had the chance. By some miracle, I was starting to like Samson.

"Bring them and the rest of Ruby's liars to my war room," Mika says to one of his guards.

The war room is hardly a war room. It is only Amalek's cafeteria, but with all the tables removed except for one in the center. Instead of a plethora of delicious dishes, there are maps spread out on the table. In-between the windows there is a large, dark blue flag pinned to the wall. The flag has black stripes and a white skull in the center with two crossed muskets below it. I can remember seeing it many times during training.

"Sit," the guard who escorted us in says. Ruby and I do as we are told and he leaves us alone. It's uncomfortably quiet.

"Ruby, how are you alive?"

She sits on the edge of her seat, as if to be as far from me as possible. She is afraid of me, but she sits up straight and stares forward trying to hide it.

"I saw the Berserkers go to you."

"I...don't know. They came to me, but they did nothing but stare and sniff at me. They treated me as if I was one of them."

"What are you talking about?"

"I mean the oxygen chamber healed my symptoms, but what if I still have the virus? Berserkers don't attack each other"

"It's ironic, isn't it?" Mika says as he walks into the room. "Everyone is so horrified of them, yet they won't even attack their own kind. Perhaps it is not them who are the real monsters." He rubs his neck and looks into my eyes. He sits across from Ruby and I with his flag behind him like a glamour shot backdrop.

I stare back, undaunted by his gaze. I remember many people that I've killed since I joined Nightshade, the ones they allowed me to keep in my memories. I can still see their faces. From war lords and rebel leaders to high-ranking government officials and politicians and occasionally a reporter or prostitute who probably knew too much. I never asked who wanted them dead or why. I just did what I was told to do, and I was damn good at it. "You're right. I am a monster, but so are you."

A vein on his forehead flashes down to his brow like a lightning bolt. He leans forward. "I am a hero protecting my people."

"What happened to the women who served my friends and I yesterday? What about all the children who were running through the streets that morning? You killed them all, didn't you? You weren't protecting your people when you killed them. They were innocent."

"None of them were innocent," he roars and pounds on the table with his fist. "They all came here with one mission, wipe us out."

"One could argue that I tried to kill you for the same reason."

He looks as if he's about to speak, but then doesn't.

"What does it matter? You're both liars and killers," Ruby says.

Mika grins. "And you are right there with us. Did you tell him how you knew there would be over fifty people working on my wall when you blew it up?"

"I did it for our daughter, you son-of-a-bitch," she says.

He chuckles and snorts. "Then where is she, Ruby? I sure as hell don't see her."

She gets up and leans towards him with a clenched fist.

"While you guys are fighting, the Cubans and Ottomans are building an army of trained Fangs and Berserkers," a man I don't recognize says. He's tall and lanky. His face is wrinkled and his hairline is receding, yet his wiry mustache makes his lip look like a teenager's. His right arm is limp and deformed and hangs in a sling around his shoulder, but his legs are long and he speeds through the room like he's on a special mission to get to Mika. His shirt is like Mika's and I wonder if it once belonged to someone he killed as well. Reynolds, Wesley, and Red enter the room behind him.

"Slo-mo," Ruby says.

"Good to see you again," he says, but I can't tell if it's sarcasm or genuine. His face is so rubbery, it's hard to read.

"He's right," Mika says. "As cliché as it is, we need to set aside our differences and work together. Have a seat, gentlemen."

They sit down next to Ruby and I. Slo-mo sits next to Mika.

"This war is about to be lost. I have been defending two fronts for too long, and a third that's cold, but keeps trying to assassinate me. The States don't realize how much they need me...or us. If we fail, they will fail. And if Big Al takes this whole country, our forces overseas will be crippled, and the Ottoman confederacy will be unstoppable. They will take over the whole world."

"We need to unite with the U.S. Maybe I can help. Maybe I can convince them," I say.

"I agree we need to unite," Reynolds says.

Mika is quiet for a moment. "Now is not the time," he says and looks at me. "You failed your mission to kill me. They will not be so keen on listening to you"

I can feel Wesley, Red, and Reynolds gawking at me. I liked it better when they didn't know I was on a mission to kill. I ignore their leers and look at Ruby.

"Mika, you need to put aside your hunger for power and territory—"

"It was never about power," Mika interrupts furiously. "It was always about the people." The little black beads in his eyes are beginning to drown. "The U.S. military was fighting half the world away. They left no one to defend the people. You know I warned them. I even tried to form my militia under their banners, under their rules. I won battles for them, and what thanks did I get? Assassination attempts on me and my family. So I formed my own nation, and I protected my people. But even so, the time will come when I must give up my power and give my land back, and I will do so willingly for my people. But now is not the time, we have more pressing issues. Slo-mo tell them."

"The Cuban government has officially joined the Caliphate, and they are now building an army to attack us." He talks almost as fast as he walks.

"How many men?" I ask.

"They don't need men. They have something better: the infected. And soon they will be upon us."

"A dead bee can still sting, but they figured out how to make dead men march. We don't stand a chance in hell," Red says.

"There is a way to stop them," Mika says.

"Don't tell me you plan on building another wall," Ruby says.

"No, I'm talking about a cure. If we could cure the infection, we could neutralize their entire army in an instant."

"Unless you have 50,000 hyperbaric chambers and a way to lure every Fang and Berserker into them, then you're out of luck," I say.

"What if we could turn the earth into a giant hyperbaric chamber?" Mika says with a smirk.

"How?" I say.

"There is a Cuban scientist in Miami working on a large-scale, oxygen concentrator. In theory, it would have the power to increase oxygen levels in the atmosphere from the current level of 20% to 50%."

"And that's enough to cure Fangs and Berserkers?" Reynolds says.

"It's enough to change the world. Berserkers and Fangs would be cured; humans and animals would heal faster, live longer, and grow taller. Plants would bloom fuller and, in turn, create more oxygen."

"*The restoration of all things,*" Wesley says to himself, as if he just had an epiphany. "It will be like the days before the flood."

"Why are you telling this to us?" Ruby says. I was wondering the same thing.

"You know the area. You've been dealing with Fangs and Cubans for a long time and are therefore, the most qualified to retrieve the concentrator," Mika explains. "Most of all, we need The Naked Lady and you are the only ones he trusts. He may have had friends before Nightshade wiped his memory clean, but all he remembers now is training, killing, and you guys."

"My mission is over. Failure or success I need to return to Director Ira. I need to debrief."

"You will go where Ruby goes," Mika says matter-of-factly. "I see the way you look at her. I once looked at her that way."

I can feel Reynolds staring at me. I look at Ruby, but she turns away.

"And why should I go?" Ruby says.

"Because of Miranda."

"Don't you talk about my daughter."

"Our daughter," he corrects her. "She never told you. Her class was on a field trip to Miami the day the Cubans attacked Florida. They had no need to attack Miami as hard as the rest of the state. With so many Cubans living there, it was practically theirs already." When no one responds, he continues. "Slo-mo will be going with you. He has a contact in the city. You will rendezvous with this person, and he or she will help you locate the scientist."

"Wait a minute; you don't even know where this scientist is?" I say.

"All we know is he is in Miami."

"Do you even know if he will help us?" Reynolds asks.

"We know he is working on a large-scale oxygen concentrator that can cure the infection. We can only assume he wants to cure the infected as much as we do."

"What if he doesn't?" I say.

"Then kill him and steal it if you have to, but we can't keep defending against armies of dead warriors! Your success or failure might very well decide the fate of this entire war."

Mika was right. I'm sitting in the SUV with Ruby and my only friends. Slo-mo is driving us south. I have my duty to return to Nightshade, but Ruby needs me. My friends need me. This country needs me. I can't abandon them now. Mika was also right about my memory. I can remember my years of service in Nightshade, but nothing before that. I don't even know why I joined in the first place. It's like my life began in Nightshade. There is a deep desire inside me to return and find out more, but I have to help Ruby and the others first.

Slo-mo says he knows the fastest route, but the roads he takes are riddled with holes and bombarded asphalt. For a man with only one good arm, he drives the same way he walks and talks...way too fast. But if he can get us there while avoiding anything infected, then I won't complain.

Ruby is up front with Slo-mo, and as per usual I'm in the back. Wesley is with me, but he's hardly good company. He hasn't looked up from his Bible once.

"Why do you read that thing so much?" I ask.

He folds the top corner of a skinny page and closes the flimsy book. He looks up at me. I never noticed his green eyes before.

"Everyone I used to know before the war; my wife, my brother, my uncle, my mom, and dad used to read this book all the time. Not because they felt they had to, but they read it and talked about it all the time as if there was treasure inside. I thought they were all stupid and unenlightened. Yet, I was the one who was left behind in this wasteland. They escaped this war...this hell on earth. And I will take every chance I can get to find out what they knew."

"They died?"

"Their bodies did with the other billion, but their spirits didn't. God took them away so they wouldn't have to live in this mess."

"So then why the hell did he create this mess in the first place?" Reynolds says almost angrily.

"We're the ones blowing each other up and infecting each other," Wesley says back calmly.

"Can't argue with that," I say.

"Speaking of infecting each other," Slo-mo says as he swerves hard around a large pothole. "The Caliphate just tested a new version of the virus. They infected an entire city in France with one bomb. 50,000 people were turned into Berserkers in an instant."

"My God," I can't help but say.

"We have to stop them," Ruby says, and now Slo-mo is driving even faster.

When we arrive in Miami, the city is dark, even though I never saw the sun set.

"The Caliphate is here," Slo-mo says as we pass a building with black smoke pouring out from the top like a great chimney. "There are more like this throughout the city. All day and all night, they burn the People of the Book and any nonbelievers." He drives down empty side streets and through dark alleyways, avoiding the colorful neon lights of the avenues. After swerving around a fallen palm tree, Slo-mo turns down a long, ghostly street with razed building and smashed cars. For the first time, he drives slowly as he looks around.

"What is it?" Ruby asks.

"My contact is here."

"In this dump?" I say as he stops in front of a building that looks as if a wrecking ball smashed through one of the walls.

"The nice buildings are for the collaborators. If that's what you came for, feel free to put on a headband," Slo-mo answers.

"What good is it to clean the outside of your cup, if the inside is filled with blood?" Wesley says as Slo-mo puts the SUV in park and we get out.

"This is the General's territory. Be sure not to piss her off," Slo-mo says as he circles around the front of the SUV. We climb over a pile of rubble and enter through the large gash in the wall of the building. Inside the building is hollowed out, with piles of rubble and debris throughout the open foyer. The sun is clouded by so much smoke that it looks like a dim, red moon above the holes in the ceiling. To the left are steps that lead to an open aisle, which seems to be the remnants of a second story. There are masked men standing above us, looking down. In the center of the open lobby, is the tallest pile of rubble with a red couch on the top. Two men with dark sweat suits and hoods over their heads are standing in front of the debris pile. They have long, gold-colored socks that meet their rolled-up pants at the knee, and they each wear thick, gold chains. Gold masks in the shape of animals cover their faces completely. They are holding gold-colored AAC Honey Badger submachine guns in their hands, but thankfully not pointing them at us. There are two more men dressed the same sitting on the couch at the top, but they are weaponless. They sit up straight with their hands on their knees, like statues unaffected by our presence.

Sitting on the couch, in-between the stoic-looking men is a pale, thin woman with long, black hair and pretty lips. The top of her face is covered by a gold half-mask with pointed eye slits. She wears loose, flowing black pants that stop halfway down her shins and black socks after that. On top of her head is a maroon-colored beret that matches a small cropped jacket with nothing underneath but several gold chains that hang between her small breasts. She sits with her lanky legs spread and her arms around the men next to her.

"Gorilla," she says, and the man at the bottom of the pile with a gorilla mask on climbs a few steps up the rubble and reaches his free hand out to her. She grabs it. He steadies her as she climbs down the pile.

"Isn't she precious?" the General squeals. "I haven't seen a dog in so long," she says with an accent I've never heard before. It almost sounds fake or exaggerated. She scratches the back of Yoshi's ears and rubs her head. Yoshi wags her tail and licks her face without even having to stand on her hind legs. The General giggles.

She looks at us and her smile disintegrates.

"Slo-mo, you're as ugly as I remember," she says. Slo-mo shrugs his shoulders as if he knows it's true. "Times are trying. It is a high offense to bring strangers into my zone. Do you come in peace or war?" As if a signal was raised, the two men behind her lift their guns and aim them at us.

Before I can aim back at them, Ruby puts her hand on my forearm and gives a look that tells me to wait and see how this plays out. However, it could very well play out with a bullet in my chest, so I raise my gun anyways and Red does as well. The General steps directly in front of me, as if to shield her masked men with her gangly, pale body. She stares into my eyes. Her eyes are a pretty, yellowish brown that remind me of Ruby's. Even with the mask on, I can still tell she is very young.

"The last time you came to us Slo-mo, we were attacked when you left," she says still staring at me. "My animals were burned beyond recognition." Her eyes suddenly well up. "They wear prisons on their heads so that I can tell them apart, and so that their General doesn't have to look upon their poor faces any longer." As quickly as the tears came, her eyes are suddenly dry. "Lion, Eagle." The two men sitting on the couch finally move. Surprisingly swift, they run down the pile. They dart opposite ways when they reach the bottom. Each of them run to a pillar that once helped hold up a second floor, but now ends only a few feet above them. In perfect unison, they disappear behind the pillar and then reappear with assault rifles aimed at us. I realize there are now several more masked men that have stepped out of dark corners with guns raised, and the ones on the remnants of a second floor also point guns at us. When I return my eyes to the General, she is still staring at me.

"Last time, Slo-mo, one of the strangers you brought betrayed our location. And we paid more than your worth," she says almost yelling.

"Who will it be this time?" She whispers to me.

I have to remind myself that we came here for help, and if I do anything rash we might all die. I can't let Ruby die because I did something stupid, so I lower my weapon. Red lowers his as well. His hands are shaking, and I'm glad he didn't accidentally fire.

"We have only come for your help, not war," Ruby says. "Your location is safe with us."

The General gracefully steps back. She laughs and lifts her hands above her head, spreading them out like a ballerina. In unison, the masked men around her pull their guns down. The man in the lion mask and the man in the eagle mask put their guns back behind the pillars and come to her, weaponless. They lift her by the arms and carry her back up to the couch. They return to their places, sitting like statues. The man in the gorilla mask and the man in the bear mask return to their posts at the bottom of the debris pile.

"Well then, how can I help you, my dear?" the General says.

"There is someone in your city that might have a cure for the infected," Ruby says.

"It could help us win the entire war," Reynolds adds.

The General turns her head slightly and glares at him. "I was speaking to the lovely girl. Not you."

His cheeks redden and he looks if he is about to speak, but then stops himself.

"As you were saying, my dear?" The General's eyes return to Ruby.

"We need your help. We need to find the man working on a large-scale oxygen concentrator."

"There's something else, isn't there? Out with it darling, we don't have much time."

"I'm looking for my daughter. I believe she might be somewhere in the city. I have to find her."

"Look around you, sweetling. She is either dead or one of them. There are not many Free People left, and we hide in the shadows and dark alleys. As for your scientist, who may or may not exist, I cannot help you. In the unlikely event that he is in fact in this city, you have no idea what his intentions are with the device. For all you know, he could have created it for the Cuban government. My animals felt the flames of the enemy the last time we helped you, Slo-mo. I will not risk them again for such folly. Leave this place and never return."

Well, this was a waste of time.

"Wait," Slo-mo says before we leave. "There's something else...something you may believe to be worth the risk."

"You've wasted too much of my time already. Be gone." The men sitting on both sides of her stand up and look down on us with crossed arms. The two below aim their guns at us again.

"We should probably listen to her," I say, wishing I could walk as fast as Slo-mo.

"The Caliph is here," Slo-mo says.

The General's head tilts slightly and she raises a hand. The men beside her sit back down on the couch, and the men below lower their weapons.

"The Cuban government has finally been accepted into the Caliphate," Slo-mo continues. "North Korea and Russia are soon to follow. If that happens, all hope is lost. Israel, Europe, and the U.S. will be forced to submit or be destroyed, but before this happens the Caliph himself must finalize Cuba's entrance into the empire. He will be addressing this city tomorrow at the temple of the Mahdi. We have to kill him."

"There never was a scientist, was there?" I say to Slo-mo.

"No, I'm sorry for the lie, but we couldn't take the chance of you saying no."

"We can still say no," Reynolds says. "Attempting to assassinate the Mahdi is likely to get us all killed."

"I don't need you to say yes, I need The Naked Lady to."

"You tricked us to come down here for what? To use me? Kill him yourself. I'm done being a pawn."

"If Slo-mo tells it truthful and the Caliph is here. We must kill him," the General says loudly. "If we succeed, we can end the entire war in an instant. He holds all the power. We can't pass this opportunity up."

"We'll help," Ruby says. I look at her wide-eyed. I thought for sure we were about to leave Slo-mo here with the General and go back to Wauchula. She grabs my arm and looks at me softly. "We'll help."

I shrug my shoulders. "Well, what's the plan?"

"In the morning, we will decide. Tonight, we'll eat and drink for tomorrow, we die," the General says.

A few moments later, men and women each with different animal masks come out from dark corners and behind walls. Some are carrying liquor bottles and others trays of food. A boom box on the edge of the second floor balcony is playing pulsating electronic music, and there are masked people dancing next to it. I manage to grab a bottle of vodka from a man with a black rabbit mask. I take a long drink and then pass it to Red as I wipe my mouth with my sleeve. Wesley intercepts the bottle.

"You're allowed to drink? Isn't it forbidden or something?"

"There's no law against it. If I'm going to die tomorrow, I'm having a little fun tonight."

"Hell, I don't like vodka, but if Wesley is drinking then I am too," Red says and snatches the bottle from Wesley. It spills on his chin and chest.

The General is standing on the couch, flailing her lanky arms and legs around to the beat.

"I don't trust her," Reynolds says.

"Yeah, but she's not too bad to look at," Wesley says.

"Wesley, you old dog," Red says and laughs.

"We need to be planning our mission, not dancing around drinking all night," Reynolds says.

"Lighten up. The war could be over tomorrow," I say and grab the bottle from Red. The liquor feels warm and harsh as it goes down my throat and swirls around in my belly. It doesn't take long until I feel lightheaded.

I watch the General as she raises her hands and sways her hips back and forth. She laughs as she looks down at me. I wonder if she has relations with any of the masked men. She is quite attractive, but she is not Ruby. I look around for her, but she's no longer in my line of sight. I take another swig and then pass the bottle to Wesley. I walk past a man with a red rat mask shoving another with a brown horse mask. A man with big, tattoo-covered arms and a light blue, koala-shaped half-mask is trying to break them up with one hand and drinking a bottle of clear liquor with the other. I climb up the steps to what's left of the second floor. There are several open rooms on the left side. On the right, I look down at the party below. Wesley and Red are drinking with some masked men, but Reynolds is sitting on a cinder block, cleaning his shotgun with a rag.

The rooms to my left are pitch-black inside, but the third one is dimly lit by the sun or moon, I can't tell. It has no ceiling and the wall opposite the door has a hole in it. I can see the neon lights of the avenues in the far distance. Ruby is sitting against the adjacent wall, staring out into the city. Yoshi is sleeping next to her feet.

"Have you ever been here before? To this city I mean?" She says softly. Her arms are wrapped around her knees.

"If I have, I don't remember."

"It used to be so alive. You could walk the colorful streets and smell the ocean mixed with all the different types of foods. It smelled so good. Now smell." She inhales deeply. "Nothing but the stench of death and destruction."

"We have the chance to bring it back to the way it was. There's still hope," I say and sit next to her. At least she still smells good.

"I hope so. But we can never bring back the people they took."

I grab her hand. "We'll find her. I know we will."

She rests her head on my chest.

"You're sweet, but you don't know that."

I wish I could argue.

"Do you ever wonder if you have a family? Maybe a wife waiting for you to return to her?" She asks and plays with my fingers.

"Everything I want is right in front of me," I say. She looks up at me.

"That was cheesy as hell, but I'll take it." She smirks and stares at my lips. I grab her face and kiss her softly, but her lips taste so good I kiss her harder. She climbs on top of me. She grabs my shirt and pulls it off and laughs as she traces her fingers across my chest and grinds her hips against me. I grab her hair and pull her head back. She moans as I bite down on her neck. I can feel my heart thumping and my blood flowing. She tugs at the bottom of her shirt and pulls it over her head. She throws it somewhere. Possibly out of the hole in the wall for all I care. Her nipples taste even sweeter than her lips, and they harden when I bite them. Sliding my hands down, I unbutton and unzip her shorts. She unmounts me and laughs as we pull them off of her. I rush to take my pants off, but she's back on top of me before I can get them all the way down. She feels my arousal and grabs me. She lowers herself and I feel her wetness as I sink into her. She cries out and reaches her hands up above her head. It's hard to notice anything else with Ruby's body rhythmically moving up and down on me, but someone is standing at the doorway behind her. I look at Reynolds and he looks at me. He brushes his blonde hair out of his eyes and then keeps walking.

13

A cold drizzle against my skin awakens me in the morning. Ruby is lying in my arms with her head on my chest. I squeeze her tightly and wish the unruly rain would go away and we could just lie here forever, slowly forgetting all about war and Fangs.

"Good morning," Ruby says and kisses the muscles below my sternum. It tickles and I smile.

Suddenly, the man in the gorilla mask is standing at the door.

"It's time," he says and leaves just as fast as he appeared.

"I guess it's time to end a war," Ruby says optimistically. It's a tragedy to see her put her clothes back on. I could stare at her all day.

When we get downstairs, the General is sitting on her couch alone. Four masked men stand at the bottom of the couch and across from them, looking up at the General are Wesley, Red, and Slo-mo.

"Where's Reynolds?" Ruby whispers to Red, but he only shrugs his shoulders.

"The Caliph will be addressing the city at the temple of the Mahdi at 1 pm. It will be televised to the whole world. This is where we will kill him. I want the world to see it," the General says and then looks at me. "Slo-mo tells me you are a trained assassin. You may take the shot."

"What's the plan? You want me to just walk up to the front row and assassinate the most powerful man in the world?"

"Precisely. Do not miss. My Lion and my Bear will be with you in the crowd. They will be strapped with explosives. If you can't kill him, we will blow the whole street up."

"You can't do that," Wesley says.

"You can't kill innocent civilians," I agree.

"Innocent?" she says and laughs. "They all wear the banners of the Caliphate. They are all guilty."

"Most of the people here have been forced to submit," Slo-mo objects. "In dark corners of this city, there have been rumblings of rebellion against the Cuban government. The Cuban people are fed up with the regime and want nothing to do with the Caliphate, but they fear coming out of the shadows. If we succeed many will join our cause."

"Then I would advise The Naked Lady not to miss," the General says with a smirk.

"What about the rest of us?" Ruby says.

"Mika has it on good authority that the Caliphate has shipped a supply of armaments and ammunitions that arrive today. This shipment is large enough to sustain the now mixed Cuban-Ottoman army in this city for years. If the people stand a chance at taking back this city once the Caliph falls, we must destroy the shipment," Slo-mo explains.

"And how do you propose we do that?" Ruby says.

"We're going to blow it up, my dear," the General says. "We're running out of time. We must proceed."

"Wait," Ruby says. "We need Reynolds. He's an explosives expert."

"We already have a supplier."

"We need his expertise," Ruby says.

"Well, where the hell is he?" The General yells as she stands up.

"I saw him leave the building earlier," Wesley says. "I thought he was just going for some fresh air—"

Red laughs. "Ain't nothing fresh about the air in this city."

"—but when I went out to look for him I couldn't find him."

"It is not safe out there without the mark of the Sultan on your head," the General says.

"Why would he leave?" Ruby asks me. I say nothing. I don't want to tell her that he saw us last night. I'm worried she will blame herself for his disappearance. "We have to find him," Ruby demands.

"I'm sorry, my dear. We must go now." With the help of the Lion and the Bear she steps gracefully down the pile of rubble. "We only have one chance to end this war. It is now or never." She walks up to Wesley.

"You must leave your book here. It is outlawed in this city."

"I never go anywhere without it. You have your guns and your bombs, but I have the Word."

"*And coming out of his word is a sharp sword in which to strike down the nations*," the General recites. Wesley gazes at her as if he just fell in love. "I will not deny the Word is a strong weapon, but God is not welcome in this city. That book will get us all killed."

He still looks unconvinced.

The General grabs his arm and gazes into his eyes. He looks down at her hand and then back into her eyes. "It will be safer here," she says. He finally concedes with a nod. She smiles and turns to the rest of us. "In order to get anywhere near the Caliph, or to his shipment, we must wear headbands with his mark on them. We were able to get our hands on just enough—"

"No! That is where I draw the line," Wesley says. The General turns to him furiously.

"It is non-negotiable," she shouts. "I've had enough of your objections. We will be captured immediately without them." Suddenly, Wesley looks like a reprimanded puppy.

"You don't understand," I say. "We almost died refusing to wear it. We will not wear allegiance to the Caliphate even if it is only for a moment."

"If you kill the Caliph, then his name on your forehead will no longer mean anything."

"Good point," I say.

"Please, it is the only way. I don't like it either, but if we destroy the empire it won't matter anymore, and we will save millions of lives," the General says.

I look at Ruby. She raises an eyebrow and nods.

"Let's get this over with," I concede.

"I'm sorry Ruby, but I can't go. I will stay here and read...and watch the SUV," Wesley says. "You don't need me. Just kill that beast and come back." He smiles.

"We'll go without him then," Ruby says.

"Let's move," the General says.

There is a large stage set up at the end of the street in front of the brightly-lit temple with tall, white minarets around it. The main streets, and those adjacent to the temple, are so crowded with men in thobes that I don't know how I'm possibly going to get close enough to aim properly. The General seems to believe that if I kill the Caliph I won't be torn to shreds by the crowd, but seeing how many people are here in support of the Caliphate it's hard to believe. This might be a suicide mission. I look at the blue building with white trim across from the stage. It wasn't part of the plan, but I think my odds would be better getting on the roof and taking the shot from there. At this point, even getting up there seems impossible. I'm still at least three blocks away and the men around me are so squished together that they are standing shoulder to shoulder. Above, thick layers of black fumes mask the sun so much so that it appears only as a faraway star.

As I try to inconspicuously squirm my way through the crowd, I can't help but reflect on how poorly planned this mission is. Ever since I joined the ranks of Nightshade, every mission was meticulously planned out. Every action had at least 100 possible reactions that we prepared for. I trained and studied every day for a year to kill Mika...and that still failed. The one thing we couldn't have predicted was my feelings for Ruby. I know Merrick will be shocked when he finds out why I failed and probably laugh. Although, right now he's most likely just angry that I screwed up the mission. The grey-haired man with a slender face and broad shoulders was my prepping agent. He worked with me every day preparing me for whichever mission I was assigned. Over the years of training, it was only natural we would become close friends. Sometimes after a particularly long day, he would take me out to a bar, and try to coerce me to talk to women, but I never wanted to. When I joined Nightshade, all I thought about was the mission ahead. When you join Nightshade, you join knowing your past life would be erased. I guess at those bars I always assumed that I had a wife and a family, but for some reason that I may never know I still joined, and said bye to them forever. So, I vowed to only focus on the mission at hand. I know Merrick will be shocked when he finds out what really compromised my most crucial assassination to date. Every time they wipe a memory they create a new man, and I don't want to be new anymore. I don't want to ever forget Ruby. If I ever go back, I will not let them wipe my memory again.

All I have weapon-wise is my Glock, and I'm still struggling to get close enough to take a Hail Mary shot. If an arduous plan in the works for an entire year can fail because of something as simple as love, what chance does a last minute cockamamie plan have? *Perhaps it actually has more of a chance*, I think as I maneuver myself between layer and layer of men. The closer I get, the tighter it becomes. It's hot and harder to breathe with every step. The crowd moves and sways as people push and shove each other, all of them trying to get a better view of the Caliph. I didn't even realize the flow of the crowd had been moving me to the side of the street instead of forward for who knows how long. I make my way past an intersection and keep moving. If I don't make it close enough to kill the Sultan, the Lion and the Bear will finish the task, and all these people will die. I look around for the two of them, but there are plenty of others with masks or covered faces. I need to find them. They might be my only protection once I do kill the Caliph.

Suddenly, people began shouting and singing for the Mahdi to appear. I may have a headband on, but I still feel awfully out of place. I look ahead. The podium and the building across from it are still too far away. I hope to God his speech is long or I will miss my opportunity. I'm beginning to think I might have a better chance fighting my way through this crowd than trying to passivly squeeze through.

The crowd begins cheering as a man appears on the stage. *I'm running out of time.* I try to move faster as he approaches the podium. The man is wearing a cream-colored thobe with a white robe over it. His hair is covered with a white turban, but a long blonde strand has escaped from the side.

"Straighten up," he says into the microphone and his voice booms through the loud speakers. His voice sounds familiar. The whole ebb and flow of the crowd has stopped completely and every man stands still watching the podium, except for me. I continue to pry and squeeze myself in-between the bodies of the crowd, and I'm not the only one. I now see the General's men. The Lion is ahead and to the right of me, and the Bear is to my left and almost within reach.

"Prepare the way for the Mahdi," the man on the stage says. I crunch my eyes and finally recognize the speaker. It's Reynolds. "The prophesied one," he says and steps to the side allowing another man to approach the microphone as the crowd cheers. Him, I know instantly. As far back as I am, I can still spot his familiar bumpy nose.

"Brothers," Caliph Amalek says. "Today, we celebrate a new nation's submission under the protection of the Caliphate. Our armies arrive as we speak." He points off east, towards the harbor.

Armies? If the shipments are armies of men instead of armaments, Ruby and the others are in danger. I need to warn them. I need to help them.

"Together, we will bring the U.S. to its knees and force them to submit to me. I am your Mahdi, the Great Sultan prophesied in the holy book, sent by god to unite the whole world as one people. Now, bow before your master."

In an instant, 50,000 men prostrate themselves on the street. The air around me immediately cools. I want to go warn Ruby, but if I don't complete my mission all these people will die. The Lion, the Bear, and myself are the only ones still standing. We all look at each other and, in unspoken agreement, rush towards the stage as fast as we can. It's hard not to trip over the prostrate men, but I'm still able to move faster than before. I'm too far for a clean shot, but I take out my gun anyway and aim ahead. My adrenaline is spiking and I can feel my heartbeat racing. My vision is becoming hazy, and I'm filled with a familiar rage. Maybe I should just let the Lion and the Bear kill everyone. Maybe the General is right. They are all guilty.

I remember Merrick telling me to focus. 'Focus on the task. Block everything else out' he used to say. I try to focus. I narrow my eyes and steady my breathing. I focus only on taking aim, on killing the Caliph. The haze clears and everything seems to slow down around me. A few more steps and I can take the shot. I begin to pull the trigger, but Reynolds looks out with wide eyes, noticing me in an instant. He quickly shields the Caliph and leads him to a short staircase at the end of the stage. If Reynolds wants to die, I have no problem killing him first and Amalek second. But, my attention is torn away as I see the Bear pull out a detonator from his pocket in my peripheral. His thumb is hovering over the button.

I take two long strides and then spin kick his hand. The detonator goes flying and lands in-between two facedown men. We both look at it and then lock eyes. I lunge for the device, but he is closer and grabs it. I wrap my hand around his wrist, twist it, and pull his arm up towards me. I strike him in the belly and then the face as fast as I can, and he drops the detonator once again. He swings at me with his free hand, I block it, but I don't see his knee coming for my stomach. I lose my breath for a moment and let go of his wrist. His fist lands so hard on the side of my face that I fall to one knee stunned. I shake my head in an attempt to reorient my vision. He reaches again for the detonator, but I grab his ankle and pull it towards me as hard as I can. His face smashes against the asphalt and I drag him further away from the bomb trigger. I let go of him and try to sprint around, but he turns over quickly and kicks me in the stomach. He then jumps to his feet and punches me once in the chest, but I block the second and the third punches with my left arm. I lunge my right elbow into his face, and he stumbles back a step. I side kick him in the stomach and land a spinning roundhouse kick to his jaw. He tumbles to the ground and, finally, lies motionless.

I look back and the Caliph is of course already off the stage by now. I scan the crowd. The Lion is in front of me, looking in our direction. He has a bomb strapped to him as well, but instead of reaching for a detonator he uses his hand to point towards a truck behind the stage. Reynolds helps Amalek get inside and then climbs into another truck. I zig and zag through rows and rows of facedown men but it's too late. The truck is already moving away from the stage and towards the avenue ahead. I can't let him get away, but there's no way I'm going to catch up trying to weave my way through this many bodies. I look desperately around for an alternative. Extending from the intersection behind me is a narrow alley that runs parallel to the avenue for at least as far as I can see. I sprint towards it trying my hardest not to stumble. I turn into the side street and finally escape the sea of bowing men. I run past dumpsters and fire escape ladders and towards the next street, but it is already taking too long. Amalek will be out of reach soon, and the mission will be lost if I don't find a faster way. Ahead of me, perched next to a grimy dumpster, is a small blue scooter with chrome plating. I rush over to it. I'm not sure if I'll be able to catch up in this thing, but it's my only shot.

I fumble through compartments and side pockets on the seat looking for keys, but there's nothing. I'm running out of time. This can't be it. If I fail now, there won't be another chance. The Caliph will leave the country and most likely return to the war overseas. I have to do something. Maybe I can hotwire it? I've been trained to hotwire cars, I'm sure a scooter is even easier. I study the ignition, and I immediately notice a set of keys hanging from it. I don't have time for any self-loathing just yet though, so I settle for shaking my head in disgust. I turn the key and the throttle as far as it goes. I zoom by backdoors until the alley dumps me on the next street and I make a hard right and head towards the avenue, passing burnt-out traffic lights and dead palm trees.

A gaggle of lifted trucks pass by along the avenue ahead. I lean forward, but it doesn't do much to speed the scooter up. When I reach the intersection, I turn left and cut through a median in-between two palm trees until I'm following directly behind them. I can taste salt in the air as I follow along the intercoastal on my right. Ahead is a bridge that leads to a long island harbor where several humongous ships are docked.

The trucks turn right onto it. I follow them the best that I can, but it's hard to keep up. I turn onto the bridge and aim my gun ahead. Maybe I can shoot out the tires, but I don't even know which truck is the Caliph's. Suddenly, I'm blinded by several large explosions ahead. Fire and smoke are pouring out from multiple ships on the harbor. Ruby and the others must have succeeded with their mission. If I had done the same, the Caliph and four trucks full of men wouldn't be on their way to kill them.

After the trucks veer off the exit that leads to the island harbor, I lose sight of them. I follow their paths and turn down the same ramp. The road curves and then runs parallel to the water. There is a long, black ship blazing on the harbor and the black smoke is making it even darker on the island than it already was. I can barely see beyond the reach of my hands, but red glare from multiple brake lights cuts through the smog. I hear gunfire all around me, so I hop off and let the scooter coast ahead of me until it falls and slides across the ground for several feet. As fast as I can, I run across the road and towards a stack of tall cargo containers. I take cover behind them and peek out. I hear shouts and more gunfire, but I can hardly see. I struggle to focus my eyes. There is movement near the red lights, but I can't make out who is who. Instead, I run along the containers towards the bay. Following the edge of the water, I circle around and look down a long, narrow lane. Two men in thobes near the opposite end are alternating between firing rifles and taking cover. I step back a few feet and then run towards the container at the edge of the aisle. Leaping up, I'm able to grab the top of the container and pull myself up. Gunfire blasts, people shouting, and Yoshi's woofing mask the sound of my footsteps hustling along the metal storage unit. I jump down between two of the men, and before they even realize I'm there I'm striking them with fast blows to their guts and faces. Wild shots escape their rifles as they flop to the ground unconscious.

When there is a break in the surrounding gunfire, I dash ahead, sneaking past the main road. On the other side, in-between a single story building and a parking garage, there is a man with a rifle in his hands. I hurry towards him and dive forward. I land the tackle and slam him onto the ground with my shoulder dug into his chest.

"Were you born sorry?" Red says wheezing. "We're on the same side."

"Where's Ruby?" I say.

"I don't know, we were on our way out when a bunch of trucks showed up. They knew we were here. I got separated."

I hear something like a subdued voice. It's the voice of a woman. It sounds like she's struggling and her mouth is covered. I jump off of Red and run. I turn right when I reach the edge of the island and turn again onto a long wooden pier extending into the water. Towards the end is a man in a thobe dragging Ruby towards a small running boat. Amalek has his hand over her mouth and is pulling her from behind with a gun to her head.

I move fast behind them, but with a quiet step. I aim my gun ahead, but there is no way I can get a clear shot. There is another man at the wheel of the boat.

"Why do we need the girl? Let me kill her and let's get out of here before her dog comes back," the man says.

"We need her for leverage. Mika will surrender to get her back," the Caliph says and pushes her into the boat so hard she falls to the floor. He steps in behind her, still pointing his gun at her head. "In the meantime, she can be my personal slave. She's attractive enough." The boat begins moving away from the dock, but not before I leap on board. It rocks as I land and Amalek swiftly turns and points his gun at me. Before he can shoot, I whack the gun out of his hand with a turning kick. It falls into the water and I punch the Caliph in the stomach so hard he falls to the floor out of breath. The other man quickly gets up from the driver's seat and lunges for me. I hook kick his face and then follow with a fast side kick to his chest. He crashes into the steering wheel with a yelp. I point my Glock at him, but he is out cold so I don't bother. I turn to Amalek. He stares at me, clutching his stomach.

"You cannot kill me," he says and stands up. His lip is quivering, but his voice holds firm. "The world needs me."

"Do it. Or I will," Ruby says.

The sound of the gunshot resonates across the surface of the water and the Caliph's lifeless body collapses to the floor of the boat, once and for all.

14

Already the city seems brighter and the smoke thinner. It's possible it's just my imagination, but I swear I could see sunlight shining off the blue water of the bay for a moment. Yoshi is riding in the hatch of the SUV with her head sticking out of the window, and her immense tongue flapping in the wind.

"While the Caliphate struggles to find a new leader, it should be easy for the Allies to defeat the empire once and for all," Slo-mo says from the driver's seat.

"I'm sure the president has already declared victory for the U.S. and its allies," Ruby says. She is in the passenger seat resting her head against the window.

"I doubt the Commander of the Israeli forces will be so quick to join them. He seems to have better situational awareness than the other Allied leaders," Slo-mo says.

"Well, I'm still pretty optimistic," Ruby says. She looks back at me and smiles.

"I doubt the U.S. will give Mika any credit," Slo-mo says bitterly.

"If he is the man he claims to be, it won't matter to him. He will give up his power and rejoin the states," Ruby says.

"He is the man he claims to be," the General says defensively in between Red and me. Her animals are in the back sitting quietly. The Bear was furious when we picked him up. It was the news of the Caliph's death that kept him from attacking me.

Slo-mo parks in front of the General's building.

"The war is not over until every Ottoman is driven out of this city.

Today was a good day, but there is still fighting to be done," the General says and climbs out of the SUV.

When we enter the building, Wesley is sitting on the General's couch with a straight back and his hands on his knees. He is perfectly still and looks down on us eerily, but doesn't even acknowledge our presence.

"You are in my seat," the General says and walks towards the pile of rubble. "If I was in a worse mood I would have my Bear drag you off."

He says nothing. I've never seen him without his book in his hands or at least nearby. The General crunches the skin of her forehead and begins to climb the pile of rubble.

I look down in front of me. There is a single Bible page on the ground. I pick it up. It says "Zechariah 12" on the top left corner. Movement on the edge of my vision draws my attention to a pile of more ripped out pages to our left. An incoming draft swishes a few of them away. The cover is burnt and torn.

"Wait!" I call out, but it's too late. As soon as the General grips the arm of the couch to pull herself up, Wesley's head tumbles off his body and bounces down the pile of debris. His limp, decapitated body falls sideways and stays there.

"No!" Ruby shouts. She steps forward, but then catches herself and instead crouches down with her face in her palms.

"They were here. Someone betrayed our location," the General says with a stony calm.

"Reynolds," I whisper and as if summoned, he suddenly appears on the second floor watching us. Yoshi howls at him.

"Ruby, I'm sorry," he says.

She looks up at him in disbelief. "What have you done?"

"I never meant to—"

"Berserkers!" Red yells and points ahead. On the first floor underneath where Reynolds is standing, multiple Berserkers rush into the broken building like mad, hungry animals. Expanded, red muscles are bursting from their decaying skin as they move towards us. Some of them crawl, with their long arms hanging down like wild gorillas.

The Lion and the Bear immediately open fire on the rushing Berserk-ers. They kill the first wave easily, but more and more keep coming.

"We have to get out of here," I yell over the gunfire.

Red shoves me aside and fires his shotgun into the chest of an oncoming Berserker. "That was close," he says.

"He's right, let's go," Ruby says. I notice Reynolds is gone before we turn around, back towards the way we came in. There are more infected humans coming in that way. There is no way out. I go to pull out my gun, but they come in so fast I have to push kick one in the chest. Once there's a bit of clearance, I shoot it in the stomach as it stumbles back. Berserkers are all around us. As I land a right hook to a Berserkers jaw, I see Ruby cut one's neck and then spin around and roundhouse kick another's face. A female Berserker grabs me and bites at my neck. Her cheekbones are sticking out of her skin and I can see her blackened, bloody molars through holes on both sides of her face. She snaps her jaw at me, but I elbow her in the sternum and kick down on her knee, snapping it backwards. I drive my fist down on her head until she crumbles to the floor.

"There's another way out," the Lion says, between precise shots that kill two more Berserkers. It's the first time I've ever heard his voice, but it sounds oddly familiar. Yoshi's jaw is latched onto a Berserker's leg and Red fires his shotgun point-blank into its chest, turning its torso into a bloody hole. When we have some space before the next wave, the Lion retracts his rifle.

"This way," he says and leads us to the southeast corner of the building. I follow last, bringing up the rear. A single Berserker crawls at me quickly and wraps its bleeding boney, hand around my ankle and I almost trip. I hasten to balance myself and feed a bullet into its screaming mouth, which explodes out the back of its head. I can hear groans and growls of more coming. The Lion leads us down a long hallway. Halfway down, a pile of rubble blocks us from going any further.

"Down here," the Lion calls. He turns right and takes us through a door and down many turning flights of steps. At the bottom, we go through another door that leads us into a dim hall. After a turn, there is a wide, but short, flight of steps that takes us down into a long, dark tunnel. Our shoes and paws splash through the puddles on the ground and echo against the arched walls.

The Bear and the Lion switch on small flashlights and walk carefully ahead, keeping the General in-between them. Although, I don't think she needs such close protection. Before we left the main building, I saw her fight off three Berserkers and kill two of them with her gold-plated machine pistol. The rest of us follow behind. Ruby would probably kick our asses if we tried to give her the same protection.

"Where are we going?" She asks.

"This will lead us to the next street. It will dump us out at the Metrorail station. We need to move quickly. They will have the whole block surrounded and infested with an army of the infected. The whole block is connected. We'll have to cross the train platform to get to the next street," the Lion explains.

As we move further down the tunnel, I hear a door slam behind us and echo through the whole tunnel. We all stop and look back to watch the passageway. Even with the flashlights we can't see anything. Suddenly, there's a piercing scream that sounds like a man on fire. It gets louder and louder as it reverberates against the channel walls. A chorus of nasty moans, screeches, and wading footsteps at the entrance to the tunnel follow close behind.

The Lion steps forward and fires his rifle towards the noise. The blaze from the barrel lights up the tunnel in short flashes. The Berserkers are closer to us than I thought. A few of them fall back, but are quickly stumbled over and replaced by more. They claw and pull at each other trying to get further ahead.

"Run!" he yells, and we run as fast as we can the other way.

"There's too many," Red says. They are getting so close I can almost feel their breath on the back of my neck. I turn as I run and fire random shots into the darkness, but I can't tell if I hit anything. My mind is becoming cloudy again. A hazy fog fills my eyes and the growls and groans of the Berserkers are being entangled with the walls and lights. I can't tell if I hear splashing water or see it. Can I see Berserkers in front of me or hear them? I don't know which way is forward or which way to shoot. I have to stop. I hear footsteps all around...or is it heartbeats?

Someone grabs me.

"Focus," a familiar voice says. "For just a little while longer, I need you to focus," the Lion says and my vision begins to clear. All my senses are heightened as I steady my breathing and concentrate on my surroundings. I can hear the Lion's heart beating in his chest. It's steady, unlike all the other heartbeats around me. I zone in and can distinguish the inhumanly fast ones from the beats of my friends. The entire tunnel seems brighter to me now. I can see the Berserkers, almost upon us. I look into the Lion's eyes behind his mask. I feel like I've known him for a long time.

"Go," I say, but before I can get a response I dash towards the Berserkers, knowing that he will listen and lead the others away.

I focus on the erratic heartbeats in front of me. They sound as if they each are going to explode. I listen to each step as they charge towards me. The water splashes as if in slow motion.

"There are so many," is the last thing I hear Ruby say before the others are drowned out by snarls and screams of the Berserkers surrounding me. I focus my senses on the infected. I slow my heartbeat and breathe long, deep breaths as a Berserker reaches its deformed hand for me. I turn as it extends past me. I grab its wrist with my left hand and twist it. I hammer down with my right arm and break its forearm with mine. I immediately swing my pistol back up and strike the Berserker so hard in the face it unhinges its jawbone and it falls back. Another wraps its arms around me, but I use it to jump up and swing kick another in the face, spinning it to the ground. I then elbow the one behind me in the stomach until it finally lets go and I can spin around and put a bullet in his forehead. Many more

Berserkers surround me, but I center my mind and see every strike, grab, and bite coming. They are fast, but I'm focused. I throw punches, kicks, elbows, and bullets at them in a fury that they can't keep up with. For every Berserker I kill, there's another to replace it. But for every strike I dodge, I land a harder strike on another one of them. Before I know it, their dead bodies begin to stack up all around me. Incoming Berserkers must climb and stumble their way towards me. These extra few seconds to prepare only makes the slaughter easier for me. I change clips and finish off the last half-dozen with a combination of bullets and skull-crushing punches and kicks. When I put a bullet in the chest of the last one and it tumbles over and slides down the pile, I can't help but yell as loud as I can in relief and pleasure. Sweat and blood are pouring down my face. I almost don't want to leave my trophy of dead bodies, but I need to catch up to the others.

I walk to the end of the tunnel and my breathing and other senses return to normal. To my left is a narrow stairwell. I climb the steps and it takes one turn to the right before dumping me out on a train platform. At the exit is a hanging chain with a sign that says 'No Entry'. I connect the chain to the link on the other side. Now, whoever finds what I left in that tunnel will have no excuse.

"If you didn't make it, we were going to throw a grenade down there," Ruby says.

"You would have risked the structural integrity of this building. The whole place could have collapsed."

"It would have been worth it," she says and raises herself on the tip of her toes to kiss me.

"We have to go now," the Lion says.

"He's right, there might be more," Slo-mo agrees.

"Indeed there are," Reynolds says. Two men with red and white checkered ghutra scarves and marked headbands stand beside him with automatic rifles aimed at us. They have themselves planted on a platform above a wide flight of steps. "You have cut the head off of the serpent, but now the body writhes and claws for vengeance. The infected have been released and will consume this city."

I turn as I hear more Berserkers and Fangs coming from the tunnel and the Metrorail terminal. I spin around searching for another way out."

"Try all you want, but the only way out is up these steps."

"You betrayed me, Milhouse," Ruby shouts.

"I was the one betrayed," he yells back. "I loved you. I helped you. I did whatever you needed me to, and for what? For you to fall for him? A stinking Brute?" he says looking at me.

"I was your friend," I say.

"None of that matters now. The only thing that matters is the Caliphate."

"The Caliphate is over, Reynolds," I say. "It will crumble without its Caliph."

"No, you don't understand. The strongest empire the world has ever seen will not be destroyed by a mere head wound. You can't win. They will not stop until the whole world submits. There is no escape," he is practically screaming.

The agonizing wails and hurried footsteps of Berserkers are closer now. They are almost here. Hundreds of them are coming from three different directions. Yoshi is sitting next to Ruby, whining anxiously.

Reynolds stares at Ruby with bitterness.

"Let us go," Red demands.

Reynolds lifts his arms and points two pistols towards us.

"Damn it, Reynolds," I say, but Reynolds steps back and my shoulders jump as he fires both guns. The two men with ghutras drop on the platform above us and puddles of blood quickly form near their heads.

"You must go now," Reynolds says. Without arguing, we climb the steps as fast as we can. Ruby stops in front of Reynolds and looks into his eyes. "Quickly now. They're almost here."

"You don't have to do this," Ruby says.

"Go, I'm already dead...I pledged my allegiance," he says and touches the mark of the Caliph on his headband with the tip of his pistol. "There is no turning back. Now go. Hurry! And Ruby, have the girl take off her mask."

I grab Ruby's hand and pull her up the steps as Berserkers pour out of the stairwell that comes up from the tunnel and the Metrorail lanes. We run up the steps without looking back. I hear multiple gunshots followed by horrible screams. They sound so human when they die and it makes me wonder how many people the Caliphate has turned into Berserkers. We make it to the street above. Below, I hear Reynolds screaming in pain, but it ends quickly.

The streets are empty and dark around us.

"The people are hiding," the General says.

"Can you blame them?" Red asks. I can hear hordes of Berserkers in the distance, and the ones down below are starting up the steps.

"He didn't give us much time," Slo-mo says.

"Down that alley. It will lead us back to your vehicle. We need to leave this city," the Lion says and nods at the Bear. The Bear steps in front of the General and pounds his fist on his chest.

"It is my honor to die for you, General," he says, bows, and then runs towards the stairs.

"What in tarnation is he doing?" Red says. I notice the detonator in the Bear's hand. He runs down the steps and out of sight.

"Into the alley, now!" I yell and we run into the protection of the buildings as the Bear explodes the bomb strapped around him, shaking the ground and everything around us. He gives us a good head start, but as soon as we make it halfway down the alley, more Berserkers follow behind us. We keep running ahead. I can now see our SUV parked in front of the General's building, but suddenly a large pack of Fangs enter into the alleyway in front of us. We all stop. We're completely surrounded.

"Pick your poison," Red says darkly, but the Fangs move quicker and will surely reach us first. I'm not sure we have enough firepower to get through them all, but I aim my gun at the Fangs ahead anyway.

Yoshi growls and barks at them, patiently waiting to pounce on the first one that gets close enough.

"Move out of the way," a strange man yells from the end of the aisle. He has straight, black hair down to his shoulders and a matching mustache that curls up at the end. His tattooed belly jiggles as he runs behind the Fangs. He waves his colorful arm. "Get out of the way. They're not coming for you."

There's no time to question him. We all hug the brick and cement walls on either side of the lane. As the Fangs get closer, I pray we were right to trust this stranger so easily but I don't suppose we had much of a choice. Ruby is across from me with her back and arms plastered against the wall. I shut my eyes as hard as I can, as if my eyelids can protect me. The vicious pack stampedes by us and I open my eyes, mercifully unscathed by the hoard. The Fangs pounce onto the Berserkers, biting and tearing at their faces and throats. But the Berserkers fight back. I watch a Berserker grab a Fang that looks like a giant husky by its tail and swing it against the wall, pulverizing its head in an instant. Another rips a Fang in half, but there are more Fangs than Berserkers. A muscular Fang with a fat bulldog's face jumps on a Berserker's shoulders and rips the back of its neck off with one bite. Two others tear at a brown-haired teenage girl's stomach until it screeches and falls dead on the ground. There's blood and guts everywhere and it's impossible to tell which is human and which is dog, but it isn't long until the Fangs have killed all the Berserkers.

"Why didn't they kill us?" Ruby asks the long-haired man, still panting slightly.

"I've been capturing Fangs for some time and training them," he says in a raspy, Cuban accent. "I tell them who to attack."

"Why did you save us?" I say.

"The Cuban people are fighting back. We never wanted to join the Caliphate. Our government forced us. We're reclaiming this city. The Caliph is dead, and we will get rid of all collaborators as well."

The Fangs are feasting on the corpses.

"They are going to eat well tonight," the Cuban man says with a croaky laugh. He sticks his pinkies in his mouth and blows out a loud, high-pitched whistle. The Fangs look up from their dinner. *"Vamonos! There are plenty more Berserkers to find,"* he says. He continues down the alley and the Fangs follow him in neat lines.

We exit the alley with raised guns, making sure to check both ways for Berserkers. As soon as it's clear, we make a run for the SUV.

"Come on, we have to get out of the city," Ruby says.

"I can't leave. This is my home. I am staying to take back my city," the General says. Ruby steps in front of her. She brings her hands up to the General's face and lifts the mask off her. She has high cheekbones and a small, curved nose that match Ruby's but her skin is milky white and with the mask off she looks even younger than she actually is. Ruby smiles and her eyes look as if they're about to erupt into streams of salty water.

"Miranda, it's too dangerous," Ruby chokes out as she palms the side of the General's face.

"Don't try and play 'Mommy' now," she says and backs away from Ruby's touch. "I've survived by myself for four years. I don't need you."

"Maybe you don't, but I need you. I've been searching for you for a long time and I won't lose you again. I'm staying with you."

"I don't think—,"

"I know it's been a few years, but I'm sure you remember just how stubborn I can be," Ruby interrupts her. "And I'm sure you can use an extra gun." Miranda finally concedes with a reluctant nod.

"Well, if you're staying, then I am too," I say and smile.

"No," the Lion says sharply. "You cannot. If you stay, you will die." He takes off his mask.

"Merrick," I say.

15

I can finally see daylight again as Merrick drives me further away from Miami. If anyone else had ordered me to go with them or face death I wouldn't have bought it, but I trust Merrick more than any other man. I'm still worried about Ruby and the others. I know they can defend themselves, but that doesn't help the pit in my stomach.

"Where are we going?" I ask.

"Sarasota."

"Why would I die if I stayed in Miami? Would you have killed me?"

Merrick laughs and flares his pointy nose. "Why would I kill you?"

"Because I never returned to Nightshade after I failed my mission. Isn't that why you infiltrated the General's organization? To bring me back or kill me?"

"You didn't fail your mission. You passed it with flying colors," Merrick says matter-of-factly.

"What are you talking about?"

Merrick loops around a wide pothole on the highway. The road is imprisoned on both sides by miles of swampland.

"There's a lot you don't know. Sometimes when a mission is of particularly high importance, it is imperative to keep vital information away from even the assassin himself. You see, your mission from the very beginning was to kill the Caliph."

"Wait a minute. What about Mika? Why send me to kill him?"

"We never wanted to kill Mika. If we killed him, we would have created a martyr and only further divided his country from the U.S. In fact, we need him in power. You may not like him, but he is every bit as honest as he is ruthless. When the time is right, we truly believe he will give up his power. A successor might not do the same...and no one can deny he has helped immensely in saving the homeland from the Caliphate."

"So, you knew I wouldn't kill him? Then that means you must have known...that I would fall for Ruby. That couldn't have been part of the plan?"

"It may be hard for you to believe right now, but yes. You needed to fall for her so that you wouldn't kill Mika, but rather join his cause. And you needed to fall for her to follow the Caliph when he captured her, because she needed to be the one to tell you to fire. We planned for thousands of scenarios and thousands of results. This was the only way to kill the Caliph and end the war once and for all."

I lean back on the headrest and watch us zoom by thickets of saw palmetto and tall gumbo-limbo trees. Their red bark branches stretch out and curve upwards like fingers holding up dense bushes of leaves to the heavens.

"Did Ruby know? Was she a part of it the whole time?"

"That doesn't matter. What matters is that you succeeded in killing the Caliph."

"It matters to me," I shout and slam my fist on the dashboard so hard that if there was an airbag it might have deployed in my face. "Was she a part of it or not?"

Merrick sighs. "You know Ruby. Do you really think she would have let the Caliph capture her so easily?"

His answer feels like a jab to my gut. It was all a lie. Everything she did was exactly what she needed to do to get me to fall for her. Every look, every smile, even our night together was a lie. Before Merrick and I left Miami, Ruby wouldn't even look at me in the eyes. She knew I was going to find out the truth. I'm so infuriated and confused my brain feels like it's turning to mud. Merrick was my trainer and friend for so long. He was once the man I trusted most in this world, but even withheld information from me. I thought I had friends, but I don't. I'm completely alone, but it's better this way. I don't need friends to be a killer.

"Why all the schemes? Why not just tell me to kill the Caliph?"

"Which is better, a killer who kills because he is ordered to do so...or a killer who kills to protect those he loves? Every time we wipe an agent's memory, we create a new man. When we do this, we must also create a man with a purpose. Mindless drones are not as effective. It is true that feelings and emotions can sometimes lead an agent astray, but it can also help fuel an agent's desire to complete a mission. I'm sorry that I didn't tell you, but in order for you to truly develop genuine feelings for her, I couldn't."

"So instead of emotionless drones, you create emotionally-manipulated ones? You screwed with my emotions and feelings all for your own benefit."

"Not my benefit, but the whole world's. Yes, you were lied to. We held information from you and possibly caused you some heartbreak, but that is a small price to pay for the end of the war. With the Caliph dead, the Allies will finally win this war. All great achievements take a little sacrifice, and you have saved millions of lives. You killed the Caliph. You—"

"No I didn't! You did. I was just the weapon in your hand."

"We may have planned out thousands of different outcomes, but they were planned around you. It was your reactions and your choices that killed him. You may not have known half of it, but this was *your* mission and your success."

"I'd hardly call that comforting. I'm done with Nightshade. I'm done having my memory wiped. The war is ending. I'm retiring."

"It's not the first time you've said that."

I look at him sharply. I wonder how many times we have had this conversation before...how many versions of this that he remembers, but I don't.

"But, okay fine. You're retired, but you must return with me first."

"Why should I?"

"I already told you. If you don't, you will die"

"How will I die? Will they send someone to kill me if I don't return?"

"There's so much you don't know."

"Then enlighten me."

"There is a rage you always feel deep inside. You've never been able to explain it. At times it seems uncontrollable, doesn't it?"

I nod, but I don't understand how he can know that.

"But when you do control it, when you focus all that rage unto the task at hand, you become stronger and faster and more precise than any other human on this planet. Everything around you seems to slow down and all your senses become more powerful."

I wonder if he feels the same rage.

"When you focus, you can become the world's deadliest weapon. However, if that anger isn't controlled you become a danger to yourself and those around you. There is only one person who can help you focus and control the anger within."

"You," I roll my eyes and guess.

"Correct. You've known me as your trainer, but I am so much more. I am your ground. I was assigned to you when you joined Nightshade and have been with you ever since. That is why I had to infiltrate the General's organization. To help you focus and finish the mission completely."

"So, you're with me now. We didn't have to leave. With you by my side we can help them take back Miami."

"There's more to it than that. I can help focus and control your rage, but only for so long without your dosage. You've already been gone too long and if I don't get you back, it will completely take over."

"What are you talking about? Dosage of what?"

"Oxygen."

"What do you mean?"

"Don't you already know that concentrated oxygen keeps the virus from becoming fully systematic? Without regular doses you will become a—"

"Wait a minute. Are you saying that I'm..."

"Yes, you are a Berserker."

"No. That's not possible. I don't remember...when?"

"The director will explain more when we get there. For now, you have to try and focus. None of our agents have ever gone this long without treatment."

"But I thought oxygen cures the infection permanently?"

"Yes, but only in an oxygen-enriched atmosphere. In our current atmosphere, it's only days after treatment before the effects of the virus take over again."

"Ruby."

"What about her?"

"She was..." I try to picture her face, but I can only see it for a moment. It evaporates into a cloud of mist around me. My thoughts are jungled together. I can't tell the difference between my senses. Merrick has become nothing more than a dark silhouette in front of me.

"Focus on Ruby," but I can't tell if I heard, saw, or felt his words. "You still love her."

"She betrayed me," I yell. The fury I feel inside me is so hot that it burns everything around me. In a flash, it all turns to flames. I can see Ruby in the flames.

"I need to save her. She's infected too," I try to say, but my lips and tongue are too hot. I can't put it into words. All that comes out are desperate moans and grunts. "You did this to me," I murmur at the flaming shadow in front of me, but it doesn't understand. I want to kill it. I don't know what it is anymore, but if I tear it apart and feel it die in my hands I think the burning will stop. I reach for it, but it's too fast. It grabs me and strikes me.

"Focus," it says, but it's too late for that. I reach for its head and squeeze it as hard as I can. *Die!* But instead it spins around me. I lose my grip and hear or feel a thump on my head. Everything becomes a bit dimmer, and then I feel it again. The fires are dying down. *Yes! Kill me and quench this terrible burning...*

...I take a heavy breath as if it was my first. I'm lying on an inclined gurney in a bright white room. My vision seems to have returned to normal again. Thankfully, nothing is burning. It feels so strange that everything is normal when what seemed to be only a few moments ago the entire world was ablaze around me. I don't know where I am. I look around. My arms are restrained to my sides by metal bars. I try to pull free, but they're too tight.

A door to my right opens and a middle-aged man in a fitted, ink-blue suit with peak lapels walks in. He closes the door behind him and walks to a seat in front of me without even looking in my direction. He sits down and pulls a small, swivel desk over and opens a thin laptop. He pulls glasses out from the inside of his breast pocket and stares intently at the computer screen. He has black stubble on his face with neat, intentional edges that follow parallel to his sharp jawline. His black hair is short, neat, and faded on the side up to a long hard-part.

"How are you feeling? Everything is clearer I trust?" He questions, finally looking up at me with piercing, ocean-colored eyes.

"Why am I restrained?" I sound calmer than I mean too.

"We're not going to get anywhere if we just keep responding to questions with more questions. Answer mine and I will be obliged to answer yours in return," he says with a sly smile.

"I'm feeling fine. Everything is clear."

"Good. You almost killed Merrick, but he got you here just in time. This is an oxygen-concentrated room. You should return to normal soon. Until then, for my safety and your own, you will remain restrained."

"I don't remember being infected."

"Just as you don't remember meeting me, but in fact you did. Four years ago you came to Nightshade, hoping desperately to join my organization. You were only twenty-two and your military record was average at best, but you had something only a few others had. You had the willingness to forget."

"Forget what?"

"Your past. You lost your family. They were taken from you when the first billion died. I, being the generous, caring man that I am, offered you a new life...a chance to forget the pain you felt. But before we wiped your memory and took away all that pain, I infected you with the third prototype of the virus. It had the potential to make you stronger, faster, and more alert than a normal human. With it, and your painful memories gone, you could become the perfect soldier, an unstoppable killing machine. My virus has changed the world and you willingly chose to be infected," he says with a high-pitched giggle.

"Your virus?"

That sly smirk returns to his face and he bounces his eyebrows. "Yes, it's mine. I created it. Brilliant, isn't it?"

"You've turned hundreds of thousands of people into mad beasts just so you could create a weapon like me?"

"I created something that could make man better. Great scientists know that every great discovery takes trial and error, and every experiment has side effects. The first prototype killed a billion people. The second, I gave to the ambitious Cuban government hell-bent on destroying the U.S. for eighty years of oppression. But all that one did was kill more humans and create the creatures you call Fangs, but I had no use for dogs and dead men. So, I kept working and created you."

"You killed the billion? You're responsible for killing my family?"

"Mystery solved," he says with a shrill, mocking tone. "And that's what brought you to me. I told you it was brilliant. I am brilliant."

"You're a monster!" I shout and try to get out of my restraints as hard as I can, but it's a futile effort.

"No, I'm a scientist," he smiles. "Working for the greater good."

"You killed over a billion people!"

"How many creatures had to die to create man? Trillions? You wouldn't call evolution a monster, but a necessary force to wipe out the weak for the sake of the strong. I have created a stronger, faster, more agile man."

"Who goes berserk after only a few days. It's not brilliant. It's stupid."

"It's not stupid!" he stands up and shouts. His chair falls backwards. His face is steaming, but he quickly gathers himself and calms down. "It is brilliant. I am brilliant. You just don't understand. Madness is only a temporary side effect. You see, I own the only large-scale oxygen concentrator in the world. So don't worry, I will use it to cure all of the infected. I will create a new world where humans and animals will live longer and grow bigger and stronger and heal more quickly and in turn, plants and trees will multiply and grow bigger and greener and pump out more oxygen. It will be a new world, a paradise...and I will have created it. The world will worship me, and my genius will finally receive the credit it deserves."

I can't help but laugh loudly and his grin dissipates instantly. "Even if you cure the infection and restore the earth, they will call you a beast when they find out what you've done and how many people you have killed."

"Yes and they will praise the beast. Do you think that I will turn the earth into a paradise before I destroy all the nations who have opposed me? You agents of Nightshade think you work for the U.S. but you don't. The U.S. and Allied leaders laughed in my face and nearly destroyed my career when I came to them with my ideas of creating a perfect man and a new world." Waves rage in his eyes. "Their small minds couldn't understand that people had to die for the sake of science and progress," he is almost shouting again. "But I didn't give up. I found supporters of my cause and together we revived the Ottoman Empire. And now that you have killed that fool Amalek for me, I will take my place as their rightful king and wipe out all those who doubted me."

"No I won't let you. I will kill you, just as I killed the Caliph."

The director laughs.

"You know, I was going to wipe your memory again like the last time I told you all of this, but I think I would enjoy it more to see you try."

He leans over and presses a button on his computer and suddenly my restraints unlock. I rub my wrists and stare at him curiously.

"You just going to sit there, or are you going to come kill me? Do you need Merrick to help you? He's been listening the whole time."

Merrick promptly bursts through the door. "Ira, you of all people should know that someone is always listening," he says to the director.

"I did know, but it doesn't matter. You can't stop me. It's time for me to finally reveal myself. It is my destiny to rule this world." He puts up his fists in a challenge. "What are you waiting for?"

Merrick lunges at him throwing quick punches, but the director blocks them all with ease and lands a fast jab to Merrick's face. I hop off the gurney and charge towards him. Merrick and I throw dozens of punches and kicks at him, but he dodges or blocks every one of them in a frenzied dance. He's so fast. Even though we're the ones attacking, we step backwards every time he steps forward. He lands occasional jabs to my face and torso that hurt more than they should. The harder I try to hit him, the easier it seems for him to block my strikes and hit me instead. I can feel blood dripping down my cheek.

"Focus," Merrick pants desperately. Ira lets out a rascally giggle, grabs his arm, jumps, and drives down a furious punch to the ridge above Merrick's eyes. He crashes to the floor, knocking over the desk and Ira's computer.

"Come on," director Ira yells at me. I blitz at him once more, trying to stay focused on his moves. He swings at me, but I move out of the way and strike at him faster than he can block until I drill a straight punch to his solar plexus. He stumbles backwards and struggles for air. He stares at me, as if I'm the first person who's ever struck him. Now is my chance. I lunge forward with my fist raised, but he spins and hook kicks my head so hard I fall to the ground. The room is spinning and I can't see straight. I have to close my eyes to stop the spinning...

16

"Get up. We have to go," Merrick says. He's crouching beside me and shaking me by the arm.

"Where's Ira?"

Merrick helps me up. "He's gone. The whole place has been evacuated. This is the last oxygen-concentrated building left in the world. We have to leave now."

"Why would we leave? We should stay and build up my strength."

"He's going to destroy it. Once destroyed, his agents will not be able to stop him."

I take a step, but almost fall. Merrick grabs my arm to help steady me. "Are you okay?"

"Yeah. My head just hurts. Let's go."

We leave the room and hustle down a long, white hallway with light brown doors on both sides. At the end is a swinging double door that takes us into an open lobby.

"Wait here," Merrick says and climbs over a curved receptionist counter. Behind it is a small dark room. Merrick goes inside and returns moments later with two handguns. He hands me back my Glock. "Sorry I had to take this from you, but you probably would have killed me."

"How long do I have, until I try to kill you again?"

"With me keeping you focused, give or take 5 days."

"Brilliant," I say shaking my head.

We leave through the front door and once again must bear the scorching Florida sun. I begin to sweat as we go around the building to a small parking lot where the SUV is parked. We quickly get in, and Merrick pulls out onto a two-lane street that leads to a highway ahead. I remember this street well. There are restaurants and bars and a large movie theatre at the end, all in perfect condition, untouched by war. If only there were people here there would be no need to rebuild.

"I always thought it strange that the Cubans never attacked this place, but now I know why. The director controls the whole world now," Merrick says.

"Not yet. We can still stop him. If we can find his large-scale oxygen concentrator, we can cure the infected. We can wipe out half his army instantly."

"We need Mika."

"Mika? For what?" I say annoyed.

"Mika knows a lot. We used that to our advantage in Nightshade, but his intelligence on enemy movements and missions is commendable. He can help us locate the concentrator, and possibly assist with its retrieval."

"I have no interest in working with Mika."

"Do you expect to find it, kill Ira, and defeat his armies in less than five days all by ourselves? Like it or not, we need his help."

"There has to be another way"

Suddenly, the windows of the SUV and the ground begin to shake and there are multiple explosions behind us. I turn around and see the building engulfed in flames. I turn to Merrick.

He gives me an "I-told-you-so" look. "I vote we keep listening to me."

"Fine, we'll go see Mika," I say begrudgingly.

Merrick turns onto a highway and then quickly takes a right onto another that leads to the interstate ahead. The on-ramp is just a pile of broken asphalt, so Merrick drives passed it. We're both quiet for a long time. I rest my head against my window. I try to picture the family I used to have, but all I can picture is Ruby. I don't want to think about her though. She lied to me and for what? So that I could do Ira's work for him? Now he'll take over the Ottoman Empire and unleash the full force of hell on the world. I just want to find him and kill him. Which makes me wonder...

"How is Ira so strong?" I ask. "The two of us couldn't even touch him."

"He's patient zero. He infected himself a long time ago."

"And that makes him stronger?"

"You already know that oxygen neutralizes the virus. That includes the extra strength and speed you've been able to harness from it. But him...somehow he doesn't lose it when he's in an oxygen-rich atmosphere. He's had it for so long that he's been able to train himself to keep his mind and his strength at the same time."

"So, what then? I have to stay away from oxygen to defeat him?"

"Or," he says and casually points to a black bag in-between the seats.

I unzip it and look inside. There are two submachine guns, multiple magazine clips of different sizes, and what looks like an explosive of some kind. I smile. "I suppose these might help beat him."

Merrick laughs. "No, not the guns. Ira is too smart to allow himself to be shot. Look in the side pocket, that one."

I look inside. There are three syringes filled with some sort of blue liquid.

"What is it?"

"You've heard of a large-scale concentrator. That's a micro-scale one. Inside are microscopic capsules full of oxygen. These are so highly-concentrated it should be enough to neutralize his virus, at least for a short time. If we let the virus manifest in you, your strength will return. And if we inject him with one of these, we may be able to level the playing field."

"That's risky. I may try to kill you again," I say with a smirk.

We drive northeast on a long, two-lane road for a while. Old farms line both sides until we pass through a small, deserted town. An unimposing pack of Fangs come out of a broken courthouse to watch us as we drive through extinguished traffic lights. Merrick finally turns right and follows along a big lake until the road curves around and throws us onto a major highway. I recognize the road. Mika's mobile home park is up ahead. He veers off the thoroughfare and onto the lengthy road that will lead us to Mika.

"We're here to see Mika," Merrick says, stating the obvious to a couple of armed guards at the gatehouse. One of them grabs a large satellite phone and holds it up to his ear.

"I still don't think we should see Mika," I say low enough so the guards won't hear me.

"What choice do we have?"

I shrug.

"Go ahead. Mika's been expecting you," the guard says and presses a button on the inside of their little guard shack. The fenced gate rolls open and we drive down the main road of the mobile home park. It looks much different than the first time I came here.

Instead of kids playing in the street, there are soldiers running and singing cadence. Instead of men in thobes, there are men and women in black uniforms with the flags of Mika, and instead of lifted trucks there are armored Humvees with U.S. flags on them. No one pays us any mind as we park next to the clubhouse. Mika's flag flies high above the clubhouse, as does the U.S. flag. A couple officers walking out of the building give us a nod of acknowledgement and continue past us.

"This doesn't look like a rebel base anymore," I say.

"Except for this guy."

There is an olive-skinned guard at the door who has a long beard and shaggy hair. We have to tilt our heads up to look at his blue and black painted face. He is wearing the signature Mika uniform, although his veiny muscles look like they barely fit inside his shirt. He is carrying an M16 rifle in his hands and has two belts of rifle bullets strapped across his chest like a vest. As if that wasn't enough for a one man army, he also has a tool belt around his waist with a pistol and several knives holstered in it.

"Mika's personal guard," Merrick whispers as we walk up to the man.

He looks down at us curiously and then lifts his wrist to his mouth. "They're here. Only two of them, sir," he says with a desert accent. He watches us for a moment, presumably waiting for a reply. "You may enter," he says and continues staring forward.

We enter through the foyer. No one is around, but I can hear multiple voices speaking in Mika's war room.

Inside, there are four men and one woman all seated on the same side of the table. They all become quiet and look up at us as we walk in. Aside from Mika and a short bald man to the left of him, everyone is wearing American officer uniforms. On the wall behind them, in-between the windows, Mika's flag is pinned right beneath a U.S. flag. I don't know if it's on purpose, but the U.S. flag is a little bigger.

"Mika, we need—" Merrick begins to say, but Mika holds up his hand.

"Throughout history the rules of war have always repeated that tired, old phrase 'don't kill the messenger.' But when the Persian messengers came to the Greeks offering submission or death, the Greeks pushed them into black pits that some say never ended. Now, the director of Nightshade has taken control of the largest empire the world has ever known and he sends his messengers to us. What do you think I will do when you offer me submission? Do you really believe I will take it? Or will I throw you both into a pit?"

"We are not—"

"I will not submit!" Mika roars and stands up.

"Mika, it will be better if we hear their terms," the man to Mika's right says calmly. He's older than Mika, with a clean-shaved face and a white, high and tight haircut. He wears a black tie and a black jacket with many pins and metals on his lapels. "You'll have to excuse *General* Mika. His army has just suffered great losses. Big Al is at our doorstep and he has finally conceded to working with the U.S. I am General Hammer. I am the highest ranking official here and you may address your terms to me."

Merrick and I look at each other and then back at them.

"There are no terms," Merrick says. "We escaped the grasp of the director when we learned of his true intentions."

Mika snorts. "Why should I believe you?"

"We have no reason to lie," I say. "I killed the Caliph."

"So that Ira could take his place," Mika snaps back. "And he already has made the Caliphate even stronger. We received word this morning that Russia and North Korea have joined the empire. Allied forces have lost western Europe, and the entirety of the U.S. territories, except for Florida."

"I didn't kill the Caliph for the director. I didn't even know it was part of my mission. I killed him because I thought it would help destroy the Caliphate and end the war. The director had everything mapped out for his specific purposes and he had us all fooled. You were just as much a part of his plan as I was. But if we tell the world what he did, if we tell his people that he was responsible for the billion and for the Berserkers and the Fangs, the people will revolt just like the Cubans are doing. We can defeat him from the inside out."

General Hammer looks at Mika, who is staring at me as if he is carved from stone.

"Perhaps you should watch this," General Hammer says and uses a remote to turn on a large projector at the end of the table. On the screen to our left appears a large altar with a great crowd amassed below its steps. It looks ancient, with large Ionic columns and high relief frieze on both sides depicting mythological warfare.

"This was recorded only an hour ago and sent out on all satellite frequencies. The entire world saw this."

"Where is it?" I ask.

"In Miami, not too far from where you were a few days ago. This is the altar of Pergamon. Originally in western Turkey, it was taken down and reconstructed piece by piece in Germany. Adolf Hitler announced his 'Final Solution' from the top of those steps. It was once again taken down and reconstructed in Miami recently, by order of the Caliph.

Listen," Mika says.

Ira finally saunters onto the stage. He is wearing the same suit that he had on in Sarasota. He is actually quite dashing. He walks towards the center podium and faces his crowd.

"I am the one who destroyed one billion nonbelievers," his voice booms in Arabic. "I purged this world of one billion infidels. One billion enemies that would seek to destroy our empire. I am the one that built this empire and formed its armies. I killed Amalek because he belonged to me and his life was mine to take. He played his role well, but I will take us farther than he ever could. I am the one who was prophesied by the great messenger to lead us to supreme victory. Europe has fallen. My armies move to secure the U.S. as we speak, and together with our new subjects, North Korea and Russia, we will march on Israel and destroy the Allies once and for all!"

The whole crowd sounds like thunder as it cheers, and then every one of them bows down in front of a smirking Ira.

General Hammer turns the projector off. "As you can see they have already accepted him as their leader. Perhaps you didn't know killing the Caliph was helping him. Nonetheless, the empire is even stronger now"

"Even when we thought we were winning, we were actually losing. The confederate armies are now on our doorstep. They have pushed us back so far that there is nowhere else to go. Florida is our last stronghold. What hope do we have left?" Mika says firmly and stares out the window. Sunlight glimmers off of the blue lake behind the clubhouse.

"Florida is our last hope; you said it yourself. The oxygen concentrator is here. If we can get our forces to control it, we might have a chance," I say.

"It won't be easy. Miami is already a warzone again," Mika says.

"I don't think we have a choice. We'll assemble a team. Selise will lead it," General Hammer says matter-of-factly.

"No," Mika hastens to counter. "I will lead the team."

"Out of the question, we need you here. Half the men at this location here are yours and won't take orders from anyone else."

"They will listen to whoever I instruct them to. My daughter is in Miami. I am going."

"If you go, you will be giving up your territory once and for all."

Mika sits back in his chair and puts his hands on his head. He lets out a long exhale and looks at me.

"I have always said I would relinquish my power at the right time. I don't know if this is the right time, but I need to go to Miami."

General Hammer exchanges a glance with his team. "Then go, and hurry. I will hold this position for as long as I can, but as you know we're low on manpower and resources. The success of this mission may determine the whole war."

"We will leave in the morning," Mika says to Merrick and I. "Get some rest. You can stay in the blue house on the corner. I'll have food brought over later."

Merrick and I leave and he takes the SUV over to the house. I sit down in the grass near the lake as the sun begins to dip towards the horizon. Fireflies dot the orange and purple sky around me like tiny bright stars.

"Ira-ish," Mika says from behind me. He comes and sits down next to me. "I know you didn't intentionally help him. I know Nightshade wiped your memory countless times and Ira was so secretive you probably didn't even know him, but what about Merrick?"

"No, he didn't know either."

"How can you be sure? He was your ground and your trainer. I know how Nightshade operates. He lied to you just as much as Ira did, didn't he? All so you could complete their mission. He manipulated you every step of the way."

I try to think of a response, but I can't. I trained with Merrick day in and day out for years, but that hardly means I know him. And Mika's right, he didn't tell me about the true intent of the mission.

"He saved us from Berserkers when we were betrayed by Reynolds.

And he saved me when the director had me held captive yesterday."

"Perhaps that was all part of their plan."

"Are you saying I could still be working for Ira now?"

"Just watch your back," Mika says and uses my shoulder to push himself up. "If I sense that you are working for him, even if you don't know it. I won't be afraid to kill you." He goes back to the clubhouse where a short, stocky, familiar-looking man is waiting for him.

Even if Mika is right, and all of this is part of the director's plan, then any reaction I have could be a part of it too. Even Mika coming to speak with me just now could have been planned. No matter what I do, it could be exactly what they want me to do.

I push myself up and wipe the dirt off the back of my pants and my hands. I march to the blue house. Merrick throws a pair of black pants and a matching blue shirt at me as I walk in.

"Do you believe this? Mika wants us dressing like his men." He laughs.

"I guess he needs every man he can get."

"Do you think we can trust him?"

"Merrick, I don't know who to trust. I don't even know what's real anymore."

He sits down on a cot and is quiet for a long time. As much as I don't want to dress in Mika's colors, it's refreshing to put on clean threads.

Suddenly, Merrick pops up. "Come on. Let's go."

"Go where?"

"I'm going to take you to the truth. Bring your gun. We might run into Fangs."

No one stops us when we leave the mobile home park. The guard at the gatehouse is a different one than earlier. He looks us up and down, and then waves us through.

"Apparently Mika's colors still have clout," Merrick says.

It's completely dark out when we make it to a small, deserted island town just south of Sarasota. Merrick drives us down the main avenue. There are tall palm trees lining both sides, some of which are bent and hanging over the road. Old-fashioned shops and restaurants stretch along the road. The ones that are still standing look as if they had been broken into and looted a long time ago. We drive passed them until the road curves and we pull up to a cathedral with tall, white steeples and wide steps that lead to large, brown doors below a carved mural depicting what seems to be Judgement Day.

"What are we doing here?" I ask with a yawn.

"Do you remember when we were training and you asked me who you were before you joined Nightshade?"

I nod.

"And I told you no operative was permitted to know under any circumstance. It would jeopardize our careers in Nightshade and possibly our lives to give even the smallest hint of your past life."

"What's your point?"

"I'm going to show you who you used to be. It's the only way for you to trust me and to know that we are both no longer a part of it."

We get out of the vehicle, but Merrick keeps it running, allowing the lights to shine on the front doors of the church. I begin to walk up the steps.

"If you tell me I was a priest, Wesley is going to roll over in his grave,"

"Not up there. Follow me," Merrick says and leads me around the side of the cathedral. There is a rundown cemetery and he stops in front of a group of three tombstones, two large and one slightly smaller positioned next to them. He hands me the flashlight and I shine it on the gravestones.

"Are these people supposed to mean something to me?" I ask, hesitantly turning over the names in my mind.

"When you joined Nightshade we didn't just want you to forget who you were, but we needed the world to forget you too. We had to fake your death."

"How did I go?"

"You shot yourself."

"What? You couldn't come up with something better than that?" I ask.

"It was the most believable story and for the most part it was true. You fought in Afghanistan and then in Syria. When you got back, your wife and your daughter were mysteriously killed with the rest of the billion. It would be only natural that you had extreme PTSD and wanted to end your life. The only difference was instead of ending your life forever with a bullet, you started a new one with Nightshade."

"Wait, you said wife and daughter?"

"Yes, we put your fake grave right next to them."

I study the stones closer under the light.

"Grace was my wife? And Tilda...my daughter?"

"Yes. They must have been lovely. You once told me you had seen terrors in war that no man should have to see, but the thing that broke you was seeing their lifeless bodies fall before you."

"So...for that you took my memory?"

"You came to Nightshade wanting to forget. You knew what you were doing."

"Was that the recruiting process? Take everything from someone until they want to forget?"

"No Danny, I didn't know."

"I'm not Danny or Daniel or whatever that gravestone says," I shout. "Call me Brute."

"For what it's worth, I'm sorry," Merrick says and walks back to the idling vehicle.

I fall to my knees and study every letter of the gravestones trying to feel something. But the only thing I feel is anger, hot and familiar inside me. I'm angry because I want to be sad, but I feel nothing for them. Ira took everything from me. I want to remember how they looked, how they smelled. I want to remember if they were happy and if I was good to them or not. When I try to think of Grace and picture her in my mind, the woman looking back at me is Ruby. A husband would remember every single detail of his wife, wouldn't he? I was a husband...and I was a father. How could I have been a father and not have a single idea what my daughter was like?

In-between the two gravestones I can see something shift. Two red eyes are peering back at me through the darkness.

17

I point the flashlight towards the two red eyes staring at me from beyond the tombstones. A large, white Fang with pointy ears and a long snout approaches me, displaying his jagged teeth. I slowly reach for my pistol and pull it out. I aim at him.

"I don't want to kill you," I muse sadly. "Before they infected you, you were probably a good boy."

It roars as it unexpectedly leaps onto me. I drop my gun and all I can do is hold the beast away and keep it from snapping my face off. All of a sudden, it shakes its head, squealing and crying. It falls off me as Merrick stabs it repeatedly in its back.

"Merrick! It's dead."

He stops stabbing the Fang and looks up at me, breathing heavily. He nods. "Right." He sheaths his knife and reaches out a hand. I take it and he helps pull me up. There's rustling in the darkness around us, but the wind is not blowing.

"There are others. We have to go," Merrick says.

"I couldn't agree more."

We run towards the SUV. From the sound of their big paws crunching on leaves and twigs and their bodies swishing through bushes, I can tell there are at least ten of them following us. We climb into the SUV and shut the doors. A Fang that looks like an enflamed border collie jumps up and smashes itself into the windshield. Multiple cracks instantly form. Another one dashes towards my door. It has the face of a bulldog, but is at least double the size of one.

"Go, damn it," I say.

The SUV begins to roll forward slowly.

"Faster for God's sakes!"

"I can't, they're ripping the tires to shreds."

"What?" I say. The charging Fang slams itself into my door headfirst so hard the window drops down and I hear it shatter inside the doorframe. "We've got to get out of here." There are Fangs all around, biting and eating the tires as if they were fresh meat.

"We're stuck," Merrick says.

A Fang stands up on its hind-legs and claws in through my window. I lean towards Merrick, barely avoiding its drool-spraying snaps. I slide the barrel of my pistol under the base of its snout and fire. Bits of brain and blood splatter on the ceiling. I shove the Fang out of the window, but there are nine more ready to replace him.

"We're not going to last long in here," says Merrick as two smaller Fangs leap and ram themselves against his door.

"Out there isn't much better," I say.

A loud shotgun blasts nearby and two Fangs, along with Merrick's side-view mirror, are blown to bits. I look up. Standing in front of the church doors is a man holding a double-barrel shotgun. He aims and fires again, quickly killing another Fang by my door.

A few of the others turn and run towards the man. He fires again and kills another Fang. Merrick and I leap out of the SUV and shoot the rest before they can get up the steps to him.

"Damn Fangs. I just cleaned these steps yesterday," the old man says. He has thinning, white hair and white bushy eyebrows, but only a few deep wrinkles on the sides of his mouth. "There's more around. You'll want to come inside."

He limps quickly and decidedly towards the church doors, while Merrick and I stare at him curiously.

"Well, come on. You'll be safe," he assures us.

We climb passed the carcasses and he leads us into the narthex. He shuts the door behind us, metal cringing as he locks it. It's dark inside. He brings us through tall, brown, double doors and into the nave. It smells of incense and there are small candles lit all around. He takes us down the aisle, passing many rows of brown, wooden pews.

"You can sleep here for the night. The Fangs can't get in," the old man says.

At the end of the aisle are marble steps with a red rug draped over them. The steps lead to a plain, marble altar with a gold-colored menorah resting on it. In front of the seven dancing flames are a gold-colored wine cup and a basket of bread. Looming over the altar is a large, bronze crucifix. The old man struggles his way up the steps. We follow him.

"Come; join me for a cup of coffee. I just found a coffee maker in one of the shops, and enough beans to last a year. I've been meaning to try it out. Oh, and take some bread as well." He opens a side door and turns back, waiting for us as we step in front of the alter, staring at the crusty bread. My stomach rumbles. Merrick reaches for a piece, but then stops.

"This isn't the body of some dead God, is it?"

"No, a living one," the white eye-browed man speaks with a small smirk. Smaller wrinkles bunch up around his lips. "You'd be wise to have some."

Merrick studies the bread some more, but hunger wins and he grabs two pieces. I do the same, and we follow the man into a small breakroom. There is a long, plastic table across from an extended counter with a coffee maker on top and a sink built into it. There are tan, metal chairs surrounding the table.

"Please, make yourselves comfortable," he says and begins to make a pot of coffee. "My name is Father Bartholomeus, but you can just call me Bart. I never cared much for titles."

Merrick and I sit cautiously at the table beside each other.

"You don't look much like a priest," I say, testing.

Bart turns around. "Why? Because I'm wearing khaki shorts and a t-shirt instead of robes? Nah, it's too hot for that." He circles around the table and sits across from us. "And besides, who wants to parade around in all those fancy robes and ornamentation? I keep my clothes like I keep my chapel. Simple and humble."

I'm satisfied with that answer and finish my bread in only a few bites. It's soft with a warm, flaky crust.

"How is it that you're alive out here by yourself?" Merrick asks.

"I may be old, but believe it or not I can take care of myself. There are several other survivors in town. We grow vegetables and wheat. We do just fine."

"Why not leave here? Head North?"

"Nah, what for? We have a radio. The war consumes the four corners of the world now. We're much safer here, where no one knows to look for us." He gets up and shuffles his way to the coffee pot. He pulls out three mugs from the cupboard above the sink. He pours coffee into each mug and then serves us. "Hold on." He shuffles back to the counter and grabs his mug. He then pulls out a half empty bottle of bourbon from the cabinet and brings it to the table. "It may not be the blood of Christ, but it will make you feel alright," he says and pours some into each mug before he sits.

"I saw you looking at my cemetery. Did you lose someone in the Rapture?"

"I hate to rain on your parade, but it wasn't the Rapture. It was an enormous slaughter by a mad man," I say.

"One truth doesn't negate the other. Their bodies may have died, but their spirits did not."

"What kind of God would kill a billion people?"

"A merciful one. They died instantly and painlessly, but their spirits live in peace having been taken from the horrors of this war. Don't worry Daniel. You will see Grace and Tilda again."

I look at him suspiciously. "You knew me and my family?"

"Them, I knew well. You on the other hand never came to mass, so our paths didn't cross until their funeral. I tried to help you with your grief, but you told me what you were going to do, so I knew you wouldn't remember me. I tried to stop you. I told you that they were with God now because of their faith."

"If that's true, why are you still here?" Merrick challenges, his face blank. He stares at Bart and sips his bourbon-spiked coffee.

"*No one can serve two masters. You can only love one and hate the other.* I wasn't always meek and humble. I used to say I loved the Lord, but what I really loved was my status. I loved the purple and gold robes with dazzling jewels embroidered into them. I loved my altar to be adorned with the finest ornaments and my crucifixes to be heavy with gold. And I loved most of all, sitting on my chair above the entire congregation. I knew the Word inside and out, but I didn't live it. So here I am now, left behind in the war of the dogs. But I do not have fear, because I know it will be over one day and good will triumph over evil."

"Don't be so sure. The Caliph dies and another takes his place. We may not be able to defeat the empire," Merrick says.

"No, you're wrong. I read the end of the book," he says, patting his hand on a little, black Bible. "We win."

"I wish I could share your optimism, but the only hope we have lies with the two of us...and we're stuck here with no wheels," I say. I sip my hot coffee. It burns my mouth and my throat on its way down.

"Ah...you're on a mission?"

"One that could tip the scales of this war in our favor," I say.

"It sounds like God has a plan for you after all," Bart says and winks at me. "Far be it from me to get in your way. Come along."

He leads us into a hallway. There are children's drawings taped to the walls. I study some of them. Crayon-colored drawings of crosses and stone slabs with scribble on them are towards the front, but as I keep walking some of the drawings show children with their families in the park or at church. One picture has stick figure drawings of a mom, dad, and a little girl in a green and red garden. I look at the name.

"Sorry Daniel, I don't have anything from your daughter. That was a long time ago," says Bart. He puts a gentle hand on my shoulder.

"Come on."

At the end of the hallway is a door that leads back outside.

"I have a car out there; it was donated to the church by a widow in my flock. I have no use for it. Our community is small. Everything we need is close by." I flash the light through the window pane on the door. It illuminates a beautiful Ferrari sports car with red candy paint and black wheels.

"Are you serious?" I say.

"Like I said, I have no interest in flashy things anymore. The keys are inside. Be quick. Fangs are still around."

"Thank you, Bart," I say.

Merrick and I rush through the door and down a small flight of steps. I climb into the passenger seat and shut my door. Merrick flips down the visor and catches a set of keys that falls from it. The engine roars as he turns the correct one.

"This is what I'm talking about," Merrick says. He shifts into drive and peels out of the parking lot.

By the time we make it back to the mobile home park, the sun is beginning to rise. Streaks of orange and purple clouds stretch across the blue sky above.

A young guard steps out of the gatehouse to watch us as we pull up. He keeps his hand on his holstered pistol. He bends over and looks at us curiously through the window. He's wearing a U.S. patch on his ACU uniform.

"Nice car," he says and looks at our clothes. "All of Mika's Guard have been given U.S.-issued uniforms. See your commanding officer, and you will be given integration instructions."

Merrick nods and the young soldier allows us access inside. Merrick speeds down the main road. Everyone turns to look at us.

"Do you think we have time for a nap?" I say. Even though I fell asleep in the car, I'm still exhausted.

"Apparently not." He points to Mika and two other heavily-armed men standing in front of the blue house. They all wear Mika's colors.

I recognize the tall, muscular Arab who watched the door of the clubhouse. The other one is short and stocky and I feel like I have seen him before. They both have long beards. All three of them stare at us as we park in the grass driveway.

"I see you traded in the SUV," Mika says as we get out of the sports car.

"We didn't have much of a choice," Merrick says. "Where's the team?"

Mika curves his lips and shows his yellow, gapped teeth. "You're looking at it."

"You can't be serious. Where are all your troops? We can't go into Miami and steal the concentrator with only five men," I say.

"My troops need to stay here. Big Al is on his way. General Hammer needs all the help he can get. We have contacts with the Free People in Miami. They will help us."

"Whatever you say," I agree with a roll of my eyes and I have to remind myself that I don't want to see Ruby again.

"We'll take my van. We don't want to attract attention," Mika says.

"Let's go," Merrick says. Mika gets in the driver's seat and Merrick climbs in the passenger seat. I open the sliding van door on the side. I look at the short, stocky man. He looks so familiar.

"Mo the Mute!" I finally realize. "I almost didn't recognize you with that beard. How the hell did you escape the Cubans?"

He stares at me for a moment and then climbs into the van and sits on the bench that lies parallel to the wall, completely ignoring me.

"Good talk," I say.

"He doesn't speak much," the tall guard explains and steps in. He sits next to Mo the Mute.

"I know. I know." I climb in and sit across from them.

Mika drives us out of the mobile home park and heads south. Mo the Mute holds his M16 and stares at me.

"If you won't talk to me, you don't get to stare at me either," I say. He says nothing and looks away for a moment, but then returns his gaze to me.

"Relax," The tall one says. He has to lean forward so his head won't hit the ceiling. "It means he likes you."

Mo the Mute smiles big and winks at me.

"I'm Luca by the way."

"Yeah whatever," I say. "So what's the plan?" I ask loudly enough for Mika to hear. "Do we know where the oxygen concentrator is?"

"What is it with you Nightshade guys and plans?" Mika says. "The plan is to meet up with my daughter and Ruby and then together we'll find the concentrator."

"That's very comforting," Merrick says sarcastically.

"Watch your mouth; I took power with a plan like that. I didn't need to go over every step for years in order to succeed. All you really need is power of will and loyal men; with that you can achieve anything."

Then we should stay away from Ruby, I want to say, but I stay quiet.

"It won't be easy though. Last I hear the city is divided into four zones. The Ottomans control the Northeast, Cuban nationalists who have rebelled against the Caliphate and want Florida for themselves are in the Northwest, and the Free People are in the Southwest. I may not have an intricate plan, but I am always well-informed of any situation I get myself into."

"That's three," Merrick says.

"What?"

"You said the city was divided into four zones. You only mentioned three."

"The last zone is South Beach, but it's completely overrun by Berserkers."

"Well whatever the plan is or isn't, if we run into Ira...he's mine to kill," I say.

Luca laughs and holds his belly. "You can't call that. You're not the only one who lost someone you loved because of him. If I see him I will kill him, and there is nothing you can do about it."

"Neither of you should get your hopes up. I doubt he will be staying in Miami for much longer," Mika says. "He thinks eventually Big Al will take it back, and if we fail this mission, he will be right."

"No, he'll be where the concentrator is," I say. "He knows we're coming for it."

After we've been driving for a while, Luca opens a backpack and hands out dry crackers and nuts with bottles of water. I eat them slowly, not knowing when my next meal will be.

"So who did you lose?" Luca asks with crackers in his mouth and crumbs littering his beard.

"My wife and my daughter, but I can't even remember them anymore. You?"

"I lost my fiancé and my parents in the billion. My twin sister died when the Cubans bombed Florida, and my brother was killed at the Battle of Hackensack."

"I'm sorry."

"Don't be. We've all lost someone," Mika says.

"I can still see her face when I close my eyes," Luca says and shuts them with a grin. "She had big dimples when she smiled and long, flowing blonde hair...and she had a beautiful set of tits." He opens his eyes and laughs so loudly that we all laugh and even Mo the Mute lets out a noise.

I wish that I could remember my family. I'm so angry with the person that I used to be. Danny was a coward who ran away because he was weak. And just when I thought I was gaining a new family, Wesley was killed, Reynolds betrayed us all, and Ruby lied to me. My head is a jumbled mess. *I wish I could forget th—No! I don't want to forget anymore.*

When we can see Miami up ahead from the highway Mo the Mute and Luca paint their faces with dark blue and black paint.

"What's the point of that?" I say.

"Our little country doesn't exist anymore. It was short-lived but glorious. So when I kill Ira, I want him to see Mika's colors before he dies."

As we move into the city, the sky becomes dark and murky again and right away I can smell death in the air. Gunfire blazes in the distance. We curve around a long boulevard and turn onto a connecting street. I watch several people running along the sidewalks with rifles in their hands. They turn down an intersecting street and disappear into the darkness. We continue further until we recognize the General's street. It's dark and empty. Mika parks in front of her building.

I'm nervous. I don't know if I will lose control of my anger when I see Ruby. Mika must be too because he just sits there studying the building. It still looks as broken and half-destroyed as it did before. There is some light emanating from the inside and I can hear music playing, but we don't move.

"Are we going to go in or sit in here for all eternity?" I say.

"Just wait," Mika says. I roll my eyes and sigh.

At least ten minutes pass before Mika finally says, "Okay let's move," but before he can fully open his door an enormous explosion inside the building sends a shockwave that slams his door shut and shatters his window. The van rocks and I'm knocked to the ground. I hold my head trying to quiet the loud ringing in my ears.

18

"**M**iranda," Mika says and gets out of the van. He hurries to the building, and we all follow him inside with raised guns.

Smoke and debris make it impossible to see more than a few feet in front of me.

"Miranda...Ruby," Mika calls out as we search the lobby for any survivors.

As the smoke clears, I scan the ground for bodies hoping I don't see Ruby's. I don't see any. There are no bodies, not even any limbs lying around. I look at Merrick. He shrugs his shoulders.

"There's no one here," Mika says.

"Oh yes there is," Luca says and suddenly I'm aware of the men and women surrounding us with raised guns.

"Dad! You tripped my alarm for nothing," the General says as she enters the foyer from the northeast corner. She is wearing baggy, white pants, a white sports bra, and white boots. Her hair is tied up into little double buns, and she is wearing several gold chains with varying thickness around her neck. She runs up and hugs Mika.

We lower our guns and so do the General's men and women.

"What happened?" Mika asks.

"Gendarmerie was snooping around here yesterday. We figured they would be back so we moved two buildings down and set up proximity remote bombs in the building. They were set for ten minutes. It's a good thing you waited so long to come in."

Mika looks at me and winks.

"Jesus Miranda, I was afraid you were dead," Mika says and hugs her again. "You're so tall now."

"Come on, Dad. I'll take you to my building. The explosion will bring unwanted attention. Let's move."

We follow the General, the Gorilla, and the rest of her soldiers out of the building and down the street perpendicular to the road where the van is parked. All the soldiers disperse into neighboring buildings, except for the Gorilla, who joins us as we follow the General into a small apartment building that is for the most part still intact. There are some shattered windows and a hole in one corner of the roof. We go inside and climb four flights of steps. Most of the apartments have no doors and are dark and empty inside, except for a couple that have armed soldiers watching the street below.

"Most of these rooms on this floor are unoccupied. Find a place and sleep where you like," the General says.

One of the window guards fires a couple of loud rifle shots towards the street below.

"That is, if you can sleep through gunfire," The General says.

"What was that?" I say.

"There are always a few Berserkers around or gendarmerie. We don't have to worry about the *Nacionales*. They don't really come to our zone." She stops and listens for a moment. "It was probably a lone Berserker."

We continue to the end of the hall to an apartment separate from all the others. It's the only one with a door still intact. Inside is an open room with a big, brown desk near open windows. Ruby is sitting behind it and Yoshi is lying next to her. She stands up when she notices us walk in. She's wearing a maroon V-neck and her black hair is in a high, straight ponytail. I hate to think it, but she looks radiant.

"Mika, what are you doing here?" She says.

"Sorry we set off your bomb, but we have urgent business. We need to find the large-scale oxygen concentrator."

"That's a myth," Ruby says.

"It's not a myth," I interject angrily. "It's here." She won't even look at me.

"Mother, if that's true we need to find it," the General says.

"*If* it's true," Ruby clarifies.

"It is true. Ira himself told me so," I say.

"Then why come to us? We obviously didn't even know it existed," Ruby snaps back. She folds her arms.

"You and Miranda have troops. And she knows this city," Mika answers.

"You have more soldiers than I do," Ruby points out.

"No. Not anymore. I gave it all up. My land, my power, and all my men save these two. I gave it all back to the U.S."

Ruby chuckles. "I can hardly believe you would give up anything."

"We didn't come to argue damn it. We came to end a war," Mika says.

She walks over to the window behind her and stares out for what seems like forever. Then she spins around and looks at the General. "What about Captain Morales?" she says.

"He hasn't been by in a while, but if the concentrator is here, he would definitely know about it."

"Send a runner to 13th. See if Red can contact him. Try Slo-Mo too on the west block," Ruby says. The General nods and she and the Gorilla leave. "As for you all, make yourselves at home as best you can. There are empty rooms down the hall."

We start to leave the makeshift office, but before I do, Ruby stops me.

"Brute," she says. "Talk with me a moment."

I'm tempted to keep walking, but I control myself and turn to her. She stares at me with round eyes that look like they've been dipped in hazelnut crème, but she says nothing.

"Can we trust Morales?" I blurt out, because I don't know what else to say.

She smirks and comes around her desk and leans on the edge. For a second, I can smell her hair. It reminds me of the night we spent together, but I try to block that rush of memory. It was all an act.

"The Cuban people are split. Not just here, but in Cuba too. Most of them are with us as Free People. Then there are the *Nacionales* who still want control of this city, but apart from the Caliphate. They are smaller in number, but well-armed and have a plethora of trained Fangs. Thankfully, they hate the Ottomans more than they hate us. So for now they leave us alone and keep the gendarmerie very busy. Then there are the collaborators. They are Cubans that still fight for the Caliphate. They are hated the most by all...Cubans, Free people and *Nacionales* alike."

"Let me guess; Morales is one of them?"

"Only in appearance. He works for them, but reports to us vital information. He gives us troop movements, warns us of raids, and if Ira's appearance hadn't been so sudden he probably could have gotten us front row seats to his speech. He is trustworthy, but extremely elusive. After all, if any Cuban finds him they will kill him as a traitor. But if the concentrator is here, he'll help us get it."

"Good, that's the only reason we are here."

She wrinkles the corners of her eyes and caves in her brows. She tenses one hand into a fist before quickly loosening it, and I know my jab landed. She starts breathing rapidly and heavily. My smirk of satisfaction disappears. I didn't mean to make her this mad. She takes a couple slow, deep breaths and unclenches her fists.

"Sit with me," she says softly and waves her hand to a couch in the adjoining room, separated only by a small, half wall with a load-bearing beam at the end. "I know you're upset with me because I didn't tell you the truth," she says matter-of-factly.

"You made me look like a fool."

"You must understand I wouldn't have done it if I didn't think it could end a world war. I didn't want to hurt you, but I had to put our feelings aside."

"Don't say that. You didn't know me. Why should you care if I got hurt or not?" I have to stop myself from shouting so Yoshi doesn't wake up.

She looks away from me. There's nothing more to say. I stand up to leave. Looking down on her, I don't know how I could've loved a person like this. I turn to leave.

"Did Merrick tell you why they choose me?"

I turn back around. "No. Maybe they knew you were my type."

"It was much more than that. It had to be me."

"Perhaps they knew you were the world's best actress."

She giggles. "You don't understand. Well, I should say you don't remember."

"Ruby, what the hell are you talking about? I don't have the patience for this right now."

"We met before, you and I...before you ever came to the community center in Wauchula."

"I knew you before?" I say and sit back down.

"Yes, when I was still married to Mika. You were on a different mission to assassinate him. It was late one night. Things were already bad between him and me at this point. We slept in different rooms. In our eyes we were already divorced, but Mika said it was better for his people to believe we were still together. After all, I was his First General. That night, I just had to try one more time to convince him to stop building that damned wall of his. It was late and I knew he was probably sleeping, but I told myself I had to talk with him one last time before betraying him and committing treason. I knew he would say no. Deep down, I think I just needed convincing myself. I needed to hear his stubbornness one more time.

"His room was upstairs. As I walked down the hall, I was thinking of what I was going to say to him. When I got to his door, I took a deep breath and reached for the knob. Before I could grab it though, I was pulled back by someone with a gloved hand over my mouth. I thought it was Mika at first, but then I felt the barrel of a silencer on my temple. The man whispered in my ear that he didn't come to kill me. He said he had come to kill Mika and that I should go back downstairs quietly and quickly. I nodded in agreement. What else could I do? But when he let me go, I turned around and looked at him. His face was pained dark green and black, so he could have been anybody, but I could never forget those eyes...your eyes. I don't know why, but I begged you not to kill him. I was so angry with Mika. I even thought I hated him, but I didn't want him dead. He is my child's father after all, and I did once love him.

"I didn't think you'd listen to me when I said it, but you did. You went back the way you came from, climbed out of the second story window, and left...just like that. I couldn't believe it. The next day, Mika left on a dangerous mission to New York, so I didn't tell him about the assassination attempt. He didn't need to be stressing over one more thing. And I never thought there was a chance you'd come around again. But a couple days later, you knocked on my front door. It was broad daylight and you didn't have face paint on, but there were those eyes again. I thought you came to finish the job, so I told you Mika wasn't here. Your eyes were dancing when you told me you didn't come for him, you came for me.

"I reached for my knife, but then you said 'I didn't come to kill you; I came to tell you you're the most beautiful woman I have ever seen.' I, of course, pulled out my knife and pressed it against your throat. You held up your hands and said 'go ahead, kill me' and some corny line about dying happy looking at me. I laughed so hard. You were so pathetic I couldn't kill you."

"That doesn't sound like me," I say, with a withering look etched on my face.

"Pathetic in a cute way."

"Is that a thing?"

She smiles. "You were unarmed, so I let you in. We talked all day. You told me you were in Nightshade and that you were ordered to kill Mika, but when you saw me you just couldn't do it. We spent every day together for a month. You had to return to Nightshade, but you said you wanted to quit and be with me. As much as I wanted you to, Mika was coming back. Even though we were divorcing, I was sure he wouldn't be happy about me being with the guy who was sent to kill him. We also both knew that Nightshade would never let you leave. They would hunt for us forever, and Mika probably would too. So I watched you leave, knowing that your memory would be wiped and you would forget all about me...while I never could.

"I never thought I would see you again until Merrick found me in Wauchula. He told me he was from Nightshade and that they of course wiped your memory after you told them what had happened and then many times after that as well. But then he told me I could see you again. I was reluctant. It would be too strange. I wondered if I could get you to fall in love with me again, but even if I could...did I really want to? They would just take you away from me again and make you forget about me all over again. I couldn't handle having to do that twice. It was hard enough the first time. I never had the luxury of forgetting about you. I told Merrick that I didn't want to see you, but he insisted. He said getting you to fall in love with me again was precisely what I had to do, but that I couldn't tell you anything. He said it was imperative that I pretend I never knew you.

"Before I could reject his proposal, he told me that you were the key to ending the war and that if I cooperated you would kill the Caliph. You had told me before all about the way Nightshade operated. So I knew it could be possible that something as seemingly insignificant as falling in love could have a huge impact on a mission. So, I put my feelings aside for a greater cause. I knew it would hurt losing you again, but if it meant saving countless lives and possibly ending this war. Then I had to do it. It wasn't acting. Nightshade knew you would fall in love with me, because you already had once before. And they knew I still loved you.

"When I saw you walk in with Mika and Merrick just now, I knew they couldn't have taken your memory again. I knew you weren't in Nightshade anymore. I am so happy that you remember me, even if it means that you have to be mad at me."

"How did you do it? If my memory was wiped many times over, how did you get me to fall for you so easily?"

"I didn't plan anything out, if that's what you mean. I didn't have to. I never stopped loving you and, somewhere deep inside, you never stopped loving me. They could erase your memories, but not your heart."

"So, it wasn't all fake?"

"No." She smiles. "The only thing I lied about was pretending not to know you. Everything else was real." She leans in and kisses my cheek. "Now go get some rest."

I don't even know how to process all of this, so I leave her and find a small apartment where Merrick, Mo the Mute, and Luca are sitting. The room is unfurnished, except for a couple of stools on opposite ends of a round coffee table.

"There he is," Luca says. He's perched on one of the stools across from Mo the Mute. Their guns are casually resting on the table, along with a deck of cards and a bottle of liquor. Merrick is standing by the window, still holding his assault rifle.

"Look what we found," Luca says and hands me the bottle of liquor. I sit down on the ground and take a big gulp. I clench my teeth as the strong whiskey slides down my throat and into my belly.

Luca laughs. "Good huh?" He grabs the bottle from me and raises it up above his wide shoulders. "To the end of the war," he cheers and chugs nearly a quarter of the bottle.

"It's not the first time I've drank to the end of the war," I say. "Spoiler alert: It didn't end that time. Things just got worse."

"Mika believes we really have a chance now to turn the tide." He hands me the bottle again. I take another shot. "The new Commander of the Israeli forces; they call him The Lion. He has yet to lose a single battle, and all the allied forces are uniting under his banners."

"Yeah only because they lost all their lands to Ira and all those fools under his spell."

"Don't worry. We'll get it all back. You know the Israeli Commander rides into battle on a white horse? Mika really believes in him."

"Well, we're going to need more than Mika's faith to win this war. We have to find that concentrator," I say.

"Let's hope it's still here."

"If it's not, then we'll go wherever it is. We'll do whatever it takes," I say.

"We may not have the time," Mika says as he walks in behind me. "Ira is already beginning to send waves of Berserkers into Israel and, with his new alliances, they will march soon. The Allies don't stand much of a chance if we don't find this thing soon."

"No one stands much of a chance as long as Ira is still alive. He is always three steps ahead," Merrick says. "He's planned all of this out for so long. He probably knows what we're going to do next before we even do."

"How do you stop a man like that?" Luca says, slurring his words.

"We have to be unpredictable," Mika answers.

I don't know if it's because of the whiskey or because of how tired I am, but my head is swimming. I can't focus on the conversation anymore. I leave the small studio apartment and search for an empty one. After passing a couple of armed Free People, I finally find one that's relatively secluded. It's dark inside. The only furniture is a small couch that I bump into as I stumble across the room. I plop myself down and immediately feel a broken spring digging into my back, but it still feels good to be lying down.

My head is fuzzy. I think of what Mika said, but how can we be unpredictable when Ira has most likely planned out every possible course of our actions? Maybe Luca is right and the man on the white horse will save us all. All these thoughts of war are making my head spin. I need to clear my mind and sleep, but I can't stop thinking about...

"Ruby?" I say. With help from the dim light in the hall, I can see her standing silhouetted in the doorway. She's on top of me before I can say anything else. She kisses me so hard it hurts my mouth.

"I've missed you terribly," she says and bites my neck. She bites so hard I think she breaks my skin. She tears my shirt off and starts clawing at my chest.

"Okay, okay not so hard," I mumble, but then I see that her eyes are as red as blood.

19

I try to grab Ruby's arms and hold her, but she's incredibly strong. She claws at my neck and face and leans in to bite me again. I push her off me and she falls to the ground. I need something to restrain her. I look around, but I can hardly see, and Ruby jumps back on me before I can find anything.

She starts pounding on my chest. I try to restrain her by wrapping my arms around her and squeezing her tight against me. I yell in agony as she bites down on the side of my jawbone. I can feel blood streaming down my neck, but Ruby doesn't let go. I try to reach with one hand and feel around on the ground, knowing I left my Glock somewhere nearby.

She finally lets go. She sits up and takes deep, heavy breaths, as if she had been drowning and just came up for air. There is blood smeared on her lips and chin. She then keels over with her eyes closed, taking more deep breaths. I notice a syringe sticking in her back and Merrick standing over her. I sit up.

The General and the Gorilla rush into the room a moment later.

"What did you do to her?" she yells.

"I filled her with a high dose of oxygen," Merrick answers.

I hold my jaw. It's throbbing and bloody.

"It will keep the virus at bay for a few days," Merrick continues.

"Virus? What are you talking about?"

"Yes. She's infected."

The General lifts a shaky hand to cover her dropped jaw.

"She'll be fine," Merrick says. "Do you have a medic? The Brute needs stitches."

The General bends over and examines my wound. "I can stitch him up. No problem."

"Wait," I say. "How old are you again?"

"I'm almost seventeen. I've lived in a warzone for the last three years. I've stitched up a lot worse. Gorilla go and fetch my kit and some vodka."

As fast as the Gorilla leaves, he comes back again with a small container and a bottle. The General grabs the bottle and pours some on her hands before passing it to me. I swallow as much as I can fit in my stomach before wanting to hurl.

"Gorilla, flash the light on his face," she says and he does.

"Wait, you're not even going to turn on the light?"

"If any gendarmerie are around we don't want them knowing we're here," Mika says as he walks in with Luca and Mo the Mute trailing behind him.

"Look this way," the General says with a needle in her hands.

"Just do it," I growl and look at her. Piercing pain runs through my body and down to my toes as she pokes the needle through my skin.

"What are we going to do with them?" Luca says in such a way that makes me very aware of the assault rifle in his hands.

"What do you mean?" The General asks, still focused on her stitch-ing.

"It's not safe to have two infected around."

"Two?" Mika says.

"She infected him. You can already see the red forming in his eyes," Luca says. Now everyone is staring at my eyes.

"That's impossible. The virus doesn't move that quick," Mika says.

"What's the difference? It's only a matter of time before he attacks us like she attacked him."

"I'm no threat to you. Nightshade infected me a long time ago. With oxygen supplementation, I can harness the good effects of the virus without going mad."

"And Ruby will be fine too. I gave her a highly-concentrated dose," Merrick adds.

Miranda finishes the last stich and cuts the thread.

"I think we need to kill them," Luca says.

"Don't be ridiculous," Mika waves him away. "Merrick, how long until the effects of the oxygen wear off?"

"You mean how long until they try to kill us?" Luca says and points his weapon at Ruby. Mo the Mute points his at me, and just as quickly the Gorilla is pointing a golden Honey Badger at Luca, and the General is aiming a heavy machine pistol at Luca. I stand up weaponless, but seeing the rifle pointed at Ruby fills me with rage.

"Calm down and focus," Merrick says to me. I count my breaths and compose myself. He waves for me to sit. I only listen because I realize what he is going to say.

"You see," he says. "I can control him."

"Yeah? Well, what about her?" Luca challenges. Sweat drips down from his temple to his cheek.

"It doesn't matter. You will not harm her. That's an order," Mika says. "You've obviously had too much to drink. I think you both need some rest."

Mo the Mute quickly retracts his gun, but Luca keeps his targeting Ruby. Mika stares at him with a glowering glare. Yoshi begins to growl, prowling in the doorway. Luca looks nervously at Yoshi and finally lowers his rifle. After Yoshi gallops to Ruby's side, Luca leaves with Mo the Mute.

"You see, I can control my Brutes too. You must forgive them. They've seen many friends either torn apart by Berserkers or live long enough to become one. They are trained to shoot infected on sight. Perhaps it would be best if we did separate."

"You mean Ruby and I should leave."

"What other choice do we have?" Mika says.

"We can't just make them go away; she's my mother."

Ruby sits up and is now breathing steadily. Miranda sits next to her and rubs her back. "Are you okay?"

"I think so."

"I won't let them send you away," the General says.

Ruby looks at her and smiles. "I know I said I would never leave you again; but if me staying puts you in danger, then I'll separate willingly."

"Where will you go?" the General asks.

"We will have to find the concentrator ourselves. Just the two of us," I say.

"You mean three," Merrick says "Who else can keep you focused?"

"Come on, Gorilla. Let's pack them some dried meat and nuts. Oh, and throw in that bottle of scotch Red brought us."

"Get some rest and head out in the morning," Mika says. Everyone leaves, except for Merrick, who watches the street below from the window.

I wrap my arms around Ruby and she rests her head on my shoulder.

"I guess we were wrong. The infected do attack each other," I say.

"I wasn't attacking you; it was the opposite. I was trying to get to you, but no matter how hard I tried I couldn't reach you. You were the only thing not on fire. I tried so hard." She sounds as if she's about to cry. I hold her tighter.

"It's okay," I say.

She looks up at my face and reaches her hand up. I back away at first, but then let her gently circle my wound with her fingers. "I am so sorry."

"Don't be. I hear chicks dig scars."

She smiles. "I don't want to ever feel that way again. It was so maddening. I felt like my whole body was burning, and I couldn't focus on anything. I tried to scream for help, but I couldn't. All those Berserkers out there are just suffering people. We have to help them and the dogs too." She reaches her hand out and pets Yoshi on the head.

"We will soon."

"We'll go see Red in the morning. Perhaps he can get us a meeting with Morales, and hopefully he can get us into Zone 1."

I fall asleep for a few hours with Ruby lying on top of me. The constant darkness of the city makes it hard to tell if it's morning or not, but at some point Merrick is ready to go. Ruby walks across the hall and I watch her lean over the General and kiss her on the head. She grabs the small bag full of dried beef and nuts that the General left by the door.

"Okay, let's go," she whispers.

I find my pistol on the floor, and Merrick grabs his bag of weapons and ammunition, and wears it on his back. Yoshi follows us down the steps and out onto the street.

It seems to be empty.

"Red is a few blocks north this way," Ruby says.

We follow the sidewalk. There is an intersection ahead. The broken street lamp squeaks as it sways with the salty breeze.

"Hold it right there." A man with an M16 comes out from behind the corner building of the intersection. "Wait for my signal," he says. He clicks a tiny, bright flashlight a couple times. Within a few seconds, another small, white light flashes far down the avenue and a moment later, multiple flashes shine even further down. "Okay, go ahead. Be careful. There has been Berserker activity that way, and a gendarmerie patrol unit was spotted in the area just yesterday."

We continue past the intersection and keep heading north. We move cautiously forward with our guns aimed ahead. I follow in the rear and occasionally look behind. Even though Ruby and Merrick check every alley and dark, intersecting street we pass, I do too. After a couple of blocks, Yoshi begins growling. We all stop.

"Berserkers! Move," Merrick shouts, and we scurry like exposed roaches into a dark space in-between two warehouses.

"Did they see us?" I ask as I back against the wall.

"I don't know, but we'll find out soon. They're heading this way."

"How many did you see?" Ruby asks.

"At least four," Merrick says. He racks the slide of his rifle and aims towards the entryway of the alley.

"No," Ruby and I say, almost in unison.

"They are still people," Ruby says.

"People that will eat our faces if they have the chance."

"They don't know what they're doing. If you kill them, we can't cure them," Ruby says.

I can hear they're rapid, harsh breaths and painful groans as they rush down the street in our direction. Their steps are hurried and heavy, but they stop right before crossing the alley. I take a deep breath...and then they appear. They gaze in our direction with wide, haunting eyes, like curious animals. Their faces are drooping and torn, and I can see bones and enflamed muscles protruding from their bodies. Bright red rashes ooze with white and green pus on their necks and faces. The sight and smell of them makes me want to vomit.

Merrick aims at them and Yoshi snarls.

"Wait," Ruby says. "I think they're leaving."

She's right; they continue past us hastily as if they have somewhere to be. We all exhale in relief. After waiting a few moments, Merrick glances outside.

"I think we're clear."

We leave the alley and continue north. We make a few turns until we reach a park. The road curves around the park and, at the north end, are a series of cheap-looking housing buildings. There's a fence around the complex, but most of it is bent over or has large gaps in it. The middle building is the only one that is fully intact, but it is dark and looks empty. Before we get too close, Ruby stops us.

There is a black van pulling up to the middle building with a red and yellow crest on the hood. It has a yellow stripe going around it with white Arabic letters inside and a flashing turret light on the top.

"Gendarmerie," Ruby says.

"Looks like it's the only one, probably just a patrol unit," Merrick says. "Let's wait here until it passes.

It doesn't pass. Instead, it parks in front of the middle building.

"Why is it stopping?" I say.

"They must know Free People are here," Merrick says.

"We have to warn Red," Ruby says.

"I think they already know," I say and point to the top floor. Someone is standing by one of the windows, holding something large over their shoulder. A light flashes from the object and, a second later, an explosion blows the van into the air. It lands completely engulfed in flames. There are people standing at the windows on each floor, cheering.

We start to make our way over, and as soon as we get close, there are guns aiming at us from the windows above. Before we can even duck, someone shouts 'Ruby' and all the pointing barrels disappear. Moments later, the front door of the building opens and several men and women holding battle rifles and shotguns pour out. The last one out has a round face with freckles and light red hair.

"Well, I'll be," Red says looking at us. "I never thought I'd see you again, Brute. You're looking beautiful as ever, Ruby." He scratches Yoshi behind her big floppy ears.

"Nice shot," she says nodding towards the van.

Red smiles. "Like eatin' fish in a barrel."

"I don't think that's how the expression goes," I say.

"What were they doing here?" Merrick asks.

"Well...I'm not entirely sure, but I reckon there will be more."

"Do you have a runner to send word to Miranda and the other groups?" Ruby says.

"You're not going back?"

"No. We're on urgent business. We don't have time to go back."

"Urgent business, huh? What kind of urgent business?"

"We have to find Captain Morales," I say.

Red's eyes slide to the ground and he rubs the back of his neck.

"What is it?" Ruby asks.

"Captain Morales is dead."

20

Captain Morales is dead and so is our hope of finding the large-scale oxygen concentrator.

"He was captured by the Cuban *Nacionales*," Red explains. "They thought he was a collaborator. I imagine they didn't give him a quick death. We tried to send word that he was actually an informant for us, but it was too late. His body was hanging upside down from the tallest building in zone 3."

"How are we supposed to find the concentrator now?" Ruby says.

"Well I have an idea, but you're not going to like it," Red says.

"Red, we need to cure the infection or we all die. It doesn't matter if I don't like it."

"Well in that case, it just so happens that I have acquired a few gendarmerie uniforms recently," he says with a wide grin.

"I hope you're not talking about those ones," I say, looking at the burning van.

Red snorts. "No, we intercepted a squad yesterday that wouldn't leave us alone. We got them by less entertaining means, but at least we can use their stuff now."

"You have three uniforms we can wear?" Merrick asks.

"No, I have four. I'm coming with you."

"I don't think that's a good idea," Ruby says. "The reason we left—"

"I haven't shown you the best part yet," Red interrupts. "Follow me."

He leads us around and through a long walkway in-between the buildings. There's a cement courtyard behind them, with a van parked in it that looks exactly like the one out front, minus the flames. It's fully intact, except for a few bullet holes towards the back of the driver's side.

"This beauty is fully loaded," Red says. His voice is brimming with excitement and his lips are pulled back from ear to ear. He knocks on the side of the van with a knuckle. "It's got an armor-plated hull, reinforced windshield, and windows with a pull-down bullet-proof shield. And the best part..." He walks around the back and opens the double doors. There's a heavy machine gun on a short tripod pointing at us. There is a black box on the side feeding a belt of long, thick bullets into the feedway. As fast as Red opened the doors, he slams them shut.

"The van and the uniforms can get us hassle-free access into zone 1. From there, we can try finding Ira and the concentrator. And it's all yours for the low price of taking me with you."

"I'm sorry. we can't," Ruby says, but before Red can respond, I grab her by the arm and lead her out of earshot. Yoshi follows at her heels.

"What are you doing? We can't refuse this offer. Without the van and the uniforms, we'll be spotted before we make it two blocks past the border."

"Then we'll steal our own van and uniforms."

"Ruby, there's no time. Ira will be leaving soon; he has no reason to stay. Big Al is on his way down and will secure this city for him if we don't stop them now."

"I will not take the chance of losing control and hurting or possibly killing my friend."

I look at red. He is wearing a silver Wesson Razorback pistol on his hip and a knife on the other side. Holstered across his back is a 12-gauge pump action shotgun.

"Um...I think he'll be fine," I say.

"I don't know. I would never forgive myself if I hurt him or anyone else I love."

"Why don't we let him decide for himself?" I say.

She thinks for a moment and then nods in agreement. I grab her hand and lead her back to Red and Merrick.

"You can come with us," She says.

"Yes!"

"However, you need to know something..."

"You two are infected," Red says.

"How did you know that?" Ruby stammers, shocked.

"Merrick just told me."

We both look at Merrick. He shrugs his shoulders.

"I didn't know it was a secret," he says with a smile.

"It doesn't matter. I'm coming with you anyway. The faster we get the concentrator, the faster we can get you guys cured, right?"

"Agreed. Let's get dressed and get moving," Merrick says.

Red takes us into the building. It's hot inside. There are a few armed men, but most of the people inside are mothers, children, and elderly. We climb the steps. Each floor is overstuffed with people in the halls. I hear Arabic, Turkish, English, and Spanish being spoken in the busy hallways.

"Many have escaped the Caliphate and found refuge here," Red explains. "We don't have enough space for all of them, but I don't have the heart to turn them away. To turn them back to a government that infects its own people and butchers anyone who doesn't bend the knee would be cruel."

"We can bring some to our building. We have room," Ruby says.

"I don't know. It's a hot zone down there, and we have a lot of wounded."

I'm sweating by the time we make it to the fifth level. There are only armed men and women on this floor, and not as many. One of them is standing in the hall, on guard. Two others are playing cards on the floor and another is propped up against the wall, sleeping.

"Most of the fighting men and women have given up there quarters for refugees," Red says and then leads us to his apartment. He enters slowly and as quietly as he can. It's dark inside. "I let those that gave up their rooms take turns sleeping in my bed," Red whispers.

The apartment is a single room, with a single mattress against the far wall. There is a man sleeping on it. A submachine gun lies next to him.

"Ruby, you can change in there," Red says and points to a small bathroom.

Merrick, Red, and I change in the main room. The uniform is all black with a patch on the chest of their yellow and red emblem. It's too tight, but I won't complain if it will get us into zone 1. Thankfully Ruby's is too, and I'm amazed at how she manages to make even a police uniform look sexy. Merrick smacks me in the chest and snaps me out of my ogling.

We climb back down the steps, and it's even warmer with the uniform on. My hair is wet and I feel sweat dripping down my back when we reach the bottom. Outside isn't much better, but at least it's less stuffy.

An armed boy with skin tanned by the desert sun and a patchy, black beard comes up to us. He looks about eighteen and his eyes are so dark it seems as if he's wearing black paint around them. He is holding an Uzi submachine gun in his hands. Yoshi barks at him.

"Ruby, it is good to see you again," he says. His accent is similar to Luca's.

"You as well Muhamet. On guard duty?" Ruby asks him.

"Yes. I'm happy to do it," he says with a wide smile.

"Muhamet is a refugee. He was forced to fight in the Caliph's army since he was twelve years old," Red explains as we walk towards the van. I look back. Muhamet is standing at the door of the building watching us. He smirks at me, winks, and then disappears back inside the building.

"Do you trust all the refugees so easily? Couldn't some of them be disguised as a refugee and still be working for the Caliphate?" I say.

Red stops. It looks like he's contemplating what I said. "Maybe you're right, but I ain't one to judge. It would be wrong for me to turn any away. Unless you got a third option?"

"No. I suppose I would do the same," I say looking at the building.

Without warning, a bright flash blinds my eyes for a second as fire explodes out of the second floor windows. Fire and black smoke consume the second floor and within seconds starts ascending to the floors above.

"No!" Red shouts and tries to run towards the entrance. Ruby and I grab him and pull him back.

"There's nothing you can do," I say. I hear sirens in the distance.

"The gendarmerie is coming. They planned this. We have to leave," I say.

Jet-black waves swoosh from the tips of the flames that now consume the top floor.

"I have to save them," Red screams helplessly. Tears are streaming down his cheeks and dripping off his chin.

Several people are jumping from the top floor and smashing against the pavement in front of us. We pull Red towards the van. The sirens are getting closer.

"We have to go," Ruby says. "They're almost here."

We try to help Red into the van, but he escapes from our grasp and runs inside the burning building. Ruby and I chase after him.

"You can't go in there," I hear Merrick yell, but it's too late. Ruby and I follow Red inside. I didn't think it could get any hotter than it was before, but now it's so hot I can barely breathe. The flaming ceiling above makes me wonder if this is real or if the infection is taking over my mind again. Judging by the dismayed look on Ruby's, face she must be thinking the same thing. I grab her hand and we follow Red down the hallway and into the stairwell. Above the first flight of steps, I can see nothing but blackness flowing in enormous, puffy clouds. I can hear the flames crackling above. We don't have to hold Red back because he stops himself and retreats his foot from the first step.

"Is there another way up?" I ask, hoping he says no. I know going up is suicide.

"This is the only way," he says somberly.

"This building is going to collapse. We have to leave," Ruby says gently.

When we turn back, the hallway is so cloudy that it's hard to see two feet ahead. I can hear Ruby and Red coughing in front of me. The black smoke and orange flames are knitting together with the grey walls and whitewashed floors. I can't tell which way is out anymore.

"Focus," I tell myself, as I stop to steady my balance. I have to close my eyes to stop the spinning room. I listen for the footsteps and coughing in front of me, and I carefully step towards them. There's something else though. The sound of a young girl crying, but it's quickly drowned out by my own choking and hacking. My throat feels as if I swallowed a spoonful of fire. When I clear my throat, I try to listen again. I can't tell if I imagined the crying. I keep moving forward. I hear it again. It's there, up ahead. I pick up my pace. The crying is to my right now. I turn into a blazing room. It's closer now, directly in front of me. I open my eyes, but it's useless. Black smoke and fire is all I can see. I'm so disoriented I have to close my eyes again.

"Please, help me," someone begs. This voice sounds like a young woman. "And my little girl." The little girl is sobbing, and the young mother is crying too.

"Where are you?" I struggle to say in-between coughs. I reach blindly out for them. "Grab my hand," I say.

"Please, help us," the young woman repeats.

Someone finally grabs me, but it's from behind. The strong hands begin to pull me backwards.

"No! Save the girl and child," I shout. I'm too weak to fight back.

"There's no time," Merrick says. "The building is collapsing."

"Then leave me and save them."

He drags me out into the hall.

"Stop, you son-of-a-bitch!"

"I'm sorry, but you're more important. They can't help me stop this war like you can."

"Focus, focus, focus," I tell myself so that I can stop him, but in reality Merrick is the only one who can focus me.

He finally, pulls me outside. I cough and inhale as much fresh air as I can. Ruby quickly comes to my side, and my vision begins to clear. She helps me move away from the large chunks of flaming debris that are falling off the building. With my arm around her shoulder, we walk over to the van and she puts me in the back with Red. Ruby gets in the passenger seat and Merrick takes the wheel. I watch as the top floors begin to collapse onto the ones below and, within seconds, a cloud of smoke and flaming debris consumes us.

"Go!" Ruby shouts.

"I can't see anything," Merrick yells back, but he drives forward anyway. I can feel the ground rumbling and hear the building crushing itself. My heart breaks as I think of the woman and her little girl. *I could have saved them.* The gravestones of my family creep into my mind, and I can't help but wonder if they felt any pain when they died. *Did they cry out for me?*

Merrick keeps driving and we finally escape the fiery cloud. He takes us north on a long boulevard that runs parallel to the bay.

"You guys shouldn't have gone in," Merrick says almost inaudibly.

"We survived, didn't we?" I say.

"Yeah, you survived that particular moment of stupidity, but the lack of oxygen in the building has most likely sped up the virus in both of you. Now there is even less time before the madness takes over again," Merrick explains.

Across the bay is the Miami Beach peninsula. We pass a bridge that once led to South Beach, but is now broken. There is a large gap in the middle, making it un-crossable.

"Zone 2," Red says to me. "The Free People had to blow up two of the bridges to keep the Berserkers out. Unfortunately, some are bold enough to swim over and others can still trek down from the north."

"Should we really be going this way then?" Merrick says.

"It's the fastest way to Zone 1," Ruby says. "Just keep driving."

"This road passes through Little Haiti," Merrick says.

"So?"

"Little Haiti is Zone 3. The last thing we want is to be caught by Cuban Nationalists dressed like this," Merrick says.

"It may be Zone 3, but you won't find anyone there. The Caliphate gassed it with the virus. They evacuated just in time. The Free People found out about it, thanks to Morales. We tipped the Cubans off and they were able to evacuate most of their people. The only thing we might find there is a few Berserkers."

"Let's hope you're right."

We continue driving north.

"Wait a minute. What is this?" I question. Ahead of us are multiple police vans and trucks forming a barricade across the boulevard. Light blue and red flashing lights pierce the black sky.

"It's a checkpoint," Merrick explains.

"Can we turn around?"

"No, it's too late. They've already seen us. It will look suspicious if we do."

"Well we can't go through," I say.

"We have to," Merrick says.

"It'll be okay," Ruby says. "We'll just say we're coming back from patrol."

"Just let me do the talking," Merrick demands.

"You won't hear a peep from me," Red says.

When we pull up, there are several soldiers in full body armor and blue and white ACU's. Their faces are covered except for their eyes, and they are holding AR-15s. Their helmets have the Caliphate slogan written across their foreheads and the black flag of the empire is sewn onto their arms.

I can feel a bead of sweat rolling down my face. One of them waves us through, past the first wall of trucks. I breathe a long sigh of relief and wipe the dampness off my face. There are more trucks and another barrier wall across the avenue. Several more armed men stand in front of them. One of them raises his hand at us and we stop.

One of the soldiers comes up to Merrick's window. It's not difficult to notice his finger resting on the trigger of his rifle. I slowly reach for my gun and keep my hand on it. The soldier bends over and flashes a light on us.

"Where are you coming from?" the soldier says in Turkish, and I understand.

"South of Zone 4 near Coral Gables. We were checking out possible terrorist activity," Merrick responds without even a hint of an American accent.

The guard studies Merrick's face. "Let me check your unit number," he says. He goes to the back of the van, looks at the tail, and then walks back to Merrick's window. "Unit 14?" he says and looks at a piece of paper. "Your patrol was only supposed to be six hours. You've been gone for more than a day. We assumed you weren't coming back."

"Yes, there was a lot of activity down there. We were tracking a possible terror suspect, but the trail went flat."

The soldier stares at us for what seems like forever. My armpits and palms are sweating. "Okay, move along."

Merrick begins to pull away.

"Wait, stop!" the soldier orders. Merrick slams on the brakes. The others are now all looking at us.

"You have some bullet holes near your wheel well," the soldier says.

"Yes, like I said there was a lot of activity. Some Free People saw us on 16th and opened fire."

"Free People?" the soldier says suspiciously and then signals the others over.

"You've given us away," Ruby's voice breaks and I tighten my hand on the grip of my pistol.

21

"Go, now!" Ruby says. All the soldiers are pointing their rifles towards us.

"Get down," Merrick commands and slams his foot on the gas pedal. The tires squeal and bullets begin to pelt the van's armor. Merrick lowers himself and drives straight ahead. A couple soldiers have to jump out of the way as the van smashes through the front ends of two parked trucks that are facing each other.

"Watch out," I yell and Merrick lifts his head and turns the van hard so only the back of the van smashes against the Jersey wall in front of it. The impact spins us forward again, and Merrick finally regains control and continues forward up the avenue.

"All of Zone 1 is going to be looking for us now," Ruby groans and scratches Yoshi's head. Yoshi hides her face underneath her paws in-between the front seats, but the rest of her body hangs out in front of me. She's quietly whining.

"What gave us away?" Merrick asks.

"The Turks don't acknowledge us as 'Free People'. They call us *alfiran*: rats," Ruby explains.

Behind I can see the flashing lights of two police vans that are chasing us and, within seconds, a third.

"How are they gaining on us so easily? Can't this thing go any faster?" I ask.

"Not all of the trucks are as heavily equipped as this beauty," Red says, grabbing his shotgun. "We should take advantage of it. Take the machine gun."

"With pleasure," I say and sit behind it with my legs extended and my feet resting against the legs of the tripod. I press my shoulder against the gunstock and wrap my hand tightly against the grip, with my finger on the trigger. I pull back the charging handle and nod at Red, who is waiting to open the back doors.

"I'm waiting for them to get closer," Red says.

"I can hit them. Just open the door."

"If you say so." He swings the doors open and quickly moves out of the way. I immediately begin firing. I can feel the power of the gun flow through my whole body as the massive bullets spit out faster than anyone could count. The bullets tear through the asphalt of the street behind our van until I raise the barrel and finally hit the van on my left. The quick bullets rip a hole through the grill almost instantly and the windshield cracks and breaks apart until the driver swerves and spins out of control. When it finally stops, I can see flames coming out of the engine.

Red cheers. "Nice shooting! Two more to go."

The other two vans are much closer now. Red is on one knee near the door, but before he fires his shotgun, one of the doors on the back of our van swings shut. He fires and blasts the door off. It bounces off one of the pursuing vans.

"They're going to ram us," Red warns, but the van slams hard into the tail of the driver's side before we can brace ourselves. Merrick swerves out of control and I fall, gripping down on the trigger. I shoot wildly and put holes in the corner of the roof. Merrick turns back hard to straighten the van. I stop shooting and push myself back up to a sitting position, just in time to see Red tumble out of the van and roll onto the street. I watch powerlessly as the further van's front bumper smashes Red's head in and then drives over the rest of his body.

The van is in my sights. Savage thoughts burn through my body. I scream and press the trigger, but now the two vans have blurred into one and the buildings melt and swallow them, turning everything into a liquid blob of colors and sounds. I keep firing, aiming wildly at all the colors swirling in front of me. I aim for the white letters that I've seen on so many foreheads, but I can feel our van twist and turn until the white letters turn to red. These letters are different. They're right in front of my eyes. They spell out the word *focus*. Everything behind them is black. I stare at it and concentrate on each letter; then the blackness fades and all the colors and sounds begin to separate back into their proper places. I can no longer see the word, but hear it.

"Focus," Merrick says again, and I stop firing as I realize there are no longer any police vans behind us. Everything is clearer now, but my heart is pounding and I gasp for air. All I can think about is Red falling out of the van. I want to kill every gendarmerie in this city. I can feel my strength growing inside my muscles and bones. I feel like I can rip a man to shreds with my bare hands.

"Did I get them?" I shout, but the only answer I get is the sound of Ruby crying and pounding her fists against the dashboard. We are driving through a skinny, colorless alley that our vehicle barely fits into.

"Both of you focus your anger and sadness into strength. Focus on your surroundings. Use that anger flowing through you to enhance all your senses," Merrick says.

"I don't know how!" Ruby shouts and claws at her own skin.

"Take a deep breath and listen to my words. Focus...focus."

I take another deep breath and let the rage flow through my body and augment each of my senses like a euphoric blast. The dark alley becomes lighter, and I can see the red brick wall of the warehouse we pass. I can hear the dust spin and whirl underneath the tires, and I can feel every ounce of blood circulating through my body.

"They're watching us," Ruby says. I listen. I hear it too. I can hear a voice whisper "Gendarmerie is here" in Spanish, somewhere above us. I hear a couple pairs of footsteps quickly pitter-patting on the rooftops above.

"We're in Zone 2," I say when I notice small, black writing on a brick that says *Viva Cuba Libre.*

Merrick slows down as we exit the alley. Men armed with Carbine 15s are now jogging beside us on both sides, and there is a line of men ahead, all aiming their short barrel rifles at us. Merrick stops before them.

"What are you doing? Run through them," I say.

"No," Ruby says. "They're not our enemies."

"Enemy or not, they have armor-piercing bullets. We wouldn't make it very far," Merrick assures me.

A Cuban soldier waves us forward with a flashlight. The beam leads to an open garage. It's pitch black inside and two soldiers smash the headlights of the van before we enter.

"That can't be good," I say. When the door shuts behind us, I can't see anything, but I can hear breaths and heartbeats outside the van.

"How many?" Merrick asks.

"I hear so many hearts thumping. I can't tell," Ruby says frantically and covers her ears with her hands.

"It's okay, Ruby. You just need to learn to zone in on what you need to hear, see, or smell and block out the rest." I grab her hands from behind her and lower them. "Just listen. Take a deep breath and focus." She turns her head slightly and then again and again, over and over, as she counts each new heartbeat.

"There are over a hundred in the building," she says almost excitedly as if she just solved a puzzle.

"132 to be exact," I say. "We're not getting out of here."

"How many down here?"

"Thirty-three," I say and listen intently to the breaths and heartbeats of those around us. They're beating so fast they sound like they are going to blast out of their chests. "They're Berserkers," I say.

"What?" Merrick says and whips his head around to study my face. "Are you sure?"

"He's right," Ruby confirms.

Suddenly, a series of ceiling lights turn on one by one, until I can see that we're in the center of a long parking garage. I immediately notice dozens of Berserkers standing around the van, each one chained by the neck to a separate pillar. They're all staring at us. The one closest to us is a boy no older than fifteen. The muscles on his face are bulging so much that they are caving in his nose and have dislocated his jaw so that it's hanging and deformed. Drool is seeping out from it. His stomach is round and bloated, but his chest looks concaved next to his swollen arms and shoulders. His skin is torn and, in some parts, is hanging off of him like a piece of bloody cloth.

We sit silently in the van for a while.

"What are we supposed to do?" I say, finally breaking the tense silence.

"I don't know. If they want us, they can come get us. I'll take my chances in here with my guns and armor," Merrick says.

"We should have kept our other clothes with us. We have to let the Cubans know we're not gendarmerie."

"They'll never believe us," Ruby says.

"Well, we can't just sit here forever," I say.

There's an old, bronze-skinned man walking along the wall ahead of us. As he walks by them, the Berserkers turn to watch. Some of them reach an arm out for him, but he walks just far enough to remain out of their grasp. He's a small man, with dark hair speckled white and parted on the left. His hair sweeps over his small forehead and underneath it he is wearing dark sunglasses with large, beige rims. He has a white, short-sleeved button-down with a palm tree pattern and beige shorts that show off his skinny legs. He shuffles slowly ahead in crème-colored socks and thong sandals. When he is in front of us, he makes a right angle turn and walks straight up to Merrick's window. The infected boy reaches for him and grunts, but the old man is a few inches out of reach. He taps on the window with one knuckle. Merrick slides it down.

The old man swirls around a hard candy in his mouth and clears his throat. "Are you going to sit here the whole day, or what?" He says slowly as if he's trying to pronounce each word without a Cuban accent, but fails miserably. "Come. Follow me upstairs. Leave your weapons inside your van." He clears his throat again and shuffles back the way he came. We look at each other. Merrick shrugs his shoulders.

"I'm afraid it's our only option," he says and climbs out of the van. Ruby, Yoshi, and I follow him, making sure not to get in range of the Berserkers grasps. The boy's eyes follow me and he leans forward as far as his neck brace will allow him. He pushes all his weight forward, and the collar sinks into his red, puffed up neck. He gags and chokes furiously, but doesn't retreat. Every Berserker we pass does the same thing. I can feel the hairs on my neck stiffen. I jump back as one reaches for me, and Yoshi barks at it.

"They can't get you if you stay close to this wall," the old man says calmly. We skim the cement wall until we reach a door. The lock echoes as he opens it, and he sluggishly leads us up the steps. If I knew where I was going, I would hurry past him.

The old man is practically gasping for air when we make it to the first floor. We enter a small atrium with some doors in front and to our sides. He opens the second one and leads us down a short, dim passage. Towards the end, there is a guard standing next to a door holding a Carbine SBR. He looks straight ahead and doesn't even move, but I can hear his heart beating faster as we get closer. He doesn't look at us as we enter the room he's guarding. The room is poorly lit and the air is damp. Aside from three stools, a metal chair, and a small, wooden table, the room is unfurnished. There are a dozen, armed soldiers inside. I see their eyes following Yoshi and hear their heartbeats increasing. Some of them begin to shift back and forth on their feet. They are scared of her. We can use their fear to our advantage. I look at each one, planning how I can kill them and escape. All I need is for one to get close enough to me, so that I can grab a gun or a knife. With Merrick, Ruby, and Yoshi by my side, we stand a good chance.

The single chair is facing the three stools that are in line with the table. I can see sharp knives and tools on the top of the table.

"Please, have a seat," the old man says.

"If you mean to scare us with those torture devices, don't bother," Ruby says. "I've had Fangs with sharper teeth bite me."

She wants them to know we're infected, but she played that card too soon.

"Then perhaps I will chain you in the basement with the others," he says. When she doesn't respond he says, "Please sit."

"We're not gendarmerie," I say as I sit in-between Merrick and Ruby. The old Cuban man sits across from us. Yoshi sits next to Ruby.

"I know you're not. If I thought you were, I would have released the locks on the Berserkers' neck's downstairs." He laughs. "We just heard a police van barreled through a checkpoint. It's only logical to assume that some 'Free People' had stolen it and attempted to very subtly break into Zone 1."

"Yeah well, we were kind of just winging it," I say honestly.

"Why did you bring us here if you knew we weren't gendarmerie?" Ruby questions.

The old man pulls out a pack of cigarettes from his shirt pocket. His hand shakes slightly as he brings a cigarette to his mouth and rests it between his lips. One of the armed guards walks over and lights his cigarette with a match. He sucks on it and then releases a puff of white smoke from his nose. "Perhaps I just wanted new friends. I'm Oswardo; everyone here calls me *Abuelo*. That's Juan-Carlos." He points to a guard behind him. "That's Ernesto, Jorge, Alejandro, and that's—"

"You didn't bring us here to make friends," Ruby says sharply.

Abuelo turns back around and reads her face. He takes another hit of his cigarette. "You know, we have much in common." He points to her with the two fingers holding the cigarette. "You see we both seek freedom from the Caliphate."

"Maybe you should have never joined them in the first place," I say.

"Not all of us wanted to. In fact, most of the Cuban people opposed it. But thanks to the U.S., our government had more guns than we did."

"What is it that you want from us?" Ruby says.

"I want your help. The *Nacionales* and the Free People need to join together."

"For what? To help you take Miami and the rest of Florida for yourselves? You wiped away the entire population of Florida in one attack. You're just as guilty as the Caliphate. You're all slaves to Ira," I say. I'm studying the knives on the table with my peripheral vision. I can grab some and have them in the necks of *Abuelo* and at least two soldiers before they even know what happened.

Abuelo chuckles and raises his finger at me. "Out of all of us, you did the bidding of Ira the most. I know who you are Naked Lady. You worked for him. You killed for him."

I can feel Ruby looking at me.

"I didn't know. If I would have known the monster he was, I wouldn't have."

"We too wish we could take back the things we unknowingly did for him, but we cannot. All we can do now is come together and take back our freedom," *Abuelo* says.

"We are not going to help you take Miami for yourselves," Ruby says.

"That is not what we wish. We only wish for Cuba back. We will give back whatever our government took illegally and set up a new government with the Allies permission. We will pay whatever reparations we have to and help to restore Florida. The Cuban people are with me. We are sick and tired of corrupt leaders taking advantage of us and sending us into wars on the wrong side."

"You'll give Miami back to the Free People if we help you?"

"Yes, we are all Free People. There should be no borders between us. No differences. You have a lot of people and we have a lot of weapons. We can help each other."

"How can we help?" Merrick says.

"We need your van."

"For what?" I say.

"We have intel that says the Caliphate is shipping something big out of the city very soon. They are posting a lot of security to this shipment, so it must be something important. We want to steal it from them."

I look at Ruby. "It could be the oxygen concentrator."

"We were thinking the same thing," *Abuelo* says. "We want to steal it, but we need a gendarmerie van. As you probably know, it's the only way to cure the infection.

"Hold on, since when do you Cubans want to cure the infection? You are the ones that brought it to Florida in the first place," Ruby says.

"Like I said, it was the government, not us. We opposed them, but had no power to stop them. Did you see all those Berserkers downstairs? Those are Cuban people who are sick. The boy, he is my youngest grandson, Pedrito." I can see the angst in his eyes. "He is a good boy. He always helped his *abuelita* clean the house. He wants to be a doctor someday. I have to cure him and the others. Think about it, if we cured them we would have more men to fight." He wipes his face and the corner of his eyes with a small tissue that he retrieved from inside his pocket.

"If we say no, will you let us leave?" I ask warily.

"Yes, we are friends now. You are not captives, even if you refuse us."

"You can't have our van," Ruby says. "But we will join your mission and help you steal the concentrator."

"It's a deal," *Abuelo* says with a smile. His teeth are yellowish-brown.

"Do you have a plan?" I say.

"It's not great, but it's better than yours."

22

There is no more Zone 3 or Zone 4. Now, it is called the 'Free Zone' and thanks to *Abuelo's* intelligence, we know the motorcade that is transporting the large-scale oxygen concentrator must pass through it to get to the harbor.

I'm sitting in the driver's seat of the van at the edge of a small path facing a short street. There's a little Cuban café with bright blue walls across the way from us. Aside from the sign on the top being a bit unleveled, it looks otherwise unscathed by war. I wish it was open. My eyelids are feeling awfully heavy.

Yoshi gripes in the back.

"I know girl. No one wanted to ride with us," I say.

"Can't blame them though," Ruby says. She has a sawn-off shotgun on her lap. The only one brave enough to ride with two Berserkers and a Fang was Merrick, but they need him elsewhere.

Parked next to us is a semi-truck that barely fits into the alley with our van. Big-eared Ernesto is in the driver's seat. After the first two vans and the truck carrying the concentrator pass us by, Ernesto will pull the truck out blocking, the last two vans of the motorcade.

"How much time?" I say. The waiting is killing me.

"Ten minutes," she says. "Remember to let the motorcade make their turn before you pull out, so they don't realize we replaced the other vans."

"But once I make the turn, won't they realize there is only one van behind them instead of two?" I say. There are still parts of this plan I don't understand. It took so long for Mika and his men and the General to show up, that *Abuelo* had to rush through his explanation of the plan.

"By the time they realize there is only one van behind them, it will be too late. They will already be on the ramp."

"Okay but what about the two vans that Ernesto blocks? Won't they just turn around and find another way? Not to mention they will alert the others."

"Were you paying attention at all?"

"No, I was undressing you with my mind."

"Don't be an ass," she says, but smiles anyway. "After the truck with the concentrator in it passes us, they turn right at the next street. Once they do, Ernesto will pull his truck out and block the two trailing vans. Then Miranda, Luca, Mo the Mute, Juan-Carlos, and Alejandro will trap them in with two vehicles. Both gendarmerie vans will have at least four armed soldiers, so they will be outnumbered in that fight. Then on the next street, the first van will pass the ramp to the highway. As soon as it does, Merrick will detonate the bomb. It will destroy the first van and block the rest of the motorcade from continuing down that route. Instead, they will be forced to change direction by going onto the highway and we will be right behind them."

"This is the part that confuses me. We will have only five miles to somehow get rid of the second van and force the truck onto the exit that we want them to take and we have to do all of that without doing any damage to the oxygen concentrator?"

"Four miles," she corrects me.

"Oh good, I didn't want it to be too easy."

"I hope you're a good driver," she says.

"I can't remember the last time I drove, literally. Maybe you should take the wheel, and I'll handle the machine gun."

"You blacked out the last time."

"Only because of Red."

"I wish he was with us."

"Me too," I say.

"Here they come. Get ready," Ruby says.

I grip the steering wheel tighter as the first gendarmerie van passes by. Hopefully, they didn't see us. The whole plan would crumble and we would be sitting ducks. Exactly six seconds pass before the next van drives by, just as *Abuelo* predicted.

Six more seconds until the concentrator passes.

"I can't see when they turn on the next street," I say suddenly. "How will I know when to go?"

"Just wait for Ernesto. Hopefully he times it right. We'll only have a few seconds to replace them without being noticed."

"This plan is shit," I say.

The box truck passes.

"Here we go," Ruby says. "We don't want to damage the truck either. We're going to need it for transport."

I can see the third van approaching. The driver looks at me. His eyes widen, but it's too late. Ernesto speeds the semi-truck across the street blocking the rest of the motorcade.

"Go now!" Ruby says. I hit the gas pedal and turn right. I swerve side to side.

"Straighten out," Ruby says. I'm beginning to think I've never driven a car before, but I manage to straighten the van.

"Turn right now. And don't go too fast. We don't want them to suspect anything until they're on the ramp," Ruby says. I turn right and try to drive as straight as possible. I match the distance of the vans ahead. The four-lane street merges into two lanes as we approach the highway to the north.

"They're wondering where the fourth van is about...now," Ruby says.

"And they're about to find out."

The first van passes the on-ramp. Out of nowhere, a car comes and smashes into its side. It immediately explodes from the inside, causing a massive fireball that consumes both vehicles.

"Come on. Take the bait," Ruby says. It seems there is still room for the motorcade to squeeze through. I'm praying they won't notice it.

Turkish chatter comes through the CB radio that I didn't even notice we had.

"They're asking if we should squeeze through," I say. I pick up the mike. "Negative, take the highway. The rats are attacking. They took out our rear van," I say in Turkish, not quite as well as Merrick would have said. I wonder how many languages I can speak.

There's no reply. Hopefully, they didn't notice my accent.

"Do we have a plan B?" I say to Ruby, but then the second van veers onto the on-ramp that curves around until it merges onto the highway. After six seconds, the truck carrying the concentrator follows the van towards the highway.

"You can speed up," Ruby says. "We're on our own now." I accelerate and curve around the on ramp, until I'm right on the truck's tail. "Four miles," Ruby reminds me as soon as we merge onto the six-lane freeway raised above the city.

I push hard on the gas and try to pass the truck, but it swerves and blocks me. Every attempt I make, the driver obstructs my path.

"Unit 3, what are you doing? Stay in formation."

"Negative. I know a faster route."

"Stay in your position," another voice says. "What is your I.D. number?"

"Just pass him already," Ruby says.

I throw down the microphone and attempt to pass the truck on his right side, but as soon as he swerves to thwart me, I put the gas pedal to the floor and veer left. The driver looks at us curiously as we pass them.

"Get close to the van, on the side," Ruby says.

I drive as close as I can to the left tail of the van. Ruby sticks the sawn-off shotgun out the window and aims. She fires. It causes the van to swerve to the right and then speed up ahead of us, but it barely puts a dent in their armor.

"Assistance needed. We are under attack."

I shut off the CB radio.

"We're never going to get through that armor. Try ramming it," Ruby says.

"Ruby, get down!" I shout. The back doors of the van in front of us swing open and I see a soldier manning their machine gun. He begins firing at us. The bullets smash against the front end and I swerve hard to the right, clipping the cement guard rail.

"Go, go, go," Ruby says. I speed up and try to pass it, but it turns hard to the right. Ruby and I duck down as the machine gun barrel swings directly in front of us. The bullets rip through and shatter the windshield. I turn the wheel to the left and veer out of the path of the machine gun's bullets. The truck behind us rams into our tail, but I hold the steering wheel as tight as I can and speed up until we are next to the van. Ruby fires her shotgun at the driver's side window of the police van. It turns sharply and bangs against the guard rail.

"Nice shot," I say. It gives me enough time to pass the van.

"Get on that machine gun."

Ruby rushes to the back and opens the doors.

"Be careful, I swear to God if you fall out..."

She mounts the gun.

"What are you waiting for?"

"I can't fire, the truck is tailing right behind the van. I can't take the chance of damaging the concentrator."

"Well we have to do something. We're almost to the exit," I say.

"Get me closer."

I look through the side view mirror and line up so that I'm directly in front of the van. I hold my breath and slam on the brakes. The van rams into us and I immediately press the gas pedal. The motorcade keeps moving forward, bumper to bumper.

"How's that?" I say.

"Good enough," Ruby affirms and fires the heavy gun. The bullets rip through the armor on the hood and destroy the windshield. She keeps firing until the van turns hard and the truck behind it barrels through its tail end, causing the van to spin out of control until it slams against the rail. I can see white smoke coming from its engine.

Ruby comes back to the front, but lets out a shriek of pain before she drops into the passenger seat.

"What is it?" I say and look through the rear-view mirror. The soldier in the passenger seat of the truck is waving a pistol around and trying to shoot at us. I look back over at Ruby. There's blood everywhere. My face turns pale and I feel a cold sweat on my shoulders and face.

"It's okay," she says with clenched teeth. "It's just my shoulder. We have to get this truck off now."

I look ahead. The off-ramp to the next exit is coming up. It's where the Free People will trap the truck and intercept it. I do the only thing I can think to do. I hit my brake until we're side by side with the truck. It bumps into me trying to move us, but I hold on tight to the steering wheel and turn into it. I look over at them and wonder if we look as frantic as they do. The one in the passenger seat tries to reach over with his pistol. He steadies his aim at us.

The exit is only a moment away.

I turn the wheel as hard as I can to the right.

"Come on," I shout and push the van off the exit just in time. The guardrail divides us and the side of our van scrapes against it. I stomp on the brakes.

The other van smashes through the metal guardrail of the circular off-ramp and flies down to the street below. It turns on its side in the air and lands on its passenger door. Sparks fly as metal scrapes against pavement until it comes to a stop in the intersection.

I take a deep breath and finally let go of the steering wheel. Little bits of it are glued to my sweaty hands.

"Take off your shirt," Ruby says.

"Ruby, I'm flattered, but I don't think now is the right time for –"

"To stop the bleeding."

"Oh...right."

"Just give me the damn shirt."

I quickly take it off and help her wrap it around her shoulder. Down below, I see Free People surrounding the overturned truck. Merrick is one of them. I turn the van around and drive down the ramp. I wonder how we're going to get that truck flipped right-side up, but I'm so relieved we were able to finally get the concentrator. If we didn't have the help of the Cubans and the Free People, it would have been much more difficult to achieve.

"Wait a minute," I say. "Ira plans everything out. He always seems to be two steps ahead. Wasn't that was too easy?" I make a U-turn when the ramp dumps me out in the wrong direction on the street below. I can see Merrick and a few others going to open the back of the flipped truck.

"Easy? I have a bullet in my shoulder that says otherwise."

"But that's how Ira works. He puts you through so many hoops you can't possibly think that someone is ahead of you, but he always is. He has everything planned."

"You're thinking too much. There's no way he could predict we would join with the Cubans and try to steal his concentrator. Not to mention the fact that we almost died doing it."

I pull up and park behind the crowd of Free People surrounding the truck. Merrick, Luca, and a couple others are trying to cut the lock on the door.

"How did the Cubans know the route of the motorcade?"

"Are you saying *Abuelo* is working for Ira?" Ruby says.

"No, but I'm saying Ira let them find out about it."

"So, then what? The oxygen concentrator is not in the truck?"

Merrick cuts the lock open and grabs the handle of the sliding door.

"Merrick, no!" I shout as I get out of the van, but it's too late. As he slides the door open, the truck explodes into a great ball of fire consuming at least a dozen Free People standing around it.

I push my way through gawking Free People until I'm stepping over charred, dismembered bodies around the flaming van. The only one who can stop the fury from taking over is now dead. I find his body.

There is a large piece of shrapnel buried in his skull between his eyes.

We should have known better. How could we be so foolish to think we could outmaneuver Ira? The world only recently discovered who he is and that was only because he allowed himself to be revealed. He is too smart, and he knows me too well. He knows how I think, because he created how I think. He and the concentrator are undoubtedly long gone. This whole ploy was probably just for his amusement.

I turn to look for Ruby. She's hugging the General tight. She probably feared the worst when she saw the truck blow up. Yoshi stands on her hind legs, trying to hug them too, but she towers over them and nearly knocks them over. Ruby laughs, and for a moment my anger subsides. Mika and Mo the Mute are with them.

"I'm sorry," Ruby says as I walk back over.

"As far as I can remember, he was my oldest friend in the world," I say.

"Don't feel too bad for him," Mika says. "Our fate is about to be much worse. I just received word that General Hammer has fallen. Big Al is on his way here with a million Berserkers. And even though Ira is not with his armies, the Caliphate is sending 100 million more to storm the Allies in Israel. The war is over. We lost."

"Must we bend the knee?" the General says.

"Never," Mika almost shouts. "They can take my head, but I will not submit."

"And mine as well?" the General asks. Mika stares at her appalled, as if he hadn't thought of that. He looks as if he's about to burst into tears. He grabs her and holds her tight. "It is better to die as Free People, sweetheart, than to submit to evil."

"Wait a minute," Ruby says. "You said Ira is not with his armies? Then where is he?"

"As far as I know, he is still here. If he had left I would have known about it. I still have friends all over this city."

"Then the concentrator is still here. Brute, you said it yourself. Where Ira is, the concentrator will be," Ruby says.

"Maybe I did, but what does it matter? We can't find it if he's always a step ahead of us."

"Perhaps we have to look where no one would think to look. Where we have no influence and no one can help us," Mika muses.

"Zone 2," Ruby says.

"Zone 2 is completely overrun by Berserkers and Fangs. To even get there we would have to cross the north bridge which belongs to the Caliphate. We would never survive," Miranda says.

"No, but the Brute and I could," Ruby says.

"I can't go," I say. Ruby shoots me a surprised look. "Without Merrick to focus me, I will lose control of my mind."

"Then you'll fit right in," Mika says with a mischievous grin.

"Brute, we are the only ones who won't be harmed by the Berserkers."

"That's a theory and a shaky one at best."

"Maybe so, but it's our only shot," Ruby says. "Merrick gave me the last two oxygen injections. He said to save them in case we run into Ira, but if you lose control we can use one."

"No, that'll only weaken my abilities. If we must do this, I will have to figure out how to focus myself," I say.

"So, what's the plan? How do we get you guys into Zone 2?" Mika asks.

"No, no more plans. Everything we've planned has gone to shit. We can't out plan Ira. The only way we can beat him is to have no plan at all," I say.

"Then what do you suggest we do? Just walk around South Beach and ask the Berserkers if they've seen a large-scale oxygen concentrator?" Ruby says.

"No, but I think I know where to look first," I say. "General, we need all the troops you can muster. Tell Oswardo the same. If you guys can help us get over that bridge. Ruby and I can handle the rest."

"We'll gather all the Free People we can. It's time to stop hiding. We will get you through the barricade and destroy all the gendarmerie strongholds in the city. We can't face Big Al's armies and the gendarmerie at the same time," Mika says.

23

Halfway across the bridge, steel-infused, cement Jersey barriers are laid out width wise on both sides of the gendarmerie barricade barring the Free People or the Berserkers on the other side from crossing. In-between the short, cement walls are two armored trucks and several heavy, machine guns lined up on both sides.

I hand the binoculars to Ruby.

"There's no way we'll get any vehicles past. We'll have to go by foot. How many do you see?" I ask.

"There's at least five...no six."

"Six isn't so bad."

"They are heavily armed, and there could be more inside those trucks."

"Hopefully the others can bring enough Free People to this fight," I say. "I still think we should take a boat across." We are standing halfway down a street that leads to the entrance of the bridge.

"Too many patrols guard the waters. We won't stand a chance," Ruby says. She has a white bandage on her shoulder that the General placed there after she removed the bullet and cleaned her wound.

We're both wearing hand-me-downs that *Abuelo* gave us after we washed in his building. Ruby is wearing a black t-shirt that stops just above her belly button and white shorts that are snug around her toned legs. She has an Uzi submachine gun hanging from a strap. On her other side is a small, leather satchel with the oxygen injections inside.

Abuelo gave me one of his dead son's grey jeans and a clean, white t-shirt. I'm carrying a loaded AR-15, my pistol, and Merrick's bag of ammo clips on my back. Yoshi sits patiently beside Ruby, sniffing the smog. She whines eagerly as an old, brown car splattered with bullet holes pulls up behind us.

The General is hanging out of the window in a red sports bra, hair neatly pulled into double buns parted straight down the middle. She has glitter painted on half of her face, from her forehead down to her chin. When the car stops, she swings her legs around and hops out. She's wearing baggy, gold pants and black boots. She reaches back into the window and pulls out a machine pistol with an extended clip in each hand. She holds them up and grins at us. The Gorilla climbs out of the driver's seat and two others get out of the back. All of them are wearing gold-colored track suits, white sneakers, and gold Honey Badger submachine guns around their necks.

Seconds later, two more cars pull up with Mika, Mo the Mute, Alejandro, Umberto, and six others I don't know. They are all carrying assault rifles or submachine guns. I notice the two cars both have a long rag hanging out of their gas tanks.

"Is this it?" I ask, already annoyed. "It's not enough. There are only six of them, but they are a long way across that bridge and they have heavy machine guns."

"You forget who really rules this city," the General says and winks at me. "Listen."

In the distance, I can hear what sounds like a mob of people singing and cheering. I turn and look down the street. There are at least 500 Free People marching towards us. When they reach our group, I realize that most of them are only armed with sticks, chains, rocks, and several Molotov cocktails. Only fifty or so have either submachine guns or pistols. One of them hands the General and Mika a brick each, and then lights the rags hanging out of the cars' gas tanks. Mika and the General each place their brick in one of the cars. They place it on the gas pedals, and the cars accelerate onward past the intersection and down the bridge. The mob begins to march forward.

The General and her masked men get in her car and drive forward with the mob. The General and the two in the backseat hang out their windows, singing and cheering with the crowd and holding up their guns. Ruby and I follow inside the crowd.

As the speeding cars drive towards the barricade, the gendarmerie opens fire. The first car veers to the right, smashes against the cement guardrail, and then explodes. The second car makes it all the way to the Jersey barricades before it blows up. The crowd cheers and hollers.

"Attack!" I hear someone shout and the mob charges across the bridge. The machine guns roar and the front lines are immediately wiped out, but that only gets the crowd louder. I see the General firing her machine pistols forward and her men doing the same. Many people are throwing rocks and lit Molotov cocktails forward. I can hear them explode on the ground, but there are so many Free People in front of me that I can't see where they hit. The machine guns continue to rumble and soon, Ruby and I are stepping over dead bodies. We will soon be on the front line as the crowd shrinks with every .50 caliber bullet fired towards us. A few Free People jump off the sides of the bridge to avoid the immense projectiles coming at them.

The crowd applauds and shouts louder, and I can hear one less machine gun firing. We must have killed one of them. We march passed the first flaming car. We're halfway there.

I step over several bloodied Free People who are screaming and crying in agony. One is a boy no older than fifteen, calling out for his mother. I want to help him, but I have to keep moving forward.

The crowd cheers and whistles loudly again as another machine gunner is killed. More Molotov cocktails are lit and thrown, adding to the fires that blaze at the barricade. There are only two rows in front of us now. I can hear bullets smashing against the General's car. It swerves to the right, but not before the masked men on the left side takes a bullet to the chest and falls out. The General screams and shoots wildly ahead. Her car is directly in front of me now. I run towards it and climb on the trunk and up to the roof. I take a knee on top of it, aim, and fire a single burst to the head and chest of a gunner. Before the crowd finishes cheering for the kill, I set my sights on the last gunner. He ducks below the Jersey wall and fires aimlessly into the crowd, killing several more Free People and causing the car to swerve to the left. I tumble off the roof and the asphalt greets me with a hard smack.

I hold my face with my hand and rub my temples. The whole world is trembling for a moment, but when my vision clears and I look up, all I see are legs and boots marching over me. Some step on my stomach and chest. They must think I'm just another dead body. I look around for my AR, but I don't see it. I listen. I can hear it in the midst of the hurricane of guns, bullets, and explosions. Someone must have picked it up. I hear cheering, and then someone finally helps me to my feet. *Where the hell is Ruby?*

The Free People are climbing over the barricade like a violent storm. One last gendarmerie soldier keeps firing from behind an armored truck. He kills at least three more people before the mob overtakes him and beats him to death with sticks and kicks. Others open the trucks and search them. Some take the machine guns of the dead soldiers and aim back towards the way we came.

"Gendarmerie!" Someone yells. At the base of the bridge, several police trucks and vans are parked. Light blue and red lights flash through the gloomy sky. The gunfire begins again and I jump over the wall of the barricade. I duck down and push as many people as I can with me as a rocket-propelled grenade zooms over my head and explodes against one of the armored trucks. Free People are screaming. One is running around in circles, looking for something to quench the fire that engulfs him. He runs towards the side of the bridge and jumps off. I look around for Ruby in the din of frantic people. I see the General's face, and for a moment I think it's Ruby's. Her eyes are fierce and her high cheekbones are the same, but her complexion is much lighter. She pushes her way towards the wall with her guns aiming towards the incoming police.

I search the crowd for Ruby. There are so many people around me, but none of them are her. I start to panic. All the faces begin to swirl around me in a fiery splash. People are bumping into me from all sides, and some shove me out of the way. There's another explosion nearby and more screams, but I don't know where it is. I see fire everywhere. Someone grabs me and pulls me close to them. I focus my eyes and see Mika's ugly face in front of me. His hands are gripping my shirt.

He's saying something to me, but I can't hear him. He's hard enough to hear without machine gunfire and explosions all around. I try to read his lips. "We'll take back the city. Go kill the beast," I think he says. Then he points to the other side of the bridge. I look over and see Ruby. Suddenly Mika is gone, swallowed up in the sea of people. On the other side of the barricade, Ruby is watching the Free People begin to take their city back. Her shoulders glisten with sweat and she holds her Uzi submachine gun in her hands. Yoshi is next to her.

I push my way through the last of the crowd and climb over the waist-high cement wall. She smiles when she sees me.

"I was beginning to think you weren't coming," she says.

"Were you going to look for me?"

"The mission is more important." She stands on the tips of her toes and kisses my cheek. "Let's move."

We walk down the rest of the bridge and towards South Beach. My head is throbbing with every bullet and explosion behind me. As we walk further into the darkness ahead, the shouts of the Free People are replaced with muffled groans, the explosions with screams of agony, and the gunfire with rapid, angry breaths.

It's so dark that the only light is from the fires spreading throughout the city proper and the small flashlight attachment on my Glock. I aim it ahead. We pass several restaurants and an old hotel on the corner that I imagine were once all once illuminated with bright, blue and pink neon lights.

"Where are we going?" Ruby says softly, as if our voices will rouse the Berserkers. But it's already too late for that. They have been watching us since we crossed the bridge. I can hear footsteps and pulsating heartbeats all around us. Yoshi hears it too. Her ears are perked up and every time something scurries by, she bares her teeth and lets out a low, steady cackle.

"I sure hope your theory is right," I say. "A group of Fangs attacked Merrick and I. They didn't seem to care that I was infected too."

"Maybe they were hungry for Merrick."

"Maybe...or maybe you're wrong."

"I'm telling you, when I was in Amalek's furnace they could sense I was one of them; they didn't hurt me."

"Perhaps, but some of these might be trained by the Caliphate...the same way the Cubans train Fangs."

I see something move fast through the light and then disappear. I aim all around, looking for whatever it was.

Ruby gasps as I shine my light onto a Berserker standing only a couple yards from us. It's at least seven feet tall. I have to shine the light up to see its face. The skin around its mouth has been torn away so it looks like it has a wide, bloody smile. There are a couple long strands of black hair on his head, but the rest of its scalp is bald and inflamed with rosy bubbles, some of which have burst, like little volcanos of pus.

It stretches out its long, beefy arms and screams so loudly my whole body shivers. It could crush all my bones with its bare hands. It steps towards us. I hold my finger steady on the trigger. It's going to take an entire clip to kill this thing.

"Don't kill him," Ruby says. "If we do, we can't heal him."

"Ruby I don't want to kill it, but my desire to not be eaten takes precedence." It takes another step, smiling eerily at me. Its eyes are protruding from their lidless holes and its belly is bloated, hairless, and in some spots, skinless.

Yoshi leaps in front of me, snarling at the giant monster. She barks so fiercely that the Berserker shields itself with its arm and then retreats backwards until Yoshi stops barking. It stays, watching us from afar.

"It's scared of Yoshi," I say and laugh.

"Perhaps it was her all along that kept them from harming me. Who's a good girl?" she says and scratches the back of her head. It seems to calm Yoshi down a bit.

"Let's keep moving," I say. I look around the next street and, as I wave my flashlight, I can now see hundreds of Berserkers surrounding us, but keeping a small distance. I lead our group east onto the next street and as we move ahead, the Berserkers seem to part for us like the Red Sea.

"Well, it seems they won't attack us as long as Yoshi is with us," Ruby says.

"Please God, let none of these zombies throw a tennis ball," I say.

We keep moving towards the coastline until I can hear the waves crashing against the shore. Then, we turn right down a wide avenue.

Yoshi whines. "I hope you know where you're going," Ruby says.

"I'm looking for the altar where Ira declared himself ruler of the world," I say. I switch my gun to my right hand to give my left arm a break.

"The Altar of Pergamon?"

"You saw it?"

"I heard about it. You think the concentrator is there?"

"At least nearby. It's the only place I know in South Beach."

"What?" She grabs my arm to stop me and the parting sea of Berserkers in front of us. "Are you kidding me? You just guessed that that's where he hid it?"

"Do you have a better idea of where it can be? Please by all means. I'm open for suggestions."

"No," she reluctantly admits. "Do you even know where it is?"

"No," I reluctantly admit. "I just remember there was a large, white building behind it."

"A white building? Hmm...did it have blue tilework over and around the entrance?"

"Yes! You know it?"

"The Museum of Modern Technology," she says.

"I think that's a pretty good place to start."

"Yeah, but we're going the wrong way. Come on, this way," she says and we turn north.

We head north for a couple of blocks and then turn left. The ionic temple surrounding the altar is almost as tall as the buildings surrounding it. It looms above us as we move to the base of the wide, marble steps that lead up to the altar. Ancient giants waging war against Pagan gods eerily rise above us in high relief. At the top of the steps, the altar is surrounded by large columns holding a square roof with griffins and gargoyles watching us from atop.

Yoshi cries in front of the steps and can't seem to figure out if she wants to sit or stand. I walk up the steps, until Ruby grabs me from behind.

"Look," she says. I turn around. There are thousands of Berserkers lying prostrate on the street in front of the altar. I feel a dark and ominous power flowing through my veins. It feels good. I want to keep climbing, but Ruby and Yoshi look so scared.

"Let's just check the museum," I say and climb down.

We circle around the wide, ancient temple and enter the tall, pink doors of the museum. The wide open foyer is dimly lit by the sunlight shining through the smoke and haze and the domed glass ceiling, although it looks more like a sliver of moonlight seeping through. Six floors are squared around the portico, with hundreds of exhibits of all sorts of machinery and technology. In the center is a large model of a world war one era bi-plane, hanging from suspension cables. Its engines are uncovered for all to see.

Straight past the plane, the foyer extends into a long hall. We follow it. Our footsteps and breaths echo off the walls.

"How are we going to find it in here?" Ruby wonders aloud. There are open rooms on both sides with more exhibits.

"We'll have to check every exhibit."

At the end of the hall is a room shaped like a pentagon. Four more halls extend from it and at the center is a small device on a pedestal, raised above a few steps.

"This is going to take forever," Ruby says. "Shall we start with this one?"

"It's too small," I say looking at the device. It's no bigger than my fist. It looks like a cellphone with some casing and wires looping around it. "Besides, Ira wouldn't have made it so obvious."

"Sometimes the most obvious places are where no one thinks to look," says a familiar voice that isn't Ruby's. Ruby and I both turn quickly. Yoshi growls and displays her vicious teeth.

"Ira," I say.

He stands at the entrance of the hall on our left. He's wearing an expensive-looking suit with a blue and white-checkered button-down underneath and a blue tie. His hair is slicked perfectly to the side and small stubble is neatly-groomed down his high cheeks and along his sharp jawline. He steps towards us, and Yoshi retreats backwards and whines.

Ruby pulls up her submachine gun to aim it at him, but I stop her.

"Don't. He's too close. He'll take it from you before you get a shot off."

Ira lets out a high-pitched snicker. "It is ironic, isn't it? This device has the power to change the world, and it has been sitting here, open to the public all along. Anyone could have walked in, turned it on, and stopped me a long time ago."

"We still can," Ruby says.

"Ah, unfortunately you're much too late," he says with a fake-looking frown. "Even if you turned it on now, my armies are still bigger than yours. There are only two cities left in the entire world that don't belong to me. You have no hope left."

"Well, then you won't mind me turning it on," I say and step up towards the pedestal.

"I'll destroy it before I let you turn it on," he yells so loudly that I stop myself from climbing further.

"What are you afraid of? You said it yourself, your armies are bigger."

"Yes and ten times as big with the concentrator off. It's not time anyway. The entire world must be mine first. All my enemies must bow down before me or be wiped out. Then I will cure the infection for all to see, and the whole world will worship me as their savior." His voice is giddy with excitement, like a child on the night before Christmas.

"It's a nice plan, but for once there was something you didn't account for," I say.

"What, you being here? Did you really think I would let you outsmart me?" He laughs obnoxiously, loud and high-pitched. "I planned for you to be here, just as I planned for Merrick to open my truck. I wish I could have seen his face the moment he realized I will always be ten steps ahead of him. Ah well, at least I'll get to see your face when I kill you."

"You're lying. You had no idea we would come here. Otherwise, you would have already destroyed it," I say.

"It doesn't matter," he says angrily. He takes off his suit jacket and his tie and throws them onto the floor. "You couldn't defeat me with Merrick at your side. What makes you think you'll fare any better with your whore and a dog?"

Ruby promptly pulls her Uzi up and attempts to aim it at Ira, but he's too fast. He charges her, grabs the gun, and kicks her in the stomach before she can pull the trigger. She lets go of the weapon as she falls backwards onto the floor. He flips the gun around and turns it towards me.

From two steps above, I kick his hand upwards and he fires a burst of bullets into the ceiling. I lift my right hand and aim my pistol at his torso. He grabs my arm and pulls it in, tucking it at his side. By the time I pull the trigger, I'm firing at the wall behind him. He hammers down his right arm, striking above my eye with the front-end of the submachine gun. I collapse like a bombed building.

He aims the barrel at me. I roll out of the way as Yoshi leaps up and bites down on his arm. He shoots wildly until she rips him around and he drops the gun with a painful grunt.

My head is throbbing. Blood and sweat are dripping from my brow into my eyes. My eyesight is contorted, but I can still see Ira on one knee, landing fast, powerful uppercuts into Yoshi's body until she squeals and lets go of him. He then spins around and kicks her in the head so hard that she falls over and doesn't get back up.

Ruby leaps off a step and pummels Ira's face with a downward punch before he can get up. He falls on his back in front of her.

I try to get up, but the rooms spins around so violently that I tumble back to the hard floor.

Focus.

Ira spins around on the floor and sweep kicks Ruby's ankles. As she falls, he gets up and unsheathes her knife in one impossibly fast motion. He falls to one knee above her and raises her knife.

Focus, damn it. I grab my pistol off the ground next to me and fire several shots towards Ira's back. I miss all of them, but Ira ducks anyway and gives Ruby the time she needs to grab and pull him down. She places her foot on his chest and then flips him over her head. She turns over, reaches into her satchel, and stabs Ira in the chest with an injection of oxygen.

I think of Merrick, my family, and all the people Ira has killed or turned into monsters. People I loved were destroyed because of him. I was destroyed because of him. I close my eyes and stand up. I take a deep breath and let my anger flow through my veins. I harness its power and focus it to all my senses. I wipe the blood from my eyes and open them. Everything is brighter and it seems time has slowed down.

My clip is empty, so I throw the pistol to the ground. Ira is back on his feet. He pulls out the syringe and smashes it on the floor. He throws quick punches towards Ruby. He's still so fast. She blocks the first few strikes, but he is able to land a hard jab to her face that forces her backwards, holding her nose. He steps towards her.

I grab her knife off the floor and swing the blade at his neck. He turns and blocks my arm and punches towards my stomach with his other fist. I swipe his arm away before his fist reaches me, but he uses the momentum to spin around and swing a hook kick at my head. I thwart the incoming strike with my forearm and straight kick him in the chest. He shuffles backwards holding his ribs.

Ruby swings her arm above him and down towards his shoulder with the second syringe in her hand. He grabs her wrist, stopping her blow and yanking her downwards. He elbows her in the jaw and she drops to the floor.

I grunt as I charge Ira with the knife and stab towards his heart. He strafes to the side, grabs me, and slams my face against the wall. As soon as I turn around, he pins my neck to the wall with his forearm and uppercuts my stomach so fast and hard I feel like my organs are turning to sludge. My mouth and throat fill up with blood and I cough out a puddle of red slime.

Ira hollers and releases my throat. I fall to one knee gasping for air and choking up more blood and saliva. I see the second syringe sticking into the back of his leg. Ruby is on her knees. He turns around and axe kicks her. She falls forward onto her hands, now bleeding from her lip and nose.

"What have you done?" Ira yells furiously at her.

"She cured you," I say and spit blood near his feet. I pick up the knife again and lunge upwards, stabbing him in the bottom of his belly. His eyes widen and his teeth clinch as I push the blade deeper into him. He stumbles backwards and I step forward. But then, he grabs my hand and stares into my eyes. I try to keep pushing forward, but I can't. He grips down so tightly on my hand that it feels like he's breaking my bones. He yanks my arm back with the blade still in my hands and pushes me backwards.

He kicks the side of my shin. I try to keep my balance on one leg, but he head-butts me and I stumble backwards. He pins me against the wall with his forearm across my chest. He twists the knife around and pushes down. I grab his forearm with my free hand and push back.

He's too strong and the knife inches towards my chest. I try to drop the knife, but he's gripping down so hard on my hand that I can't let go. I push back with all my strength, but it only makes the sharp blade enter my upper chest slower and more painfully. I shout in agony. I can hear my pain echoing through the halls.

"I'm still stronger," he says, pressing the knife deeper into me. He smiles with bloody teeth.

"But you're slower now. You can't see what's going to happen next anymore."

"I will always be one step ahead of you," he says. He pulls out the knife and raises it up above me. He hammers down, with it aiming for my neck, but Yoshi leaps up and takes him to the floor with her. She tears his neck apart like a chew toy, until there is a huge, bloody hole and his head is barely attached to his body.

"Thank God we didn't listen to Samson," I say and rest my hands on my knees, gasping for air. I help Ruby up and kiss her forehead.

"We have to get you to Miranda. You're bleeding a lot," she says.

"So are you."

"Okay, I'll get Yoshi. Grab the concentrator."

I climb up the steps and grab it.

"Come on, girl," Ruby says. "Yoshi?" Yoshi is lying on top of Ira's dead body, not moving. Ruby runs over to her and nudges her. She rolls over with a soft cry. Ruby's knife is in her belly.

"No, baby it's okay," Ruby says. She wraps her arms around Yoshi and kisses her head. Her tears soak Yoshi's fur. With one last howl, Yoshi rests her eyes forever.

24

It doesn't take us long to realize that the large-scale oxygen concentrator is solar-powered. To escape the smoke and ash that masks the Florida sun, we march several miles outside of the city to the low marshes on the outskirts of the Everglades. We brought with us the entire army of the Free People. It was easier to rally 3000 able-bodied men and woman than to get Ruby to leave Yoshi. I had to promise Ruby that we would come back to bury her.

The sun is boiling hot. Sweat is soaking the bandage on my chest, but I'm hoping the heat will charge the device quicker. There's a small screen and a tiny outline of a battery. It's only half-charged.

"Are you sure Al-menzanii's armies are coming this way?" Ruby asks Mika.

"This highway is the fastest way here. He has to come this way." About 150 yards ahead, the highway cuts through the vast marshlands. "A hundred miles of swampland on both sides of them will make their vast number useless against us. If we can hold them before they pass that tree line, we might stand a chance."

"This won't be enough to stop them. This is all the vehicles you could find?" I ask. There are eight gendarmerie vans and armored trucks lined up in two horizontal rows across the highway, and a dozen, heavy machine guns lined up extending from the shoulder lane like curved wings. They are all pointing towards the threshold of the narrow path that cuts the swamplands in half for at least 100 miles.

"Be happy with what we have. It wasn't easy getting them," the General says.

"And be happy you're not in the Valley of Megiddo. 100 million Berserkers and fifty million more Caliphate soldiers are marching on the Allies as we speak," Mika says.

I look at the battery level: 58%

"Do you think they'll try to bomb the city before they attack?" Ruby says.

"We shut down all the furnaces, but the smoke won't clear for a while. No one will be flying through that black cloud, and they shouldn't know we're here," Mika says.

A small, white golf cart drives up to us. Slo-mo is sitting in the driver's seat with dark shades on. I wish he had an extra pair. My head is beginning to ache from squinting so hard. *Abuelo* slowly pulls himself out of the passenger seat. He is wearing an obnoxiously bright, yellow polo shirt tucked into short, white shorts. He shuffles his brown sandals to us.

"Everyone is armed," he says out of breath.

Extending out horizontally from the highway, Jersey barricades stretch out side by side forming a wall as far out as the army stands. The muddy ground has sinks the wall shorter than waist-high.

"This isn't enough," I say again. "Big Al has one million Berserkers and twenty thousand troops after that."

"Haven't you ever heard of the Thermopylae pass? Their numbers won't matter in a narrow strait," Mika ensures.

"Didn't the Greeks die in the end?" Ruby counters.

"Trust me, it will work," Mika says.

"Even if it does, we'll run out of bullets before we run out of Berserkers to kill," I say.

I look at the device in my hand: 65%

Suddenly, Fangs are howling all around.

"Stop being negative, you're making the Fangs upset," Ruby says. The Cubans brought at least fifty, trained Fangs with them. Most of them look like terrifyingly large pit-bulls and rottweilers, two of which I remember hiding from at the Cuban base days ago.

"I don't think that's what they're howling at," Mika says.

"*Mira*," *Abuelo* says, pointing to the sky above the Everglades. A black cloud covering the entire sky is coming our way fast.

"What the hell is that?" I say.

Free People are beginning to panic and aiming their guns upwards. The black cloud widens as it moves closer. I can hear a chorus of squawking and chirping as the massive flock of birds fly over us.

"They're fleeing from something," Ruby says. "The infected are coming."

70% Come on damn it!

The sky clears as the birds pass us and blend into the darkness above the city. Far ahead, down the highway the stampede of Berserkers finally appears.

"They're coming. Is that concentrator ready?" Mika directs his question to me.

"Seventy-three percent," I answer.

"I was hoping we wouldn't have to fire on them," *Abuelo* says and shuffles back to the golf cart. When he is inside, Slo-mo drives them back to the eastern flank.

I can hear a choir of screams and awful moans as the horde comes rushing towards us.

"'*On that day I will strike every man with madness' declares the Lord*," I recite under my breath.

"What?" Ruby asks.

"Zechariah 12. Just something I learned from Wesley," I say. The page from his book is still in my pocket.

"Take your positions," Mika shouts.

The Free People line up side by side along the Jersey walls, aiming whatever gun they were given or took off of a dead gendarmerie.

77%

I see another swarm forming in the sky above the Berserkers. Ruby and I crouch down behind the cement wall. The Berserkers are almost to the threshold of the tree line. They stretch back as far as the eye can see.

"I don't want to kill them," Ruby says.

80%

"I don't either, but it's them or us," I say.

"Fire," I hear Mika shout, right before the stampede crosses out of the hallway in-between the trees. The heavy machine guns open fire first. It sounds like rapid thunder. A mound of dead bodies forms quickly. Some Berserkers escape past the border, but are quickly filled with bullets by the flank gunners.

83%

The hill of bodies quickly becomes a wall that extends from tree to tree across the highway. It grows almost to the height of the trees, but more and more keep coming. Climbing over or pushing through.

I wonder how many more mounds are piling up at Megiddo.

The Fangs are barking and howling ferociously as the black cloud of birds comes our way. This cloud seems different though. They fly in a thick line following the highway and, over the machine gun fire, instead of squawks and twitters I hear buzzing and insect chirps.

I swallow hard.

"Locusts," Ruby says with wide eyes.

85%

I hear men and women screaming as the giant insects descend upon us. They seem even bigger than I remember. Some of the Free People are retreating, but the rest fire frantically as they swarm over us.

"Protect the gunners!" I yell to any who will listen. Ruby fires her Uzi and I shoot my Glock towards the ones above the gunners. I put a bullet in-between the eyes of one and Ruby shoots a burst into another's underbelly, but there are many more. Several of them snatch up the gunners in their talons and eat them whole, or rip them in half and stuff them between their sharp teeth piece by piece.

We keep firing, and thankfully so do the remaining gunners, but there are less of them now and more Berserkers are beginning to break through the gate of the swamp. A dying locust smashes on the ground in front of me, still twitching its legs and head.

Another massive bug picks up a van and drops it on the right flank, smashing a couple people and a Fang to death. Another one lands right next to us. Its deafening screech turns everything else mute for a time. I step ahead of Ruby to shield her, but the beast swings its leg to my chest and I'm thrown several yards away. On the muddy ground, I hold my chest gasping for air. I watch as it thrusts its mouth towards Ruby. She seems frozen staring up at it.

From the ground, I hold my pistol up and aim at its head. Before I can fire, I hear a shotgun blast. The beast screeches in pain and turns towards Mika. He fires another shot and the bug's head explodes into chunky, dark brown goo. Its body falls to the ground. Mika is quickly off firing in another direction.

92%

I push myself up and run to Ruby, all the while firing at a locust flying above me with a soldier in its talons. It drops the soldier on his head and then dives into the marsh, flapping its broken wings and splashing mud and water. I shoot it a couple more times until it stops moving.

I grab Ruby and wrap my arms around her. Her heart is racing as fast as mine is.

"Focus," I say.

She nods. "I'm good. I'm good."

Berserkers are now pouring out of the woods on both sides of the highway, splashing their way towards us while even more climb over the pile of corpses. A few have already made it over our walls. Remains of Free People, Berserkers, and locusts are beginning to pile up on our side too.

"There are only three gunners left," I say. "We have to protect them." The last two locusts are swooping down on them. One grabs a gunner in its talons and the other fights it for the kill. I put a new clip in my gun, and Ruby and I unload on them until they crash to the ground, smashing a couple rushing Berserkers. Now the marsh between the woods and our wall is completely filled with Berserkers dashing towards us.

97%

All the remaining Free People open fire. Grenades are thrown and exploded bodies fly into the air all over, but there's too many of them. The last machine gunners are consumed by the massive horde and they start pouring over our wall. We keep firing, but they're too fast and...before I know it, they are all around us.

One of our trained Fangs is gnawing on the back of a Berserker's neck. Her snout is covered in blood. When it's finished with the kill, it leaps for another, but a Berserker grabs it out of the air and tears it in half like a piece of paper. Infected close in on me on all sides and I can no longer see Ruby.

99%

I shoot several Berserkers around me, but there are so many more. The explosions, bullets, and screams are all mixing together and sound like a loud trumpet blaring in my brain. I look at the oxygen concentrator in my hand, but can no longer read it. A filmy, colorful curtain is swirling over my eyes. I shake my head and take a deep breath.

My vision clears, but a Berserker grabs me and pulls me towards it. It screams and spits in my face. I kick hard between its legs and, as it keels over, I strike my elbow down on its forehead until it falls to the ground. I shoot another in the head and put two bullets in the chest of one that looks like a nine-year-old girl that's missing half her face.

From behind, hulk-like arms wrap around my arms and chest. I holler in agony as it presses against my knife wound. I drop my gun and the concentrator. The large Berserker bites down on my neck. I grunt and grind my teeth. I can feel the pain run down my spine.

"Focus!" I hear Ruby yell, but I can't see her. I steady my breathing and ram my elbow into its stomach until it lets go of me. I turn and hook my right fist to its face several times before it falls over and is quickly trampled on by more Berserkers and Free People alike.

I search the ground for the concentrator. It's ahead of me in the mud, but someone kicks it out of sight again.

A Berserker bumps into me and I shove it away violently. I can feel blood pouring out from my neck. I kick another Berserker and jab two more. I grab inflamed shoulders in front of me and yank it down to the ground. I shove and punch my way through several more before I see the device again through the countless moving legs and feet.

"Ruby!" I yell. She's in front of me. Berserkers are all around her, but she keeps fighting. She roundhouse kicks one, punches another, and slits another's throat. Then she spins around and fires several bursts into the bellies of three others, giving her some breathing room until one grabs her from behind.

"The concentrator!" I shout, blocking the arms of a Berserker who is trying to claw at my face. I kick it in the stomach and then spin kick it in the face, until it gets lost in the crowd. I push and shove my way towards Ruby. She finally spots the device on the ground in front of her. She plants her elbow on the Berserker's face several times until it releases her. She reaches for the concentrator, but too many Berserkers are in the way and grabbing for her. I try to push forward, but there's too many around me too, grabbing and clawing at me. I try to fight back, but they pull me and shove me to the ground. It's incredibly hot and I can barely breathe. I try to push myself up, but so many people are stepping on me. I'm sinking deeper into the mud. Blood and sweat drip from my body.

Rapid shotgun blasts fire near me and a pile of dead Berserkers form directly in front of me. I try to climb up the pile. Dead, round eyes with no lids stare at me as I crawl over them. I hear heavy machine pistols firing behind me. Mika spots me and helps me up. As soon as I get my footing, he lets go and shoots another Berserker in the chest. The General screams, and she jumps over the pile of dead, firing her machine pistols. Her arms and face are covered in blood and glitter. A dozen frenzied men, women, and children drop dead in front of her. The three of them form an open circle around me and I'm able to finally catch my breath. I'm covered in mud and blood.

"Find the concentrator," Ruby instructs hurriedly and shoots in front of her. I search the perimeter of the muddy circle.

"I don't see it," I say.

"Look under those bodies," Mika suggests. He throws his empty shotgun aside and pulls out a pistol. An infected old lady with a torn, pink sweater and a single breast hanging out grabs him. He shoves her face back and puts a bullet in her neck. Infected blood sprays out like water from a broken pipe.

I start pushing and rolling dead bodies off the top of the pile.

"Hurry, we can't hold them for much longer," Mika shouts over the mayhem. I pull another body off and drag two more out of the way. My eyes are burning, but I don't know if it's from sweat, mud, blood, or smoke. I wipe them with my sleeve and finally get to the last body in the pile. I turn it over.

"I got it!" I pick up the large-scale oxygen concentrator and lift it up like a trophy.

"Turn it on," Ruby says and fires a burst of bullets into a fat Berserker with no bottom jaw and eyeballs that are hanging from his sockets.

"Right," I say. I wipe the mud off the screen as best as I can, but my hands are so muddy it hardly makes a difference.

100%

The power button is finally lit up. I press it.

"Well?" Ruby yells. "Did you turn it on?"

"I don't know. I pressed it. Nothing's happening."

"Press it again," Mika says.

There's a sea of infected humans as far as my eyes can see in every direction. I can hear the guns of many Free People still fighting and can see dead bodies of Berserkers piling up around them, but I would guess we have lost over half our troops. I press the touchscreen power button again and again.

Nothing.

"It's not working. I think it's broken." It must have broken when I dropped it in the mud.

"Then we've lost. We're dead," Ruby says and empties her last clip. "I'm out."

"Wait a minute, wait a minute. Hold your fire!" Mika orders. "I think it's working." I look at the device in my hand. It doesn't look any different. It's not even making a sound, but Mika and the General stop shooting. All the Berserkers around us are taking long deep breaths as if they were breathing for the first time.

"Hold your fire!" Mika yells over and over again as he wades through the crowd. Gunfire around us begins to dissipate, and soon all I can hear is a million people filling their lungs with oxygen.

"What's going on?" I hear someone say.

"I can talk. Thank God, I can talk again!"

"What's happening?"

"Do you understand me?" Another asks. Ruby and Miranda are trying to calm the people around them.

"You're okay now. You're cured," the General says.

"What's happening to me?" A man grabs me with the biggest smile. "It doesn't hurt anymore." His skin looks like it's already beginning to heal.

"You're cured."

He hugs me and then looks up at the sky. "Thank you Lord!" he shouts joyfully towards the heavens. Now, everyone around us is doing the same. I smile at Ruby. She laughs as people hug her and Miranda.

"Listen up everyone," Mika projects through the bullhorn of one of the trucks. "I know you are all confused. You were all infected by the Caliphate that used you for evil, but we found the cure. You are all cured." A roar of jubilation fills the air as the crowd cheers. "The unquenchable fire that seemed it would never end is over for you, but the battle is not. Big Al is coming with an army right up that highway. He and his men are responsible for the nightmare that tormented you for so long. We have weapons for a lot of you. For those that want to join us, form lines at the big, black boxes behind me. My people will supply you. If you don't wish to fight, and just want to rest and eat and breathe, you are free to return to Miami and live."

"We want to fight!" A woman yells out in the crowd, and everyone cheers like roaring thunder.

25

I t isn't much of a fight. A million Free People overtake Big Al and his army in the center of the Florida Everglades. At least 100,000 Free People perish before they destroy the entirety of the Caliphate army. The bodies litter the highway for miles and miles. Crows and scavenger birds from a thousand miles away have gathered to fill their bellies several times over.

The smell of the bodies is overwhelming in Miami and, now that the sky is clear, the crows can be seen swarming day in and day out.

I sit by the ocean with my feet in the cold, white sand. Every once in a while, a breeze comes from the east and the smell of salt masks the stench for a moment.

Ruby comes and sits next to me. She's wearing a white sundress and she smells like flowers.

"Mika says the oxygen level has already reached thirty percent," she says. "He says it will get up to forty by the end of the year."

"I can feel it. Look," I show her the wounds on my neck and chest that Miranda patched up.

"They've already healed," Ruby says, amazed.

"I know," I say.

"You know, they say that we will live much longer now. So you're stuck with me for a long time," She says.

"I don't think I'll mind." I grab her face and kiss her.

"You know, it probably also means that our child is going to grow much taller than his father," she says and rests her hand on her stomach. She smiles.

I laugh. "Are you serious?"

She nods.

"That's fantastic!" I say and jump on her and kiss all over her belly. She laughs and pushes me off.

"Come on, let's go."

"Go where?" I say

"The new King has summoned us to Jerusalem. He wants to thank us personally for helping the Allies defeat the Caliphate. If we hadn't found the concentrator, they would have lost at Megiddo and we would all be dead."

"New King?" I say and help her up. We walk towards Ocean Avenue, which is once again alive and bustling. The people seem so happy, and many of them look and point at us. Some stop to touch our hands or give thanks.

"The Commander who rides the white horse," Ruby says. "They proclaimed him the new King, and he has invited all of us into his new kingdom."

"There's something I have to do before we go."

"Please tell me it's taking a shower," she says and scrunches her nose. "The city water is clean and running again."

"Okay two things." I laugh, rolling my eyes.

It's a bright morning on the small, island town of Venice. I'm wearing a fitted, blue-grey suit but I'm not sweating at all. There's a crisp breeze coming from the east. I stand in front of my wife and daughter's gravestones. Bart helped me remove mine when I arrived.

"I don't know if I was a good husband or a good dad to you," I say. "Whatever I was died with you. I'm made new. For what it's worth, I promise I will be a good father and a good husband to them. Now, I'm going to do something I should have done a long time ago."

The bells of the church ring loud at the top of the steeple signaling the start of Sunday service.

"Danny," Ruby calls for me. She's standing on the steps in a blue sundress with a white flower pattern. She smiles at me as I come to her.

I pick her up and kiss her as Bart welcomes in Mika, Miranda, *Abuelo* and Pedrito, Juan-Carlos, Slo-mo and many other Free People.

Before we walk in, Bart unfolds a thick, rectangular piece of paper and hands it to me.

"I found this," he says. I look at it. Sketched with bright-colored crayons is a child's drawing of a little girl and her parents standing in front of a colorful house with a big yellow sun behind it. They all have huge smiles drawn inside their circular heads. I look at Bart wondering why he gave me this.

"You were a good father," he says and points to the bottom-right corner of the paper.

In blue crayon it reads: *Tilda.*

The end.